The Missing Films

Other Doherty Mysteries

The Mill Town
The Lost Survivor

The
MISSING FILMS

A Doherty Mystery

By Sam Kafrissen

International Digital Book Publishing Industries

Florida, USA

For Luke and Lily Rose, the future

Chapter One

The client cracked his knuckles and fidgeted in his chair. Despite the comfortable temperature in the room he took out his handkerchief to wipe his brow for a second time. Doherty laced his hands behind his head and rocked back in his swivel chair, his cigarette dangling from the corner of his mouth. He had to admit he was enjoying Johnny Briggs' discomfort.

"You gotta understand something, Mr. Doherty. This kind of stuff is not my end of the business. Gus usually handles missing person cases. I do mostly investigations into infidelities and divorces with all the legal mumbo jumbo that goes along with them. To be honest with you, I wouldn't know where to begin in a situation like this."

Doherty leaned forward and tapped a quarter inch of ash into the large glass ashtray that resided on his desk. "Look, Mr. Briggs, there's something I don't get about this. You run one of the largest investigative agencies in Providence yet you've come down here to West Warwick to hire me to find a missing person. Maybe you should explain why."

Briggs twisted in his chair as the conversation once again had taken an uncomfortable turn. "Well, you see it's not just any person that's missing. It's Gus Timilty."

There was a prolonged silence in the room as this piece of information settled into Doherty's head.

"He's been gone for over a week now and nobody's seen him. I can't send any of my people out to look for him 'cause it would be bad for morale in the office if they knew Gus was AWOL. Besides, I already told most of my people that he had to take some time off to deal with a personal matter. If they had any idea he was missing who knows what effect it'd have on our operation. That's why I came to you. You know Gus as well as anybody. He always said you were the best around at finding lost people."

This last piece of info put a whole new light on why Johnny Briggs was in his office looking to hire him on a missing person case. Gus had been Doherty's mentor when he was on the police force in West Warwick. They continued to remain good friends and professional colleagues after Timilty was forced to resign from the cops. Nobody had done more to help Doherty set up his own practice or provide him with clients than Gus. On top of that, the older man always had Doherty's back in tight situations. Gus being the missing person gave this case a whole new dimension.

"So, is he taking time off to deal with a personal matter?"

"I dunno. He got a phone call about two weeks ago that got his shorts all in a twist. The only thing he let on to me was that he needed to locate some guy named Frankie DeAngelo. I'd never heard of him so I asked a couple of our junior investigators to look into it. One of them came back a few days later with some dope on a DeAngelo who lives in Cranston and does business moving hot merchandise. You know, stuff that fell off the back of a truck. No other Frankie DeAngelo popped up doing anything remotely dirty so I passed this info onto Gus. That was the last I saw of him. He left the office that same day and I haven't heard from him since. Do you think you can find him? Not having Gus around leaves a big hole in our operation."

After leaving the cops Timilty hooked on with the Briggs Investigations Agency. Within a year of joining that outfit he became a named partner. Doherty figured it was Gus' investigative skills that turned Briggs and Timilty into a first class operation. Now witnessing Johnny Briggs here in the flesh he understood why. The man was somewhere in his late forties going quickly to paunchiness. He wore his thinning dark hair laced across his scalp, but not enough to hide the pink crown on top. Although his clothes were expensive he did not wear them well. Gus Timilty was a far better face man for their partnership.

"I'll need everything you have so far on this DeAngelo character. You'll also have to sign one of my standard contracts. The fee is fifty dollars plus expenses."

For the first time since he entered the office Briggs smiled, accompanied by a chuckle. "Gus said you were kind of small time, but I didn't think you were that small. How about if I give you a hundred bucks and we forgo the contract? I don't want anybody knowing I hired you to find Gus. Truth is I don't want anybody knowing Gus is missing. I'd prefer to keep this arrangement just between you and me."

Doherty didn't say anything. He just gave Briggs a non-committal look while he finished his cigarette. When he was done he carefully stuffed the butt out in the ashtray.

"I'll make it two hundred as long as you keep this under your hat. Any of our clients find out Gus is missing we could lose their business."

Doherty remained silent. He wasn't doing it to juice up the charges or anything. It was more a case of trying to figure out if Briggs was telling him all he knew. The client took out his nose rag again and mopped his forehead for a third time. Then he stood and pulled a thick wallet out of his back pocket. He extracted a bunch of bills from it, counted out ten twenties and placed them on the desk in front of Doherty.

He looked down at the money then up at Briggs again, taking in the entirety of his new client. "I'm obligated to give you the usual spiel about how I can't break any laws in pursuit of this enterprise, and if Gus has, I can't be party to aiding and abetting him in any way."

Briggs waved his hand dismissing everything Doherty'd just said. "Yeah, yeah, I understand all that. Just do me a favor, find Gus and do it fast. We're in a jam at the company without him. This week alone a couple of clients specifically asked for his services."

"I'll do my best," Doherty said as he scooped up the two hundred and slipped them into his pants pocket.

Chapter Two

After Briggs left Doherty stashed most of the cash in the locked drawer in his filing cabinet. He pocketed the rest and then dropped down to Harry's Barbershop for a shave and a trim. Harry's was the biggest operation of its kind in West Warwick. It had five chairs rather than the usual two like most of the other shops in town. All the important business-men and shopkeepers in Arctic came to Harry's to get the latest poop on what was going on around town.

It was also Doherty's second home. Even when he didn't need any ton-sorial work or a shoeshine he often spent time in Harry's talking with his best friend, the barber Bill Fiore. If Bill was busy he would sit in one of the customer chairs reading articles in the men's magazines that were spread around the shop to occupy clients while they waited for a free barber chair. He assumed these mags were there to give the customers a manly feeling before getting their fur clipped. On those occasions when he came down to hang around Doherty purposely loitered just long enough to get under Harry's skin.

A little over a year ago Doherty'd gotten on the wrong side of the town's political boss, Judge Martin DeCenza. The Judge had used his influence with Harry's landlord to get Doherty banned from the barbershop unless he was there on business. However, when he later uncovered a nasty little secret about the Judge's role in a crooked land deal, he used it to hammer out an arrange-ment that, among other things, allowed him to hang out at Harry's whenever he wanted and for however long he wanted. He knew this circumstance was unsatisfactory to Harry, who was no fan of Doherty's in the first place.

Bill was just finishing up with an elderly gent whose hair was so sparse it barely needed cutting. Still Fiore, in his gentlemanly fashion, worked his scissors on the old guy's head as if he had full plumage. When he whisked the sheet off, the customer stood for a few moments in front of the mirror admiring his new, lacquered follicles. Doherty found himself checking for clippings on the floor to see if any hair had left the man's head. He detected only a few gray strands littering the area around the chair.

After the customer paid for his cut along with a generous tip for Bill, the barber ceremoniously offered the chair to Doherty as if it were the throne of England.

"What'll it be, Baby Huey?" Bill asked as Doherty parked his keister.

"The works if you've got the time, Beetle."

"Hey, I got all the time in the world. You know we don't get busy till late afternoon after the men get off work. Though with the mills closin' like they are, Harry's already makin' noises about layin' off a barber or two. He says the shop won't be able support five chairs much longer."

"Seems like times are tough everywhere in town. Whenever I walk up Washington or down Main I see another shop going out of business or moving somewhere else. Just last week the fellow who owns the paint store in the front of my building told me he was moving his operation to Cranston in February. Says he bought some land there and is building his own store. That'll be a big empty space to fill."

"How are things otherwise? You gettin' any business upstairs?"

Doherty shrugged under the sheet. "A little here and there. I just got a new case that'll probably keep me ahead of the bill collectors for a couple of months." He knew Fiore was acquainted with Gus Timilty from Gus' days with the cops. He'd promised Johnny Briggs to work this case on the QT so he kept details about his new client vague. The barber was sharp enough to know when Doherty didn't want to talk about a case.

Sensing this, Bill changed the subject. "What's the news on Agnes? How's her pregnancy going?"

Agnes Benvenuti was Doherty's secretary and had been since he hung out his shingle four years ago. She'd proven to be indispensible to his operation even though she only worked three days a week. Her husband Louie was a merchant marine so he wasn't in town all that often. Agnes never bothered to tell him that she was doing clerical work at Doherty and Associates. However, last spring when Louie was in port he'd gotten Agnes pregnant so she had to cut back on her time at the agency, at least until the baby was born.

"She complains about getting as big as a house; personally I think she looks pretty good. I told her being with child appeared to agree with her. She wasn't buying it."

"So what are you doin' for clerical help these days?"

Doherty hesitated, not wanting to say what he knew he had to. Fiore was too good a friend to keep in the dark about recent developments. "Rachel comes in a couple of days a week to help out. Agnes is showing her how our operation works – such as it is."

"Jesus, Huey. Are you okay with that?" Bill said stopping his cutting at this news.

Rachel Katz was a young Jewish girl from Providence that Doherty was dating last spring when they were viciously attacked by a group of Polish ex-Nazis from Pawtucket. They were men Doherty'd been tailing as part of a missing person's case he was working at the time. He was hit over the head and knocked out, but Rachel got the worst of it. The ugliest member of the group raped and beat her, which left her psychologically damaged. After it happened Doherty thought he'd never see Rachel again, even though he'd exacted a measure of revenge for the attack by shooting the rapist. Then one night several weeks later she showed up at his apartment and asked if she could spend the night. This arrangement had been going on two or three nights a week for the past few months.

"Does that mean you two are back together?" Bill asked.

"I don't know how to answer that. She's at loose ends right now. I guess you could say I'm providing her with some sort of anchor. She needs to get out of her parents' house, but she's got nowhere to go and no real income since she decided not to go back to teaching. I told her I could give her some work so she'd have some spending money – and could stay at my place any time she needed to. I didn't know what else to do."

"What about the other stuff?"

Doherty hesitated. "We don't sleep together if that's what you're asking. On days when she comes by early I give her my bed and I sleep on the couch. When she comes late at night she takes a blanket and pillow from the closet and sacks out on the couch. We haven't talked about any of that other business – not yet anyway."

"How long do you think things'll go on like this?"

"Damned if I know."

"Do you think this set-up is a good idea?"

Doherty shook his head. "I don't think any arrangement would be good under the circumstances. All I know is that I can't tell her not to come, not after what happened to her on my account. For now all I can do is take things as they come. Why don't we just leave it at that, okay?"

Bill let out a long deep breath. Instead of resuming this line of conversation he began to strop his razor for the shave. Right now Doherty needed to push thoughts about Rachel out of his head so he could focus his attention on finding Gus Timilty. Each new case gave him an excuse not to look at what was happening in his personal life. Sometimes he thought it was why he went into the investigations business in the first place.

Chapter Three

When he returned to the office he saw there was a message from Johnny Briggs on his new answering machine. Doherty installed this device shortly after Agnes began to cut back on her hours. He could no longer afford to miss any potential clients and he couldn't very well spend his days sitting by the phone waiting for calls. Now the machine took messages when there was no one in the office.

He dialed the number for Briggs and Timilty and a secretary answered. He identified himself and asked to speak with Mr. Briggs. A few seconds later Johnny Briggs' gravelly voice came on the line.

"I wasn't able to get much on that DeAngelo guy for you," Briggs said. "From what my men could scrape together he appears to be a small time grifter who fences stolen goods and wholesales hot merchandise. It sounds like he's an independent operator. As far as we could tell he doesn't have any connections to the wise guys. His current listed address is 34 Maple Street in Cranston. That's all we've been able to find on him so far." This paltry amount of info once again convinced Doherty that Gus was the real brains at Briggs and Timilty.

"It's not much, but enough for me to run with. I'll be in touch if this DeAngelo character turns out to be connected with Gus' disappearance in any way. In the meantime see if your guys can find out if DeAngelo's had any run-ins with the law. I assume you've got connections with some of the local police departments who can pass on that kind of information."

Briggs hemmed and hawed and then finally said, "I'll see what I can find out."

The next morning Doherty took his '55 Chevy Bel Air out of Denny Belanger's garage where he housed it when it was not in use. He paid a small fee each month for the garage space and did most of his food shopping at Belanger's Market as an additional payment. It was a convenient arrangement for both of them. Since most days Doherty preferred walking to town rather than driving, his car spent more time in the garage than on the road.

He didn't know Cranston all that well, only that there were a couple of main routes, Reservoir Avenue and Elmwood Avenue, which passed through it on the way into Providence. The other main drag was Park Avenue, a commercial street that crossed those big avenues and ran the length of Cranston from east to west. After leaving West Warwick he drove north on Reservoir past the new Garden City shopping complex that was just beyond the boys reformatory at Sockanosset. A few miles further on he reached the next big intersection in Cranston where Park crossed Reservoir. Not knowing exactly which way to go he chose to turn left on Park.

About a quarter mile down Park he stopped at an Atlantic station to tank up the Chevy and ask for directions to Maple Street. A feral looking character wearing a greasy baseball cap and an even greasier mechanic's suit came out to pump the gas. He was chomping on an unlit cigar that was likewise ringed with grease. Once the nozzle was in the Chevy, the grease monkey checked the oil and squeegeed the windshield and back window. While he was working on his car Doherty got out and asked for directions to Maple Street.

The attendant removed his cigar with an equally greasy paw and pointed west on Park. "It's a little ways down there in the Village," he said indicating the direction. "I think it's the first or second right after the big turnoff for Gansett. Maple is on the other side of Park from Nardolillo's Funeral Home. You can't miss it."

"Why is that place called the *Village*?"

The greasy man stuck the chewed up cigar back into the corner of his mouth and mumbled, "You'll see. It's a bunch of houses all the same." The fill-up cost him $2.50; the oil check and windshield cleaning were free.

Doherty followed the man's directions and had no problem finding Maple Street. It was actually the second right after a group of baseball fields; the first was Oak Street. The attendant's description of the houses was accurate too. Every one of them was an identical two-story, side-by-side duplex – all painted exactly the same, white with green trim. The only differences were in the mailboxes people had mounted by their doors and any little do-dads they put out front. Since each building abutted the street there wasn't much room for any kind of individualized decorations.

He parked in front of #34, which shared the space with #36. There was no screen or storm door, just the front door right out there facing the street. No signs by the door or on the mailbox indicated Frank DeAngelo or anyone else lived there. Without a doorbell, Doherty had to knock. After waiting without getting an answer, he hit the door again, louder this time. Still no response. He walked around the side of the house to the back and knocked at the back door.

"If you're looking for Frankie, he's not here," a female voice shouted from the neighboring yard. He hadn't noticed her when he turned the corner, but now saw a woman reclining on an aluminum beach chair in the adjacent space. She was sitting in a small section of the yard that was catching the last of the afternoon sun. A magazine sat on her lap.

He walked slowly over to where she was sunning herself, taking her in as he did. She was somewhere in her late twenties or early thirties and was wearing a red gingham bandana on her head that covered most, though not all of her strawberry blond hair. She had on a pair of dungarees that were turned up into cuffs just below her knees. They were accompanied by a man-tailored, blue oxford shirt, unbuttoned a couple of notches from the top and tied at her waist. A pair of white Keds without socks covered her feet.

"How did you know I was looking for Frankie DeAngelo?"

She gave him a know-it-all smile and said, "You were knocking on his door, weren't you. That was kind of a dead giveaway."

Doherty banged out a Camel and lit it as he moved closer to the woman on the folding chair. "You live here in #36?"

She laughed. "No I just sit out here in their backyard till they come home from work. Of course I live here – with my son Mark. He's at school right now. Are you a bill collector or a customer?"

"A customer?"

"You don't exactly look like one Frankie's customers. I know you aren't a friend 'cause he doesn't have any friends 'cept me. Since you're dressed better than most of the mooks that come around looking for him and you're not a bill collector, I gotta ask if you're a cop?"

Doherty ignored her question and looked around the neighborhood for few beats. "Why is this neighborhood called *the Village*?"

The girl put down her movie magazine and swung her legs over the side of the chair. They were nicely shaped, pale and lightly freckled. "It used to be called the *White Village* 'cause all the houses are painted white. It's where the people who worked at the Print Works lived. My old man was one of them. I grew up in this house. This whole neighborhood was company housing at one time. The Cranston Print Works rented these places out to their workers. Most of them are now owned by the people that live in them or by some landlord who rents them out. Whatever the reason, everybody in Cranston still calls it the Village."

Doherty was familiar with company housing. Many of the mills in West Warwick once owned a lot of residential properties surrounding them where their workers rented out apartments in duplexes just like this one. And like the Village, most of those units were now owned outright by the families who lived in them. These days people who still work in the mills have to find their own housing. The companies that run the mills stopped providing it years ago

"To answer your question, no, I'm not a cop. I'm actually looking for a guy who might've been around here recently looking for Frankie. He wouldn't have looked like a customer either."

"An older guy with gray hair. Big face. Nice smile but cold eyes. Is that the guy you mean? If it is he came by one day last week."

"Could be him. Sounds like it. Did you talk to him at all?"

The girl shook her head. "Not really. I just told him when Frankie isn't here he's usually down by the beach. Frankie told me he has a summer place near Bonnet Shores. That's somewhere down in South County, isn't it? I've never been there myself." The girl reached over to the far side of her chair and picked up a can of Black Label and took a sip. "Would you like a beer? It's kind of a hot day for October."

It was a hot day and a beer sounded like a nice idea. Plus, it would give him more time to see what he could learn from the girl about Frankie DeAngelo or Gus' whereabouts.

She got up and headed toward her back door. "Oh, by the way, there's another chair leaning up against the house if you wanna take a load off." While she was gone Doherty unfolded the other aluminum chair. It was more of the upright kind. He wiped the dust off it with his handkerchief and parked it by hers.

She returned with two more Carlings and a large bag of potato chips. She set the chips down on the grass between them and handed Doherty a can of beer. She'd already plugged it open.

"By the way, my name's Maureen Donovan. My friends all call me Moe."

"I'm Hugh Doherty. Most people just call me Doherty."

They both sipped their beers and took in the unexpected warm weather. "What do you do when you're not out here sunning yourself?" Doherty asked to make conversation.

She shaded her eyes and looked at him as if she was wondering whether she should be so friendly with a stranger. "I'm a nurse at Rhode Island Hospital. I worked the graveyard shift last night so I'm off today. My boy stays with my folks when I work at night or need a break, like today. They live just a little ways from here on the other side of Park Ave. He's only nine so he can't be left by himself. There are some pretty rough characters still living here in the Village. I have to keep a close eye on him. He's a good boy, but he could easily get in with the wrong crowd. I've already caught him a few times trying to steal cigarettes from my purse."

"Does he have a father?" Doherty was almost sorry he asked knowing that the question could change the tenor of the conversation.

"He does, sort of. My ex is a long hauler. Drives sixteen wheelers cross-country every month or so. Two years ago he took a load to Arizona and never came back. A year later I got divorce papers in the mail. He pled to adultery so the court would grant me the divorce. Turns out he had a girl out there who'd already had his baby. He's supposed to send us money every month for child support, but he's got a knack for forgetting about it whenever it suits him. There's not much I can do given that he's way the hell on the other side of the country. At least I got my folks to look after Mark and help us out when we need money. What about you? Are you married, Doherty?"

He shook his head. "No. Never even close if you want to know the truth."

"So, what do you do when you're not nosing around looking for people?"

"Not much else. That's pretty much my whole job."

"But you said you weren't a cop?"

"I'm not. I'm a private investigator. I was hired to find the older guy you mentioned a few minutes ago. So far my only lead is Frankie DeAngelo. What else can you tell me about Frankie that might help me out?"

"Damn, where to begin? Mostly he sells stuff – all kinds of stuff: TVs, radios, phonographs, kitchen appliances, paint, jewelry, hardware. You name it, Frankie's got it."

"Does he have a store or a warehouse?"

The girl shook her head. "Not as far as I know. Keeps most of his goods right here in his place. I suspect he's got another stash down at his beach house. You could say he's an enterprising fellow, except that he's also a sleazeball. But I can't complain. He's good with Mark, always giving him stuff like model airplane kits, baseballs, gloves and bats – things like that."

"What about you? Does he give you things as well?"

The girl hesitated. Doherty wondered if he'd gone too far.

"Yeah, every now and then. A scarf or some perfume. I don't like to take too much from him 'cause I know he always wants something in return."

"And?"

She looked away from Doherty and bit her lip. "I have on occasion. A girl can get lonesome living by herself with just a small boy. But Frankie DeAngelo isn't my kinda guy. Now you take somebody like this Rock Hudson," she said, holding up her movie magazine with his face on the cover. "If he were to give me a scarf or some perfume I'd jump right into his arms. I think he's just dreamy. Don't you?"

Doherty laughed to lighten the mood. "I like his movies. I especially liked him in *Giant*, but he's not exactly my type. Elizabeth Taylor, now she's a different story."

The girl drained her beer. "I'm going in for another, would you like one?"

"Sure, why not."

Moe returned with two more Carlings. She and Doherty talked about their backgrounds a little as the sun began to disappear behind some clouds. When it did the temperature took a decidedly downward turn. He could tell from the slurring that was creeping into her speech that his host was feeling the effects of the beers.

She shivered and said, "Would you like to come inside? It's starting to get cold out here."

Doherty agreed and picked up his beer and the potato chips bag and followed her into the house. The back door opened onto the kitchen, which was neatly furnished and moderately clean. He surveyed the room paying particular attention to a bleeding heart Jesus portrait on the wall above the stove. Some dried palm leaves were tied up under it. He wondered if they were left over from Palm Sunday, which passed a good six months ago. He and the girl took seats on either side of a red, Formica topped table that was surrounded by chairs with matching color seats and metal tubular frames.

"Is there anything else you can tell me about Frankie DeAngelo that might help me figure out why my guy was searching for him? You know, like was Frankie into selling something else besides hot goods?"

"Hell, Doherty, isn't selling hot goods enough to get somebody on his case?"

"The cops maybe, unless he's got them paid off. But see the guy I'm looking for isn't a cop; he's a PI like me. He wouldn't care a bit if Frankie was selling hot goods – unless some dissatisfied customer hired him to put the squeeze on Frankie."

The girl took a pack of Winston off the kitchen counter and lit one. Doherty pulled out his Camels and joined her in a smoke. "Well," she hesitated, "Frankie does sell the occasional reefer, if that's what you're talking about."

"Reefer?"

"You know, marihuana, maryjane, pot. The stuff people smoke to get high."

Doherty was not at all familiar with reefer. He remembered the time Rachel had taken him to a beatnik coffeehouse in Providence. She told him that some of the musicians who performed there occasionally blew reefer in the back room. She said she thought about trying it herself. Aside from that and hearing some Negroes in the army talk about it, Doherty had no real knowledge of the drug.

"Except from what I've read in magazines at the barbershop, I'm not really acquainted with reefer," he said almost as an apology.

The girl gave him a devilish smile. "Would you like to try some? Frankie gave me a small bag of it a while back. I keep it hidden from Mark. I'd never do it when he was around, but he'll be staying with my folks tonight."

Doherty wasn't sure where this was going. Yet under the circumstances he didn't see the harm in blowing a little reefer. He told himself that this knowledge might help him in his work someday. Moe disappeared into another room. While she was gone he took the liberty of relieving her fridge of another Black Label. A church key was attached to the handle by some string. She soon returned with a small plastic bag of what looked like ground up parsley and a corncob pipe.

"I don't really know how to roll up cigarettes, so I use this old pipe my father left here. I hope you don't mind." She held out the bag to Doherty. "Here, smell it."

He stuck his nose close to the herb-like substance. It certainly didn't smell like parsley, or tobacco.

"What do you think?" she asked.

"It's pungent all right. How do you smoke it?"

"Pretty much the same as tobacco, only you hold it in a little longer to get the full effect."

She stuffed some of the reefer into the corncob and lit it with a match. She sucked on the pipe until a large plume floated up from its bowl. She held the smoke in until she was racked by a hacking cough. Only then did she hand the pipe to Doherty. He copied what she'd done and let the smoke drift up into his sinuses and out slowly through his nose. They passed the pipe back and forth a few times each taking in a good lungful of reefer. As far as inhaling went he didn't find it any harsher than his Camels.

When the bowl was exhausted Moe placed the pipe on the table and leaned back in her chair. Her eyes were glazed over and a broad smile creased her face. For his part Doherty could feel the muscles in his neck and shoulders relax. Then the relaxation drifted down his chest, his arms and all the way to his legs. He lit a cigarette and inhaled deeply. He didn't feel all that different, though he knew he felt better than when he'd arrived.

The girl stood up and oozed her way to the refrigerator. As she passed by his chair she ran a hand across his shoulder and lightly stroked his neck. She took a container of ice cream from the freezer and handed it and a spoon to Doherty. It was a mix of vanilla, chocolate and strawberry, what was usually called harlequin. He took a heaping spoonful; ice cream had never tasted so good. He passed it over to Moe and they passed the pint container back and forth as they had the pipe.

She began to giggle. "Mark isn't going to be happy if we eat all of his ice cream," she said. "I'll have to go down to Food Town and get some more for tomorrow."

Doherty laughed but her concern over her son's ice cream allotment did not stop either of them from devouring more. The girl then got up and came over to his chair. She looked down at him then spread her legs and straddled him where he sat. At first he didn't know what to think. The drug was interfering with his reasoning process. He hadn't been with a woman since the incident with Rachel five months ago. His libido had been at rest that whole time.

She unbuttoned her oxford shirt and showed him that she wasn't wearing a bra underneath. Her breasts were small, barely more than lumps that protruded from her chest. Like her legs, her arms and chest area were sprinkled with freckles. She was thin but had strong looking shoulders. She began to unbutton his shirt and Doherty did nothing to stop her. She peeled it off his back and then slowly slipped his undershirt up over his head. Once that was done she started to gently caress the hair on his chest and stomach, stopping briefly to run her fingers over the shrapnel scar near his left shoulder; an unwelcomed souvenir from the war.

She leaned in and kissed him briefly and nestled her head into his neck. After a few minutes of kissing and nuzzling she stood up and peeled down her blue jeans and slid off her underpants along with them. Her nest hair was the same strawberry blond as that on her head. To finish the disrobing, she slid the bandana off her head and shook out her hair, which fell a few inches down below her neck.

Doherty was pretty hard by this point so when he removed his trousers and shorts she mounted him right there on the chair. He couldn't remember if he'd ever had sex in this position before and wasn't about to spend much time thinking about it. She held tightly onto the back of the chair and moved up and down, letting out small gasps as she did. He couldn't move himself but he stayed with her the whole time feeling her long strokes as they approached climax. When they were both done she stayed on his lap and grasped him tightly around the neck. He held her to him and could feel the rib bones that ran across her back.

He had no desire to move from this position, not sure how much the intensity of this experience had been brought on by the reefer or by his months of celibacy. His whole attitude about sex had been changed by Rachel's modern ways of doing things. And though Rachel was no longer part of his life in that way, he unwittingly brought her with him today.

When the girl finally extracted herself from this position she stumbled to the fridge and pulled out another can of Black Label. Standing there naked she silently motioned to Doherty to see if he wanted one. He held up the can he was already working on to say he was okay. She smiled but didn't speak. They were both too spent to utter any words. Moe picked up her clothes and drifted off to another room. While she was gone he slipped on his boxers and finished his beer accompanied by another cigarette. He heard water running. She came back a few minutes later and gave him a sweet smile. She was fully dressed except for the bandana and her bare feet. Doherty put on his clothes in a languid manner. The reefer and beer had left him in a mood he could only describe as supremely relaxed.

"I think I ought to be going," he said as he patted down his clothes to make sure they weren't entirely mussed. He'd left his sport coat in the car, so he only had his slacks and a short sleeve shirt to worry about. She came into his arms and gave him a deep tongue kiss.

"Will I see you again?" she whispered in his ear.

He pulled his face away and smiled at her. "I certainly hope so."

Driving back to West Warwick was not as difficult as he thought it would be. In fact the reefer made him feel at one with the road. He could actually sense the rub of the tires on the pavement. Cars were passing him fairly often until he realized he was barely driving at the speed limit. But he didn't care; it had been a pleasant day full of unexpected pleasures.

Once back at his apartment he took a quick shower, just in case Rachel showed up that night. He wasn't exactly feeling guilty about what had transpired in Cranston, he just didn't want her to smell sex or reefer on him. Fortunately, she didn't appear by eight so he suspected she wouldn't be there at all tonight. He heated up some leftover Chinese food and contented himself with reading more of *East of Eden*, John Steinbeck's twentieth century take on the Cain and Abel story. He liked the book much better than the movie made from it starring James Dean that he'd seen it at the Palace a few years back. Thinking about James Dean made him think about *Giant*, another movie he starred in, along with Rock Hudson. That made him think about Maureen Donovan and her movie magazine. These were the last thoughts that flitted through his head before the book collapsed on his chest and he fell asleep for the night.

Chapter Four

Doherty's experience with South County was pretty much limited to the beaches at Narragansett Pier and Scarborough, where he often went with his Quonset buddies on Sundays after the war. Back then they were all young and single, having survived their respective battles in more or less one piece. A summer afternoon at the beach checking out the young girls in their swimsuits was as pleasant as life could be. Because he was a good swimmer, Doherty loved being at the ocean. Nevertheless, he always had to be careful not to spend too much time in the sun or his white Irish skin would leave him looking like a lobster.

A year ago he was working a case for Judge DeCenza that took him down to South County to a place called Great Island in search of a missing man. His task then was to convince the missing guy to return to his real estate business in Warwick and his position as Republican Party Chairman in Kent County. The Judge's wish was for Doherty to persuade this fellow to resume his normal life so that nothing would reflect badly on the Democratic Party if he stayed missing in the weeks before a crucial statewide election. At the time DeCenza was afraid the Providence papers would lay the blame on him and his party if this Spencer Wainwright fellow remained among the missing. Once he was located, Doherty convinced Wainwright to comply with the Judge's wishes, at least until the election. After the man returned to Warwick it seemed like an open-and-shut case for which Doherty was generously remunerated. However, Wainwright went missing again two weeks later and Doherty was hired a second time to find him. On that occasion his client was the man's secretary, who was doubling as his mistress.

Subsequently things went south and Wainwright ended up dead. It turned out the deceased had gotten himself involved in a shady business deal with some Rhode Island mobsters looking to clean money through commercial real estate investments. Somewhere along the line a major land purchase had gone bad, and the girlfriend turned out to be something other than who Wainwright thought she was. She was involved all along with the very people who wanted him dead. In fact, the girl used her affair with Wainwright to set him up. It was Doherty's first murder case and one that left him with a distinctly bad taste in his mouth; a taste he carried with him today as he drove across the bridge to Great Island, past the sign telling visitors this was a private community and trespassers were not welcomed.

For old time's sake, before heading to his intended destination Doherty took a detour and swung by the deceased man's cottage. There was a For Sale sign stuck in the ground out front. The place had a new coat of paint and looked much spiffier than it did when Doherty went there searching for Wainwright. Even the small lot around the house was neatened up with some new plantings. Apparently Wainwright's less than grieving widow was intent upon ridding herself of their summer cottage.

When Doherty finally found the house he was looking for on the island it was in a much less splendid setting and more ramshackle than the Wainwright place. The cottage sat in the middle of the island on a flat, dry piece of land surrounded by browned grass. Its paint was peeling in spots and weeds were growing up through the broken shells that defined a small parking area out front.

The owner, Alex Klinoff, had been on the police force in West Warwick when Doherty was still in uniform. Back then Klinoff was living the good life despite bringing in a paltry policeman's salary. Doherty remembered him always bragging about his summer home on Great Island. It wasn't until he learned that Klinoff was a bent cop raking in a lot of dough doing outside work for the DeCenza machine that he understood how the guy could afford a place down here. Shortly before Doherty left the force Klinoff was canned for reasons that weren't entirely clear.

Once Doherty was out on his own, he lost interest in Klinoff or why he was sacked. But now he was hoping to reconnect with the former cop to see if he knew anything about Frankie DeAngelo's business interests in South County. It was a long shot, though the only play Doherty had at the moment. Since he and Klinoff were hardly pals when they were cops together, he wasn't sure the man would even talk to him now.

Doherty climbed out of the Chevy and saw no signs of anyone around the property. Still he went through the routine of knocking at Klinoff's door. He waited patiently, though like at DeAngelo's place in Cranston, he sensed from the get-go that neither Klinoff nor anyone else was at home.

A man in a neighboring yard was hosing down a boat resting on a trailer parked on its own plot of crushed shells. Doherty wandered over to see if he could scratch up something on Klinoff's whereabouts. When he got within earshot the man turned off his hose and gave him a weak smile. The neighbor was older, perhaps in his sixties. He wore a pork pie hat with a series of fishing flies attached to it, a hunting vest and loose fitting khaki pants. His face was marked by a series of broken blood vessels on his cheeks and nose.

"Do you know Alex Klinoff, the guy who lives in that house?" Doherty asked, pointing with his thumb at the neighboring cottage.

"Yep, I know him," was all the man said.

"Do you know where I can find him?"

"Works up in Wickford - in the boatyard. You'd best find him there if he isn't out fishin'."

"Does he usually come home at night?"

""Couldn't tell ya."

That was about all Doherty was going to get out of Klinoff's friendly neighbor. He thanked the man and got back into his Chevy.

Wickford was a twenty-minute drive up Route One from Great Island. He'd only been there once when he worked at Quonset before being drafted and sent overseas. Some of the married soldiers stationed at Quonset lived in government housing on the outskirts of Wickford village. After the war the housing went public and men now working at Quonset bought homes there for their new families. It was a pretty little town with a few food joints that sat right out over the watery inlet that flowed through it. A number of small commercial fishing boats went out into Rhode Island Sound from Wickford.

The town had some nice shops, a movie theater and all the other ameni-ties of a junior sized Arctic. It had grown up mostly on the business it got from the large number of people first stationed and later working at Quonset and Davisville. It was quaint enough that it now attracted some tourists in the summer and year-round residents not attached to the military bases.

Since it was near lunchtime Doherty stopped at a little seafood shack with tables that sat on a deck over the water. At a takeout window he ordered a bowl of clam chowder and a half dozen deep fried clam cakes. The space inside was chock full of locals and a few post-summer visitors. When his food was ready Doherty chose to sit at a vacant outdoor table. It was chillier than the day be-fore so he had the space to himself. This gave him time to think without the distraction of a lot of neighboring chatter.

He couldn't finish all the cakes so he returned to the girl at the window to ask for a doggy bag. While there he inquired about the location of the com-mercial boat yard. She sent him to the end of Main Street, the large avenue that was the chief artery into the village and abruptly ended at the water's edge. Although there were a fair number of boats moored there by the pier, he was told that the real working boatyard was across the waterway at the other end of the village. He retraced his route and crossed back over the small bridge that spanned the harbor. After couple of missed turns he eventually found the boatyard.

He parked the Chevy in a lot that abutted the seawall in front of a boat and boating accessories dealership. The yard was a short walk from the parking lot. There were a handful of pleasure and fishing boats out of the water propped up on stanchions. Once he was in the working yard he asked for Klinoff and was pointed in the direction of a skiff that sat up on stilts. The former cop was squatting under the boat running an electric sander along its hull. Doherty didn't think the man heard his approaching footsteps above the loud screech-ing of the tool.

When he got close Klinoff spotted him and cut off the power tool. He came out from under the boat, stretching his back as he did. Klinoff had gained a few pounds and lost an equal amount of hair since Doherty'd last seen him. Despite the coolness of the day he was sweating like a racehorse; his work clothes and skin were covered in paint dust; he did not look like a man who was enjoying his new vocation.

Doherty started to introduce himself, but was cut off when Klinoff said, "I know who you are. We were on the cops together, remember."

Doherty offered a half-hearted apology.

"What're you doin' down here? You're a little out of your jurisdiction aren't you?"

"I'm not with the West Warwick police anymore. I'm a private investigator now. My cases take me all over the state. Today one of them took me to Wickford to find you."

Klinoff responded with a harrumph but added nothing more.

"I need to talk to you about a guy named Frankie DeAngelo. Does that name ring any bells?" From the look that briefly crossed Klinoff's face he suspected it did.

"Why do you think I'd know anythin' about this chump?"

Doherty thought of how to phrase things without offending Klinoff, who had never been friendly toward him to begin with. "Because you're an ex-cop. You know what they say: once a cop, always a cop."

Klinoff picked up his sander and made a move to get back to work on the boat's hull. Doherty added a kicker. "I've been told that this DeAngelo is into a lot of illegal businesses, maybe even drugs. I heard that part of his operation is down here out of a place called Bonnet Shores. I was hoping a man with your background might be able to help me out."

Klinoff walked back and stood uncomfortably close to Doherty. "Look smart guy, I know you're only tryin' to blow smoke up my ass 'cause you think we're like blue buddies from bein' on the police together. But maybe I don't feel like singin' Old Lang Syne with you." The beads of sweat were running down the sides of Klinoff's face, carrying the paint dust with them. He was close enough that Doherty found the smell coming off him to be pretty rank. Still he stood his ground, sensing that Klinoff knew something that would help him get a line on DeAngelo.

"You haven't answered my question about Frankie DeAngelo. Do you know who he is?'"

Klinoff's face broke into a smile, almost against its will. He shook his head. "You're kinda like a dog that's got somethin' in its teeth aren't you. Look,

I can't talk right now. My boss sees me waggin' my jaws with you he'll be all over my ass. He's a little prick I could bend in half with one arm if I wanted to, but I need this job so I haveta kiss up. Why don't you meet me at a place down on 1A, not far from Bonnet Shores? The locals call it the Willows, but it's really named Twin Willows. I get off here at five. I'll meet you there about five-thirty - out on the deck. If I give you somethin' you can use, I'll let you buy me dinner."

Chapter Five

He had no problem finding the Twin Willows restaurant. It sat right on Route 1A where Klinoff said it would be. Though the place was surrounded by a couple of lovely willow trees, hence the name, it still looked like a roadhouse. The weather had turned cooler so after he parked the Chevy, Doherty retrieved his jacket from the back seat. If he and Klinoff were going to sit out on the deck he wanted to be comfortable.

Instead of going directly to the deck from the parking lot, he chose to enter through the front so he could check out the place. It was dark inside and the space had a low ceiling. A horseshoe-shaped bar dominated most of the restaurant, with a few tables for dining scattered around the edges. About a dozen people, mostly men drinking beer, were bellied up to the bar. They were all talking and laughing loudly – no doubt happy to be drinking away the end of a workday. There were a few women sitting among the men; they were receiving a lot of attention from the beery guys, some it wanted and some not.

Doherty drifted out to the deck where Klinoff was already ensconced nursing a bottle of Gansett. He took a seat on a wooden bench across from his former colleague. Klinoff was wearing his work blues with a light jacket over them and his shirtfront was still flecked with paint dust. His eyes were bloodshot, which might have been from the beer, though more likely from the paint he'd been blasting all day. He looked up and nodded at Doherty; no words of greeting were exchanged. A waitress came by shortly after Doherty parked himself and asked if he'd like a drink.

"I'll have what he's drinking," he said, pointing at Klinoff's beer.

As she began to move away from the table Klinoff said, "Hey sweetheart, can you bring me a shot of Old Smugglers along with another beer?" She gave him a wry look, clearly not pleased with being addressed as 'sweetheart'. Or maybe she had some history with him.

When she was gone Klinoff looked up from his drink and said, "You know, I never really liked you when we were on the cops together. You always seemed kind of conceited with all your war hero shit."

Doherty might have taken offense at this remark given that he'd seldom talked about the war or his role in it with the other cops. He knew the *Times* had written him up when he first came back to town, so his reputation preceded him. Doherty didn't recall doing anything to burnish it. But he was here to get information from Klinoff and wasn't about to queer things by getting into a beef about stuff that happened years ago.

"You were a good cop from what I heard. Why'd you leave the force so early?"

"I don't know," Doherty said vaguely. "I guess the job didn't turn out to be as interesting as I thought it would."

Klinoff smiled at him. "Too much dirty work for the machine, huh? I bet that didn't go down too well with a war hero like you." His allusion to how the cops were always at the beck and call of the DeCenza political machine was indeed the main reason Doherty quit the police force barely three years in. He didn't bother to respond to Klinoff's last remark, not wanting their conversation to go down that road.

"At least you got to leave on your own terms. Me, I got bumped out just when I was makin' some real dough. Changed my whole life around."

This time it would've been awkward for Doherty not to respond. "I don't understand," was all he could think of saying, keeping things cloudy while still moving them along.

The waitress arrived and dropped off the beer bottles and Klinoff's shot. He smiled at her but she didn't return the gesture. He lifted the Old Smugglers in a toast and said, "To West Warwick police days," and downed the shot in one gulp. Doherty raised his beer glass and took a swig in a half-hearted gesture of joining in the toast.

"You see, unlike like you, I was makin' some good side money doin' after-hour jobs for the machine. It didn't bother me none 'cause I knew how things were in West Warwick. And I wasn't the only cop doin' work off the books for the Judge and his people," he added defensively. Doherty sipped his beer and remained quiet.

The drinks had lowered Klinoff's defenses because he now leaned in and said, "I was workin' as a guard for this high stakes poker game. At that time it was bein' run by DeCenza's boy Tuohy. Do you know Tuohy?"

"Yeah, I know Angel. We've had some dealings over the years. I hear the Judge is thinking of running him for state rep next year."

"Jesus, you gotta be shittin' me." Doherty shook his head in response. "So anyways, I was gettin' paid good money to guard this here poker game. I mean there was nothin' to it. All I had to do was show up in my uniform, sit outside the door and make sure my sidearm was loaded. They only wanted me there in case somebody came by who had a reputation for shavin' cards or dealin' off the bottom of the deck. For the most part everythin' else was on the up and up. Just a bunch of local hot shots with money to burn."

"What happened to change all that?"

Klinoff shook his head as if to shake some bad memories out of it. "One night when I was on duty we got held up. Two guys showed up in ski masks with pistols in their hands. They got the drop on me 'cause maybe I was dozin' off a little. I don't exactly remember. Next thing I know they tied me up and gagged me. Then they went in and took all the money off the table – almost five thousand bucks according to Tuohy. And guess who got blamed for the whole thing? Yours truly. I mean there was nothin' I coulda done. I wasn't about to take a bullet over a freakin' card game."

"A week later I was fired from the force. And get this: they said they had to let me go because I was doin' private security work while still in uniform. There must've been five other guys doin' what I was doin', but because of the robbery I was out on my ass. Stood to reason the Judge was behind me gettin' shitcanned. Funny thing was he was the one that told Tuohy to make sure I wore my uniform when I was on guard duty. They thought my being there in uniform would scare away any unwanted players. But hey, when the Judge pulls your number in that town there ain't nothin' you can do about it."

"Are you living down here full-time now?"

Klinoff shook his head and took a large gulp from his beer. "After I got fired things kinda fell apart at home. I guess I was doin' a lot of drinkin' and my wife was always naggin' me about gettin' another job. I went through a long time of feelin' sorry for myself. She eventually took the kids and went back to live with her mother. Without any cash comin' in I couldn't keep ahold of the house in West Warwick. Before long the bank took it out from under me. The only thing I had left was the summer place on Great Island. So I winterized the cottage and moved down there full-time a few years ago. Now I'm livin' the bachelor life. Spendin' my days sandblastin' and paintin' the hulls on boats owned by rich assholes. It ain't like bein' a cop, but at least I'm alive. When I think about that night I realize I coulda been shot."

"Did they ever catch the guys who held up the card game?"

Klinoff leaned in even closer, close enough that Doherty could smell the whiskey on his breath. He said just above a whisper. "They were a coupla local guys who ran their mouths off about a big score they had from knockin' over the poker game. The stupid bastards were braggin' about what they'd done. Just between you and me, I heard after DeCenza's people caught up to them they was disappeared."

"And the money?"

"Tuohy got most of it back except for what those two nitwits already spent. Can you imagine rippin' off a poker game set up by the Judge in his own town and then crowin' about it? They coulda signed their own death warrants right when they took that money."

The waitress swung by again and the two men ordered another round of beers. This time she smiled at Doherty, which seemed to piss off his companion.

"Hey, do you ever see Sgt. Timilty anymore?" Klinoff asked out of the blue.

"As a matter of fact I've seen him quite a few times. He's now a partner in a big time investigations firm in Providence."

Klinoff shook his head from side to side. "He was a tough sonofabitch, but a good cop from top to bottom. That was real strange when he left the force. We all took him for a lifer."

Doherty broke the conversation for a few seconds to light up a Camel. He offered one to Klinoff but his companion waved him off. "It's actually because of Timilty, that I'm curious to find out what you know about this Frankie DeAngelo character."

"I don't follow."

"Well, like I said, Timilty works for this agency in Providence. One of his specialties is finding missing persons. It's what I do for the most part in my practice as well. Gus has been gone for a while and his partner is getting kind of antsy. So he hired me to find him. The only thing I got to go on so far is that Timilty was looking for a guy named Frankie DeAngelo. So if there's anything you can tell me about someone with that name operating down here it could help me figure out where Gus is and what he's up to."

It took Klinoff a while to digest all that Doherty had just fed him. The drinks had slowed his thinking.

"I'll tell you what I know, but this can't come back on me, understand." Doherty nodded his head in agreement. "You see I gotta live down here and I don't want nothin' that's gonna complicate my life."

He didn't know what Klinoff was hinting at with this last remark but let it slide now that the door to DeAngelo was about to open.

"First of all, everythin' I tell you comes to me secondhand. I mean I do have a police scanner at the house that I listen to from time to time just for curiosity's sake. So far nothin' about DeAngelo's ever come up on it. Given what he's doin' I figure he's payin' off people down here, possibly even some cops."

"And what is it that he's doing? I know he deals in hot goods. Is there more to it than that?"

"Yeah, if you consider drugs more serious than sellin' hot TVs and radios."

"You mean like reefer?"

"Yeah, reefer *and* smack. It's why he has a house down here. Apparently he gets most of his stuff delivered by boat. I don't know where it comes from - whether from Mexico or from right here in the U.S. I hear he's been bringin' in some large quantity."

Doherty mulled this over for a few seconds. He lowered his voice and said, "I don't see how he can be doing business like that without running afoul of the mob. It's my understanding that they pretty much control the drug traffic in this state."

"Beats me," Klinoff said. "I don't know who he gets it from or who he sells it to. But if he ain't doin' business with the wise guys then he's playin' a very dangerous game."

The wind had picked up off the water making it too cold to stay out on the deck any longer. Doherty offered to buy Klinoff dinner inside and he accepted.

They sat at the bar. Doherty had the fried flounder and Klinoff a lobster roll. They ordered another round of beers and kept their conversation to safer topics like baseball and mutual acquaintances from West Warwick days. From his tone it was evident that Klinoff missed his life back in the old mill town. As promised Doherty picked up the check for the food and all the drinks. He kept the receipt figuring he would expense it to Briggs and Timilty once the case was closed.

They shook hands out in the parking lot. As they did Klinoff said, "You know you ain't such a bad guy after all. I kinda wished we'd been friends back when we were on the force together." Although Doherty knew he would never have befriended someone as crooked as Klinoff, he couldn't help but feel sorry for him now. They agreed to keep in touch. Doherty knew they probably wouldn't unless they needed something from each other.

Chapter Six

Jack Moroni was sitting alone at a table in the back of the Shepard Tea Room when Doherty arrived. The place was filled mostly with salesgirls and housewives out on shopping excursions into downtown Providence. Moroni wore the kind of stern look on his face that must've been his stock and trade when he was handing out speeding tickets as a state cop. Doherty parked himself in a chair across from the Shepard Company's security chief and nodded a hello. Moroni was wearing a dark grey striped suit, a well-starched white shirt whose collar was biting into his thick neck and a club tie. His lacquered hair had captured a few more strands of gray since Doherty'd seen him last.

"I shouldn't even be talking to you," Moroni said. It was not the way Doherty wanted their conversation to begin.

"Why's that?"

Moroni turned his usual look into sterner overdrive, if that was possible. "Let's start with the fact that you shot and killed one of our employees last spring."

"Jesus, Moroni, the guy was a despicable human being who hurt people I cared about, including myself. Put that together with the fact he was an ex-Nazi and I'd say I did the world a favor."

"Maybe the world, but not the Shepard Company. How do you think it looked with all the papers blabbing about how Shepard's hired a Nazi to work in their store selling shoes? I'm the goddamn head of security. All anyone wanted to know was why my department hadn't done a better job of screening

Stanislaw Krykowski. I'll tell you who's probably happier than you that he's dead: the Outlet Company, that's who. Their main selling point now is, 'we don't hire Nazis'. Since the story broke we've had nothing but complaints from many of our customers as well as our suppliers, and not just the Jewish ones either."

At that moment a waitress came by to ask if the two men were going to have lunch. Moroni told her they would so she dropped off a couple of menus. She was young and pretty and gave Moroni a nice smile. Doherty was immediately jealous for no good reason.

"And, Charlene, could I have another cup of tea?" he asked as he handed her his empty cup.

"Sure, Mr. Moroni. Why don't I bring you a small pot." He gave her his approval. Doherty quickly asked for a cup of coffee as she was moving away from the table.

"Do you know all the girls who work here by name?"

"I ought to. I have to clear every one of them before they're hired. Since the events of last spring, I've been under renewed pressure to be more scrupulous about all our recently hired employees."

"I suppose I should apologize," Doherty said.

"Don't bother because I know you wouldn't mean it. And before you think I'm a total hard case, I'm glad you put Krykowski down. I was in the war too so I've got no truck with ex-Nazis living in this country. I just wish this particular ex-Nazi hadn't been an employee of our company. As far as my bosses are concerned, public relations always trump politics."

Charlene returned with a small tea cozy for Moroni. After setting it down along with Doherty's coffee she took their orders. The Shepard security man ordered the turkey club and Doherty opted for a bowl of tomato soup and a grilled cheese sandwich. Once she left Moroni poured some tea before indicating they could resume their conversation.

"I'm surprised I didn't get another introductory call from Gus Timilty. Weren't you afraid I wouldn't be willing to see you?"

Prior to connecting with the store's security chief last spring, Doherty'd used Gus as a way of getting his foot in the door at Shepard's.

"Well," he said, hesitating for a few seconds. "You see it's because of Gus that I wanted to talk to you."

"Is he in some kind of trouble?"

"I'm not sure yet. I've been hired to find him because he's missing. My assumption so far is that he's missing by choice."

Moroni looked confused. "I thought Timilty was working for some big investigations outfit over on Broad Street."

"He is. In fact it's now called Briggs and Timilty on account of Gus doing most of the important legwork."

"Wait a minute," Moroni held up his hand as if he were stopping traffic. "The Briggs in question wouldn't be a guy named Johnny Briggs, would it?"

"As a matter of fact it is. Do you know him?"

"Say no more. I knew Johnny Briggs when he was a low-rent insurance investigator working for Aetna right here in the city. We had a couple of unpleasant run-ins with them. Briggs wasn't above bending the truth on occasion to save his company a few bucks. Let's just say back then Johnny Briggs had some honesty issues."

Doherty smiled and lit up a smoke while waiting for his coffee to cool. "I get the distinct feeling that Briggs and Timilty did not go big time until Gus became a partner there. I think it's safe to say that Gus provides the kind of police connections and know-how that a guy like Briggs couldn't scratch up in a hundred years."

The food arrived and both men took a break to eat some of their lunch. Before leaving the table Charlene asked if they'd needed anything else. Doherty asked for another cup of joe.

"The reason I called you is that last time we met you made a reference to Gus having to leave the West Warwick police because of some trouble he got into involving a prostitute. I wanted to ask you for more details, but I figured one of these days I'd get the whole story directly from Gus. However, now that he's gone missing I thought it'd be a good idea to check out that angle before moving on."

Moroni was chewing his club sandwich very methodically. He did not speak until every morsel was devoured. His mother must've told him when he was a kid that it was impolite to talk with food in his mouth. Doherty waited patiently. Finally the man replied, "The way I heard it Timility was trying to get some girl out of the whoring trade. At the time she was turning tricks for a small-time pimp named Jimmy Ricks. I should mention that this pimp has since graduated into the big time. I don't know what Timility's interest was with this girl. Apparently he used his connections with some city cops to get certain charges against Ricks dropped. I assume it was in exchange for Ricks cutting the girl loose from his stable."

"Do you know if Ricks kept up his end of the deal?"

"I believe he did," Moroni said before taking another big chomp out of his sandwich. While Doherty waited again through the prolonged chewing process, he spooned up some of his tomato soup. It was house made and very good. Much better than the Campbell's he was used to.

"Do you happen to know what kind of charges Ricks was facing?"

"If I remember correctly, they had to do with trafficking drugs, not with selling women for immoral purposes. I doubt the city cops care much about prostitution as long as they continue to get paid off to look the other way. But selling drugs, that's another matter. It takes a truly crooked cop or one with a habit of his own not to take an interest in a smack dealer."

"So let me get this straight: there's a well-known pimp here in Providence selling drugs and running whores and the cops haven't done anything about him in the last five years?"

Moroni smiled for the first time, and not at Charlene. "Those things aren't my responsibility anymore. I'm no longer a state policeman. I now work as the head of security for the Shepard Company," he said with a sour tone. "My time arresting criminals like Ricks is long past. The city cops could arrest him if they wanted to, and no doubt one day they will. That is, when the Federal Hill people tell them that Ricks is no longer an asset to their organization. If, or when, that time comes, he will either end up doing time at the ACI or floating in the river. Until then he will continue to practice his various enterprises in our fair city unimpeded."

"Do you think there's still something going on between Ricks and Gus?"

"I really couldn't tell you. Gus' business with Ricks was five years ago; five years is a long time in the world of prostitution. Most girls don't last that long in the skin trade. On the other hand, the hookers I arrested often had a hard time leaving the game and getting a real life. Some don't because they can't live without the easy money, even when a substantial part of it goes to their pimps. Others stay in because they're hooked on drugs. As you can imagine, nobody has easier access to reefer and smack than pimps. If a girl gets too old and doesn't wind up in the morgue, her pimp will use her to recruit younger girls into the racket."

"Sounds like a pretty sad life. No wonder Gus was willing to use his clout to get some girl out of it. It's too bad it cost him his badge."

Moroni tilted his head in sympathy. "When you think about it there aren't a lot of other options for girls who aren't married to make the kind of money they can whoring. Some of the hookers I ran into had kids they needed to take care of. It's not a pretty picture, but it's a real one. I saw a lot of girls in similar fixes when I was with the staties. You bust them, the fines are paid, and they're back out street walking the very next night. Even the ones who do time, soon as they're released they're flatbacking again."

"If that's the case then whoever this girl was she must've meant something special to Gus - enough that she cost him his job as a police sergeant. Who knows, could be his latest search is taking him in a similar direction."

"Do you have anything else to go on?"

Doherty shook his head. "Not really. The only lead I've got so far involves a guy from Cranston named Frankie DeAngelo. From what I can tell, he's a low level booster and a fence. He unloads goods out of his apartment as well from a house down south along the shore. According to Briggs, Gus was looking hard for this DeAngelo. I recently learned that DeAngelo is in the drug trade as well, apparently as an independent operator."

"Well, for his own health I hope he's not moving any significant amount of illegal drugs. You do that in this state you're bound to get into trouble with the mob. Then you end up dead – or worse." Doherty wasn't sure what was worse than dead, but didn't want to speculate on it either.

"If you need any more help you can call me," Moroni volunteered. "I'll give you my home number because I can't afford to have anyone from the company know that I'm doing business with you. As far as they're concerned, you're still the guy who killed one of our employees."

"Is that why we had to meet here at the Tea Room instead of at your office?"

"Precisely," Moroni smiled. "And next time it may have to be even further away. I'm only helping you because Gus Timilty is a good guy and I don't want to see anything bad happen to him."

"Me either," Doherty thought but didn't say.

When he went to pay his share of the check, Mornoni told him to keep his money, that the lunch was on the house. He didn't know if dining in the Tea Room was part of Moroni's fringe benefits or the Shepard's man was picking up the check himself. He didn't bother to ask.

Chapter Seven

The next morning Doherty headed north out of West Warwick on Providence Street. Just over the line into Cranston, he stopped at a liquor store on Reservoir Avenue to pick up a pack of smokes and a six-pack of Carling Black Label, the lady's beer of choice. He turned left at Park and made his way toward the Village. A beat-up light brown Ford was parked in front of 34 Maple so he slid the Chevy in behind it and went to the door at 36.

Maureen Donovan answered after the second knock. She was wearing her all-white nurse's uniform, complete with her nametag and a little hat that sat on the top of her reddish blond hair. She was in her stocking feet. At first she was startled then pleased to see Doherty at her doorstep. "Well, aren't you a sight for sore eyes," was the first thing out of her mouth.

"May I come in?"

"Sure." She stood aside and let him pass into her side of the duplex.

He gave the kitchen a once over. A pile of dirty dishes was stacked in the sink and an open package of Wonder Bread sat on the kitchen table. The bleeding heart Jesus hadn't moved, nor emitted any more blood.

"Did you just get off work?"

Maureen looked at the clock. "No, I got off at eight but had to run a few errands before coming home. You know, pick up some food and take care of the electric bill – stuff like that. What have you got there under your arm?"

Doherty pulled the sixer of Black Label out of its paper bag and handed it to her. "Thought I'd replace the ones I drank the other day."

She looked at the clock again. It was still before noon. "Oh, what the hell, I've been up all night." She punched open the top of a can with a church key. Doherty joined her even though it was early to start drinking even by his standards.

"Nothing like a beer for breakfast," he said as he lifted his can in a toast.

"I ought have something to eat with this. I haven't had anything but coffee since seven last night. But first I've gotta get out of this uniform. Sometimes I feel like I spend my whole life in this damn thing."

"Would you like some help?" he asked, not bothering to mask his intentions.

She gave him a come-hither smile and said, "Do you get turned on by girls in uniforms?"

"Occasionally."

"I'll bet you knocked off a few of those WACs while you were in the service."

Doherty grinned. "Not too many. Most of the WACs looked like men. On the other hand, the nurses were a different story."

She crooked her finger and summoned Doherty into her bedroom. It was neat and plain with some extra throw pillows on the bed and a wooden crucifix on the wall directly over it. The room smelled of women's odors: perfume, face cream, hair spray and other female beauty aids. She turned her back to indicate she wanted him to unzip her uniform. Once he had, she let it slip slowly to the floor.

Moe was now clad only in a thin half-slip, a bra and white stockings held in place by a matching white garter belt. She put her thumbs inside the waistband of the slip and slid it off her hips. Then she raised one leg up onto the bed and began to detach her stocking from the garter belt. Doherty stepped in and relieved her of that task. He slowly rolled down each stocking over her toes and dropped them to the floor with the rest of her discarded clothes. When he was done she picked up the stockings and draped them over the footboard. Then she turned into Doherty's arms.

Before long he'd shed his clothes and they were in bed making love in a manner that felt surprisingly familiar. It was good even without the reefer and a six-pack of beers. When they were finished Doherty reached for his cigarettes, lit one and leaned back on the pillows. Maureen slid her head under his arm and rubbed her hand softly over his chest hair. As before, she stopped when her fingers wandered to the shrapnel scar just below his left shoulder. Then she reached up, took his cigarette and put it in her mouth.

"Would you like one?" he asked.

"No thanks. These non-filtered ones are too harsh for me." She handed it back to him. They lay there quietly, not wanting to think too much about what they'd just done. Doherty did his best to ignore the crucifix above his head.

"How come you're not married, a handsome guy like you?" she asked.

"I guess I haven't met the right girl yet."

"Ah, the stock-answer of every bachelor."

He shook his head. "Not every one. Some guys just don't like girls, or they don't want to be tied down. My barber's like that. He's not married and he probably has more sex than most married men."

"Is that how it is for you? More sex than most husbands."

Doherty laughed so that the smoke he'd just taken in made him cough. "To be honest with you, Moe, I haven't been with a woman like this in almost six months."

"Not counting last week?"

"You know what I mean. What about you? You ever think about getting hitched again?"

She sat up and looked at him. The covers fell from her chest and he found himself staring at her little breast buds. "It's hard to meet guys when you work a schedule like mine. Work all night, sleep all day; work all day, sleep all night. Having a son also keeps a lot of guys away. To be honest with you, except for an occasional tumble with Frankie DeAngelo, I've had a sex drought myself for some time now. That's why I was so accommodating with you. Don't get me wrong, I'm not complaining or anything. I mean I have my job, my own money and my parents to help me with Mark." She paused and then added in a quieter voice, "But a girl can get lonely sometimes."

Doherty put his arm around her and pulled her in close. They kissed as if kissing would make all their loneliness go away. It worked - at least for the moment.

"I suppose I'd like to get married again. I just haven't met the right guy. And even though I'm really enjoying this, I'm smart enough to know you're not him."

"What about all those doctors you work with at the hospital? Can't you snag one of them?" he asked as a way of removing himself from consideration.

She waved her arm dismissively. "Doctors and nurses are like oil and water. Don't get me wrong, the docs'll sleep with any nurse they can 'cause they all think they're God's gift to the world. For most of them, screwing a nurse is like putting another notch on the bedpost. Although most of the doctors are married, that doesn't stop them from flirting up the nurses. As for me, I'd never marry a doctor knowing I'd only end up like one of those wives - sitting at home while my husband was busy screwing his nurses."

"Sounds kind of sad."

"I guess. But that's the way it is at most hospitals. I find the best way to avoid all that stuff is to concentrate on my work and keep the MDs out of my pants. I've gotten pretty good at that." Doherty finished his cigarette but couldn't see an ashtray anywhere to stub it out.

"Here, give to me," she said. Maureen got out of bed and walked into the bathroom. He could hear the water running though she hadn't bothered to close the door. He slid out of bed and slowly dressed himself. When she returned she had a towel wrapped around her. She saw that he was fully dressed and went to the bureau to get some civilian clothes. She quickly put them on before carefully hanging her uniform on the closet door, brushing out the creases as she did.

"Are you hungry?" she asked.

"I could eat."

"Why don't we go for a walk? I could use the fresh air after being in the hospital all night. It'll give me a chance to show you around the neighborhood. After that I'll take you to a really good Italian restaurant for lunch. How's that sound?"

Doherty leaned down to take in his visage in the oval mirror on her bureau. He tried to straighten out his hair with his hand but wasn't having much success. Maureen giggled before handing him her comb. He thanked her and combed his hair down flat. When he was done he looked more presentable to the outside world.

She'd put on the same cuffed dungarees and Keds she'd worn last time. She accompanied them with a light sweater and a waist-length tweed coat she took off a hook by the door. It was cool out so Doherty zipped up his blue windbreaker. As they headed up Maple in the opposite direction from Park she took his arm.

They walked to the end of the street and then took a sharp left down a steep incline onto a rutted road that led to a larger thoroughfare.

"This is Dyer Avenue," Maureen explained. They turned right and continued along the much busier street. At the next corner Dyer intersected with another large street that Maureen informed him was Cranston Street. She then pointed to a large complex of buildings across the way and said, "There it is, the Cranston Print Works. The place my father has given the best years of his life to, or so he says. Have you ever seen anything like it?"

Doherty had to laugh. "As a matter of fact I have. I see mills that size everyday in West Warwick. Some of them are even bigger than this complex – or at least they were when they were still in operation."

Maureen Donovan looked disappointed so he asked her what went on at the Print Works to make her feel better.

"Cloth printing mostly. They say at one time this one plus the other mills owned by the Sprague family were the largest cloth printers in the world."

"Did your father tell you that?"

"No, we went on school field trips here. They'd take us through the plant and afterwards we'd sit in a cafeteria where they would tell us the history of the Print Works from the beginning. They made it sound like the whole industrial revolution began here."

Doherty shrugged. "I bet the people up in Lowell, Mass. might disagree with that."

"Did they ever take you on school field trips into the mills down your way?"

"No, they only took us through some dairy owned by a relative of the town's political boss. I suspect our school principals were told not to take us on field trips through the mills for fear no one would ever want to work in them once they saw what it was like. But that's neither here nor there now that most of them are closing down."

Maureen looked wistfully across the broad avenue at the Print Works complex and its signature bell tower and smoke stack. "Same thing here. They've been slowly moving parts of this operation down to North Carolina. My father is one of the old timers so he thinks he'll be able to hang on long enough to cash a pension check. For my folks' sake I hope he does. What about you, Doherty? Ever think of working in the mills when you were growing up in West Warwick?"

"Never," he answered emphatically. "My old man put in almost thirty years at the Royal Mill before his liver gave out. Don't get me wrong, lots of guys I went to school with went into the mills; some even left school early to do so. As for me, I always wanted something more out of life."

"Have you found it?"

"I guess so, thanks in part to Uncle Sam. Once the war was on and I got drafted, I saw that there was a lot more to this world than slaving away in a textile mill. I worked at Quonset Point for a while after I got out and then I was a cop for a few years. Neither one suited me like this job. I like being my own boss, even if I don't always know where my next paycheck's coming from."

They paused to take in the area around the works. A small, deteriorating church sat on Cranston Street across from the Print Works. "What's that building?" he asked.

"Oh, that's St. Bart's. I think it used to have a congregation but it hasn't been doing business since I've been alive. It was the Sprague Meeting House back in the last century when it was built. Later it was a church for the Protestants who lived in the neighborhood. We don't have too many of them around here anymore. Most people in this part of Cranston go to one of the big churches up that way," she said, pointing to a small hill on her left. "There's a large square a few blocks up Cranston Street where St. Anne's and St. Mary's face each other. St. Anne's is for the Irish, so that's where my family always went. St. Mary's is for the Italians. Kind of strange, don't you think? There being two big Catholic churches sitting right next to each other."

"You would think so, but it's the same in West Warwick. The Irish have their churches, the Italians theirs and the French-Canadians theirs. Plus every village in West Warwick has its own church. It's kind of provincial considering they're all Catholic churches."

They began to walk up Cranston Street away from the Print Works. Maureen pointed down the other part of Dyer, which was lined with side-by-side duplexes similar to the ones in the Village.

"Those were company housing for the people who worked in the plant just like mine was. This whole area was once called Spragueville after the original family that owned the Print Works. The Spragues were probably the most important family that ever lived in Cranston."

They crossed Cranston Street and she pointed to a prominent looking white mansion that neatly abutted the avenue. "That's the Sprague mansion. It was always part of our field trips. The Spragues started the original mill works and two of the Spragues served as governors of Rhode Island back in the 19th century. At one time there were two brothers who ran the mills. Then one became a U.S. Senator and the other stayed here to run the family's various operations. The one that stayed home was murdered somewhere not too far from here. Apparently his murder and the trial of the killer were really big deals back then."

"Murder usually is," Doherty said, speaking from experience.

"They say he was on his way back to the mansion from his farm just over the town line in Johnston when he was attacked by two men and bludgeoned to death. His bloody body was found lying in the snow on New Year's Day. Three brothers from this Irish family that ran a tavern that sat not too far from here were charged with the murder. One of them was convicted and got hanged for it. I've been told it was the last execution ever held here in Rhode Island."

"There must've been solid proof that the guy did it for him to be executed."

"Not according to my father. He said the guy was hanged 'cause he was Irish and his business was cutting into the Sprague's profits at their company store. He told me that this Gordon guy that got hanged had threatened the Sprague who ran the mill because Sprague used his influence to get the Irishman's tavern shut down. Supposedly it was a very popular place among the mill workers. On the field trips we were told that Sprague didn't like it that a lot of the workmen would take their lunch at this tavern where they'd knock down a few drinks before going back to work. The way my father tells it, the Spragues didn't like this Irish family because they also ran a grocery store where a lot of the wives of the workers bought their goods rather than at the company store because the prices were cheaper. For my father it's always about how the rich Yankees discriminated against us Irish back in the day."

They were standing now in front of the mansion admiring the newly painted white colonial home that stretched half a city block.

"Rumor has it that ever since then the mansion has been haunted. Some say it's by the ghost of the Sprague that got killed. Others say it's the ghost of the Irishman who was hanged for a crime he didn't commit. Those who say they've seen it think it's a woman. Possibly the wife of one of the Spragues."

"Did you ever see the ghost?"

"No. The only ghost I ever saw in the mansion was Ricky Kimball trying to slip his hand inside my blouse. I was thirteen at the time so there wasn't much for him to find. There still isn't as I'm sure you've noticed." They both laughed and Maureen took Doherty's hand and they continued down Cranston Street.

A few blocks along Maureen pointed to a brick building that abutted the street. A number of signs for professional offices adorned its façade. "That's my doctor, Dr. Cardi," she said pointing at a nameplate that read Alphonse P. Cardi, MD. "He delivered me and my sister, and he also delivered Mark. He's been our family doctor for over thirty years."

At the next big intersection they turned right, but not before she pointed out several large homes around the neighborhood. "This area used to be called Bull Town because it was where most of the overseers and supervisors at the Print Works lived. They said it was called that because a lot of them came over from England to work for the Spragues. I guess English people are sometimes referred to as bulls."

"John Bull is a symbol for England like Uncle Sam is for the U.S. I saw a lot of him on propaganda posters when I was doing combat training over there during the war," Doherty explained.

"My father says it was called Bull Town because the foremen in the plant acted like cops, always pushing the workers around and telling them what to do. I guess cops are sometimes called bulls."

"Yeah, they are, especially in prisons. During the Depression the cops who worked for the railroads that kicked hobos off trains were always referred to as railroad bulls. My uncle Patrick rode the rails for a while during the '30s.

He told me great stories about hopping freights and sleeping in hobo camps. I suspect the stories were better in the telling than in the living. But who am I to judge? Since I've been home I've heard guys talking about the war as if it was the best years of their lives."

Maureen stopped and looked hard at Doherty. "Maybe they were if the only thing they had to look forward to was going back to working in mills like our fathers."

Doherty didn't want to argue about the goodness or badness of war experiences. He knew that only one out of every five men who served in the military during the war ever saw action. So for many men being in uniform, away from home and out of harm's way was probably the best thing that ever happened to them. He knew it was true even for some guys who were in the heat of battle and lived to tell about it. They were stood drinks in bars for months afterwards as long as they had war stories to tell. It wasn't always their own war stories, but they were war stories nevertheless. There were times when he was tempted to do the same, but he didn't because it would only remind him of his buddies who didn't make it back.

They crossed over a railroad bridge and beyond it stretched acres of baseball fields. Below them was a large, full sized diamond and on the opposite side of that was another, smaller softball diamond. He realized they had walked a full circle because he could see the Village on the other side of the fields. Above the lower fields, at street level, was another baseball diamond. A group of young girls were playing kickball on that field. They wore their little gym outfits of shorts and sweatshirts. Many wore knee socks tucked into their sneakers. Maureen stopped and smiled at them.

"That was me not so long ago," she said wistfully. She pointed at the large school building across the side street from where the girls were frolicking. "That's Hugh B. Bain Junior High. My whole family went to school there. It's where Mark will go in a few years. Some of the kids I was in school with are now teachers there. Can you beat that."

The building was three stories high and much larger than the junior high in West Warwick where Doherty started his public school career. He didn't go there until halfway through eighth grade when his father could no longer afford to send him and his sister Margaret to parochial school. Although he felt out of place at first, after a while it was a welcome relief from the harsh discipline of Catholic schools. By the time he got to high school he fit right in. Now he looked back fondly on those school years.

"Were you a good student?" he asked Maureen.

She thought about the question for a moment. "Good enough. I liked science a lot, which was kind of unusual for girls back then. You know they always wanted to push us into the domestic arts or clerical stuff, but I kind of like the real subjects. Not too many girls went the science route. Some of the male teachers even tried to discourage me. I stuck with it 'cause I always wanted to be a nurse. And it wasn't just to 'help people', which I know is the stock line. I liked all the medical stuff too. I was a candy striper at Chapin Hospital when I was in high school. That's what really got me interested. My mother always encouraged me because she thought if I became a nurse I'd meet a nice doctor and marry him. Boy, was she wrong about that."

They stared at the junior high edifice for while until Moe said, "So are you hungry yet?"

"Hell, I was hungry when we left the house."

She smiled and took Doherty's hand. "Then you're in luck because Marcello's is right across the street." It was only then that he noticed a group of stores that lined the main street across from the school. In the middle of them was a place that advertised itself as Marcello's Italian Restaurant. There was a small parking lot on its left side and a three-step entrance that went into the restaurant.

It was warm inside and the whole place smelled of tomato sauce. They took off their jackets, hung them on hooks and slipped into a neighboring booth. It was nice to be inside after their walk.

A heavyset, dark skinned man wearing a white apron came to their table. He gave Maureen a big toothy grin that revealed a large gap between his front teeth. He had jet-black hair and looked like he was somewhere in his forties.

"Pasquale," Maureen said giving the man a big smile.

"Hello Moe," he replied.

"This is my friend Doherty. Doherty, this is Pasquale Marcello. He owns this joint." The name Pasquale reminded Doherty of the bakery where his mother went to work shortly after his father died. Pasquale's Bakery was now shuttered like a lot of other places in West Warwick.

Doherty shook hands with the man who said, "Please call me Pat. Moe likes to use my real name because it makes her feel like she's in an authentic Italian restaurant, like in Italy." His strong hand was meaty and calloused.

"How's that young boy of yours?" Marcello asked Maureen.

She shrugged her shoulders. "He's doing okay. School's going good but I gotta keep an eye on him when he's around the Village. I'm afraid he's going to get in with the wrong kids. You know, the ones that are always stealing stuff and breaking windows and streetlights. It's tough not having a man around." The restaurant owner gave Doherty a quick glance that he pointedly ignored.

"So what'll it be for you two?"

Doherty looked at the girl and said, "What do you recommend, Moe?"

She bit her lip and thought for a few seconds. "For lunch, I'd go with the meatball sub. Pasquale makes the best meatballs in town. He also does a terrific steak sandwich on the heal of an Italian bread."

They both ordered meatball subs. Maureen asked for a Coke with hers and Doherty opted for a bottle of Gansett.

"You know they brew that right down Cranston Street not too far from here."

"Really, I knew it was brewed in Cranston I just didn't know where."

"Yeah, when I was a kid some of my friends' fathers worked at the brewery. They probably still do. It's hard to miss. You can smell the place from a mile away."

Doherty chuckled. "And you don't drink your hometown beer."

"You noticed that, huh. I guess I prefer Black Label. Does that make me disloyal to Cranston?" He wasn't in a position to be judgmental about the girl's beer choice.

Marcello soon appeared with their drinks and sandwiches. The meatball sub was nearly a foot long and was dripping with tomato sauce. Maureen took a small container of grated cheese and sprinkled some on her sub. Doherty did likewise. Concerned about splattering red sauce all over his shirt, he carefully tucked his napkin into his collar. They were both starving so they ate greedily without much conversation. Pasquale returned little later to ask if the subs were good. They both shook their heads emphatically.

"Look, Moe. You have any real trouble with that boy of yours you bring him over here. I'll put him to work in the kitchen. That'll straighten him out."

When they were finished eating Doherty insisted upon paying the bill. While he did Maureen gave Pasquale a goodbye hug.

Next to Marcello's was a little bakery that was emitting wonderful smells of fresh dough baking. "When I was at Bain we used to stop in here every day after school to get fresh baked hermits. They were the best," she said.

"Where to now?"

She smiled and took his arm. "I got one more treat for you." They strolled down Gansett Ave toward Park until they came to small store, a shack really.

"This is Del's Lemonade. The original Del's. Have you ever had one?"

"Not really," he said. "I've seen their trucks parked by the ball fields in the summer."

"Well you're in for a real treat." Maureen ordered two small cups for them.

The frozen lemonade was like shaved Italian ice only finer, with a distinct lemon flavor to it. He found it unique and very refreshing after the meatball sub.

"C'mon, let's go sit by the field." She led him across the street and down a short incline to a small baseball field in front of the junior high. On the opposite side a section of the field was fenced off where a gym class of boys was playing softball in their gym suits. They sat on a bench and talked casually as they watched the boys.

"That's where the Little League games are played," she explained, pointing at the other diamond. "Mark just began playing this year. He's young compared to the other kids, but I think he's going to be a pretty good ball player. Did you play baseball a lot when you were young?"

"Yeah, I loved baseball. I played in high school and even went to one of those major league tryouts."

"Really," she said sounding impressed. "What happened?"

"I got drafted into the army. By the time I got back to the States my ball playing days were over. A couple of things happened over there that took my skills away."

"Like that scar on your shoulder?"

"That and one of my knees got jammed up. I couldn't run like I used to so any dreams I had about playing professionally were over."

"That's kind of sad."

"I suppose. It could've been worse. I could've tried out and had them tell me I wasn't good enough. At least this way I can always blame the war for me not making it to the majors."

"Maybe sometime you could come up and play catch with Mark." Maureen stopped abruptly, afraid she was pushing things too far. "Frankie gives him baseball stuff, but he never plays with him."

"I wouldn't mind tossing the ball around a little bit if I'm ever here when your son's not in school." That pretty much ended that line of conversation.

"Speaking of Frankie DeAngelo, I need you to give me a little more dope on him so I can get on with the business of finding my friend."

"What do you wanna know?"

"Please, Moe, don't play coy with me. Tell me about the people who come to see him – unusual people, not just his run-of-the-mill customers."

Maureen looked off into the distance where the gym class was wrapping up its softball game. "Most of the people who come to see Frankie are your typical collection of lowlifes looking to buy hot goods for cheaper than what they'd pay for them in a store. You know how things are here in Rhode Island when it comes to stolen merchandise. I try to avoid Frankie's customers if I can."

"You said *most* of the people are like that. What about the ones that aren't?"

The girl was uncertain as to what she could let on to Doherty despite their recent intimacies. "There were some colored boys who came around a few times. Boys in their twenties and thirties, not kids. We don't see many of their kind here in Cranston, especially in the Village."

"Can you describe these colored boys to me?"

Maureen bit her lower lip, not sure what she was getting herself into. "Well, the first time they came there were three of them. They were hard to miss. Parked this big cream-colored Cadillac right in front of our door. We never see cars like that in the Village either. One of the black boys was short and fat. He was almost as wide as he was tall. Had dark-skin and short hair. Another one was kinda tall and lanky, also dark. He wore a hat, like a fedora, only made out of straw with a feather in it. The third guy was very light skinned, lighter even than some Italians I know. He could've passed for white. He was good looking and was wearing one of those rags on his head."

"A do-rag. That's what they're called. Negroes wear them when they're trying to straighten their hair."

"I suppose. He must've been the boss because the fat guy opened the car door for him like he was his chauffeur or bodyguard."

"Then what did they do?"

"Nothing really. They went into Frankie's, stayed for about twenty minutes and left. While they were inside a few people from the neighborhood gathered around outside to admire their car. When they came out they weren't carrying anything from Frankie's place, which is rare. Most people come to him to buy hot goods: you know, like toasters or mix masters, TVs or suits. Something of value. These guys looked like they were leaving empty-handed, or at least without anything you could see. Mark was the one who saw them first and he called me to the window. I don't think my son'd ever seen colored men that close before. I mean he sees them on TV in baseball games and boxing matches, but there aren't any coloreds living here in Cranston. I've hardly ever seen them myself outside of the hospital."

"And that was the only time they came?"

"The whole three of them, yeah. The fat one came back maybe twice more but he wasn't driving a big fancy car those times. Just some old Chevy. It was the same thing; he'd go into Frankie's, stay for ten minutes or so and leave, not carrying any merchandise – least none that we could see."

"No other strange visitors?"

"Hell, Doherty, they're all strange, but nothing like those colored boys. Most of his customers are your usual collection of stumblebums."

"Is there any chance I can get into Frankie's place to take a quick look around? I won't take or move anything."

"Jesus, Doherty, you're not making this easy for me are you. I'm starting to think maybe you've been using me just to get at Frankie."

"Please, Moe. This is important. Frankie DeAngelo is the only lead I have right now for finding my friend."

Maureen didn't say anything. She stood up and said, "Let's go back to the house."

Chapter Eight

Conversation was at a minimum as they walked quickly back into the Village. It was still early afternoon so things were quiet around the identical duplexes. Once inside Maureen moved a chair over to one of her doorways, stepped up on it and retrieved something from the ledge above the door. When she stepped down she was holding a key in her hand.

"He gave me this just in case."

"In case of what?"

She shook her head. "He never said. All he said was I could use it to take whatever I wanted in case he didn't come back." She then led Doherty outside to DeAngelo's door. They quickly slipped inside.

Structurally Frankie DeAngelo's side of the duplex was a replica of Maureen's only in the exact opposite configuration. But that was where all similarities ended. There were boxes stacked everywhere: on his kitchen table, on all of the counter tops, even atop the refrigerator. Where there weren't boxes there were household appliances all covered in plastic. His apartment resembled a small appliance store. The only room not consumed by merchandise was the bathroom, which otherwise was a smelly mess. The downstairs bedroom was filled with boxes and was itself pretty untidy; an unmade bed sat in the center of it with dirty sheets and clothes scattered about.

Maureen stuck her head in and said, "Jesus, do you believe the condition of this shithole?" She then started for the door.

"Where're you going?"

"I'm gonna get some stuff to clean his bathroom with. No human being should have to use a bathroom like that. Don't touch anything while I'm gone."

Doherty drifted upstairs where there were two bedrooms off a short hall. The door to one was closed and padlocked from the outside. He assumed this was where DeAngelo kept his high priced goods like TVs, radios and phonographs. He walked into the other bedroom. It was devoid of boxes and almost looked lived in. The bed was unmade and probably hadn't been for some time. He wondered if this was where Moe and DeAngelo *tumbled* or whether it was at her place. As he was snooping around he heard her return. She started running water into the tub in the grungy downstairs bathroom.

Doherty opened the closet door in the second bedroom. Fortunately, the closet had a pull cord that switched on a plain light bulb. The hanging rack was jam-packed with suits of different sizes, textures and qualities. All of them were covered with plastic bags. He knelt down and examined the bottom of the closet. It was covered with shoeboxes containing new, name-brand shoes, some of high quality, others not so much. Like the suits, they were in a variety of sizes.

The shelf that ran along the top of the closet was also crammed with shoeboxes. He pulled a stool over to stand on so he could get a closer look at these. When he stepped up on it something didn't feel right. The stool wouldn't balance correctly and he was afraid it might topple over. Doherty stepped down and looked more closely at its legs. They seemed perfectly okay – none was loose and they were all of the same length. He placed the stool back into a new position but when stepped up again he had the same uneasy feeling.

Meanwhile he could hear Moe singing as she cleaned DeAngelo's bathroom. This time he moved some of the shoeboxes on the floor out of the way so he could see why the floor wasn't right. Once he had he noticed that at least three planks were loose. He took out his pocketknife and slid it into the crack of one of the loose floorboards. With some encouragement it lifted up from the others. However, it did not leave him enough space to slide his hand in. In order to do that he would have to move more shoeboxes and lift up the other loose planks. That didn't seem practical at the moment.

He returned the plank he'd pried up into its place, piled the shoeboxes back on top of it as they had been and decided to search the rest of the room instead. He slid open some drawers in a chest standing against the wall facing the bed. Inside one drawer was a large collection of cuff links, tie tacks and tie clasps. Inside another was a variety of watches, some cheap knock-offs of expensive ones, others looked like the real thing. The lower drawers held women's jewelry of various qualities. Not being an expert on jewelry, Doherty had no idea what their worth was. He assumed most of it was of the costume variety otherwise DeAngelo would have put them in the padlocked room.

Just then Maureen stuck her head in. "Have you found anything interesting?" She stood in the doorway wearing a pair of pale blue rubber gloves that stretched almost to her elbows. She saw him staring at them and said, "As a nurse I need to keep my hands soft and sanitary. I wouldn't want to bring Frankie's bathroom grime into the hospital."

"To answer your question, everything I've found here is interesting. However, I haven't found anything that could help me with my case."

"You haven't snatched any goods, have you?" She smirked. "Sorry about that. Not to be a pest or anything, but it's getting late and Mark'll be home from school soon. I don't wanna have to explain you to him."

Doherty nodded. "I understand." They descended to the first floor and out the door. Maureen made sure DeAngelo's front door was firmly locked. They stepped into her side of the duplex. He stood beside the door as she took off the rubber gloves and placed them and her cleaning materials under the kitchen sink.

"Is there anything else that Frankie told you to do 'in case'?"

Maureen hesitated for a moment. "He gave me a phone number. Said if there was any trouble here I should call this guy Jimmy." A full twenty seconds elapsed before she added, "I'll get you the number. I keep it in my address book with all my other numbers so nobody'll think it's anything special." She wrote down this Jimmy's phone number on a slip of paper and handed it to Doherty. He turned toward the door.

"Will I see you again?" she asked.

"I certainly hope so. Why don't we make a time so I don't just drop in on you unannounced like today?"

Maureen smiled. "How about next Tuesday? I've got the day off and I can arrange for Mark to go to my mother's after school."

"That sounds nice. And thanks for letting me into Frankie's place."

"Doherty, next time you come you don't have to bring a six-pack to get in the door."

"I'll remember that."

She crossed the room and slid into his arms. They embraced and kissed deeply before he left. He didn't know what this all meant and didn't want to think too deeply on it either.

Chapter Nine

I t was just after three when Doherty returned to West Warwick. He was a little wiped out from the meatball sub and the beers he'd drunk earlier in the day than he was used to. He decided to stop in at the office to see if anything was shaking. There were no notes left on either the outside desk or on his larger one in the inner office. He did a quick check of the answering machine; the only message was from Agnes asking if he wanted her for anything. Since Rachel had caught up on all the paperwork the only thing he needed from Agnes was advice on whether or not he should be getting involved with Maureen Donovan. That wasn't advice he'd solicit over the phone.

He settled himself in his office where he took a seat in his swivel chair, lit a Camel and rested his feet in their usual spot atop the desk. After a while he pulled out a note pad and began to scribble down some ideas.

Gus Timilty was forced to resign from the West Warwick PD five years ago because he got mixed up with a pimp from Providence named Jimmy Ricks. Although Doherty always intended to ask his old mentor about that business, he'd never gotten around to it. In time Gus became so enamored with his new role at Briggs and Timilty he no longer wanted to revisit his days with the police force down here.

While working on a case last spring, thanks to Gus, Doherty'd made the acquaintance of Jack Moroni, the former state cop, who was now the head of security at the Shepard Company. Moroni made it clear at their recent lunch that he thought Timilty had gotten a raw deal being let go from the force for trying to help some girl get out of the sex trade. That rescue mission cost Gus his sergeant stripes after thirteen years on the force. Now some five years later Gus suddenly disappears, ostensibly while tracking down a small-time *entrepreneur* named Frankie DeAngelo, who sold drugs as well as goods that 'fell off the back of a truck'.

Maureen Donovan informed him that Timilty recently came by DeAngelo's place looking for her neighbor just as Doherty did. Then she reluctantly disclosed that DeAngelo suggested she contact a guy named Jimmy in case something bad happened at his Cranston apartment or if he suddenly disappeared. On top of that she laid out a description of a group of Negro customers that visited at DeAngelo's place not once but three times. And each time they left carrying no visible merchandise. From her description of these men Doherty had a hunch one of the three dark-skinned visitors was Jimmy Ricks, the same pimp that Gus had helped out of a jam.

In putting these pieces together Doherty concluded that the trail Gus was following ran through Frankie DeAngelo back to Jimmy Ricks and possibly to the girl he'd rescued. If that were the case it made sense that Gus wouldn't want his partner Johnny Briggs or anyone else from their operation knowing what he was up to. The first question nagging at Doherty was why a guy as smart as Gus would put his career as a cop at risk by doing a good deed for some nameless whore and her lowlife pimp? This girl must've meant something special to Gus. Either that or she had something on him and used it to force him to go to bat for her pimp. Whoever she was she was likely the key to this whole case.

The second question is if she is still an important person in Gus' life then how does DeAngelo get linked to Ricks, her former pimp? Is there a connection between these two beyond the fact that Ricks appears to be one of DeAngelo's customers – most likely buying drugs from him? As a PI Gus would not've been interested in either man's drug transactions. There had to be something more to it for him to be so intent on finding DeAngelo. Doherty figured if he could make contact with one of these guys it would help him locate Gus. Since he'd been unable to find neither hide nor hair of DeAngelo, his best move now would be to talk with Ricks. The problem was he had no idea of how to go about doing that.

He'd lost track of time. When he looked at the clock it was almost six. Normally he would've gone home and thrown some slop together for dinner. But the situation with Gus coupled with his day at Maureen Donovan's left him feeling like he didn't want to be alone with his thoughts right now. Instead of heading to the apartment he walked up Washington to Main and ducked into Duffy's, Arctic's most popular Irish tavern in a town renowned for its Gaelic watering holes.

By this time the day shift mill workers would be into their second or third round at Duffy's. Most days a good number of the Micks who still had jobs in the mills would gather here to drink and complain about work until it was time to drag themselves home to fight with their wives. On a few occasions the wife would appear at the door looking for one of them. Or more often, she would send one of her sons to guilt pappy into stumbling home with him.

Doherty's father had spent many an evening passing a good portion of the family grocery money across the bar at Duffy's. Once he was old enough his mother would send him to fetch the old man home. Later, he refused his mother's requests, preferring to let Peter Doherty drink himself into a stupor. At least that way his father would pass out as soon as he got home saving Doherty, his sister and his mother from having to listen to him rant about how unfair life was. All those nights in taverns eventually rotted out his father's liver. Then the cancer set in.

There was a goodly crowd tonight at Duffy's. Doherty knew quite a few of the customers even though he'd never worked a day in the mills. Some of them were old enough to have worked with his father; others were guys Doherty'd gone to school with until they quit to get their working papers or went into the mills after graduating. With the bigger operations in West Warwick closing down, most of the younger men would be unemployed sooner rather than later. Because of that they drank harder and complained louder about how the town's days as an important mill town were coming to an end.

A fellow named Kevin Meany, who Doherty'd played baseball with in high school, was working the taps tonight. He bought Doherty a shot of Jameson, but didn't have time to stick around for anything more than a cursory greeting. Not being a mill boy or a cop any longer, Doherty was excluded from the talk in Duffy's. He liked it that way. It allowed him to drink in peace.

After he drained his shot and a 'Gansett chaser, he ordered a hamburger to settle his stomach and keep his next beer company. Feeling generous he stood a round for Meany and his pals so he wouldn't be a complete foreigner in Duffy's. By eight things began to get rowdy so Doherty took this as a sign for him to amble on home. Once out on the street the sobering effect of the night air persuaded him to leave the Chevy parked by the office and walk to his apartment. It wasn't far and as a rule Doherty preferred to walk whenever he could.

At home he was confronted with two sights that seriously put him off. One was of Rachel curled up asleep on his sofa. The other was of a small TV balanced atop one of his bookcases. The TV had a rabbit ear antenna on top providing some hazy reception for a comedy show that was accompanied by an annoying laugh track. Doherty'd always been pretty comfortable not having a TV in his apartment. He was aware of some of the more popular shows that now crowded the airwaves, but he still preferred reading or listening to the radio than sitting bug-eyed staring at a boob tube. Not wanting to wake Rachel, he simply lowered the volume. Before sacking out himself he found an extra blanket and threw it over her.

His day with Maureen coupled with Rachel's unexpected presence in the apartment left him in a quandary. Although they'd had a pretty active sex life before the assault, he and Rachel hadn't renewed their intimacies in the five plus months since. At first he thought the events of last spring would be a deal breaker between them. When she first returned to his life he was elated. However, things between them have been strained ever since. He couldn't figure out how he should act around her or what she wanted from him. On those rare occasions when they did spend time together they would talk about anything and everything except what had happened that night. Since the perpetrators of the attack were men he'd been tracking, Doherty couldn't help but feel responsible for Rachel's condition. There was no way he'd ever be able to escape that.

He climbed into bed and picked up the book he'd just started reading. After finishing Steinbeck's take on the Cain and Able story, he was now reading a war novel called *The Naked and the Dead*. It was the first book of its kind he'd read since being discharged in '46. It was about a platoon of American soldiers fighting against the Japs on some islands in the Pacific. He'd heard tales from guys who served in that theater and even from some who'd been captured by the Japs and put into prison camps. It didn't make him feel any better about what he'd been through in Italy, though he was glad that the fighting in the Pacific ended before guys like him got shipped over there.

One part of the book that did ring true was how the hard-nosed sergeant was the real leader of the platoon while the lieutenant just out of OCS was clueless about leading men in combat. Sometimes Doherty thought wars were designed so sergeants could show their true mettle while candy ass junior officers won decorations.

The book kept flipping back to the lives of the main characters in the U.S. before they went into the service. He liked these backstories. They gave him a sense of who these men were in the real world. It was funny when he thought about how some soldiers were very important people in civilian life, yet would be the first to cower in combat, while other guys who were nobodies back home did things in the heat of battle that were above and beyond the call of duty.

Doherty liked to think he was one of those guys and that's why the army awarded him the medals that they did. But secretly he knew he did some of the things he did in combat because he was too afraid or ashamed not to do them. War often made men do things because they were afraid of what their fellow GIs would think of them. Sometimes he was more afraid of embarrassing himself than he was of the enemy. Maybe that was real cowardice – the fear of not acting bravely in front of the men in your platoon, most of whom acted the way they did for the same reason. He guessed that was what all the training was about. Doing what you had to for men you served with even if you didn't like them and wouldn't ever be their friend outside of the army. You did it simply because you were part of a team.

While he was ruminating on these strange concepts his eyes began to flutter. He tried to push on with the novel but found himself reading the same passage over and over again. He finally gave in and flipped off the nightlight. Doherty was in a pretty deep sleep when Rachel slipped in under the covers and cuddled up beside him. He didn't know if he should do or say anything. He was also worried that she might smell Maureen on him. In the end he was too drowsy to do either so he went back to sleep.

Chapter Ten

In the morning Doherty woke to the smell of bacon cooking. His head felt a little foggy from too much alcohol and not enough sleep. He staggered to the bathroom and did his business. When he came out Rachel was standing by the stove with an apron on.

"Would you like your eggs fried or scrambled?" she asked.

"Fried, over easy please."

"You snored a lot last night. Probably from drinking too much." It was a comment Doherty'd heard his mother hurl at his father dozens of times. In her case it was usually an accusation. Rachel stated it more as a fact of life. After all, it was his bed she'd come into it without being invited so he had every right to snore as much as he wanted.

He sat down at the table in his boxers and undershirt while she served him a plate of bacon, eggs over easy and toast. She set a mug of black coffee by his elbow and then joined him with a plate of the same combo in a slightly smaller version.

They ate in silence for a while, neither one of them wanting to acknowledge that last night was the first time they slept in the same bed together in over five months. Rachel talked nervously about her work at the deli. She described how each day when she was carving up a corned beef or meatloaf she secretly fantasized about slashing her mother's throat with the carving knife. Rachel and her mother didn't get along too well and things had only gotten worse since the attack. And now, without her teacher's salary, her chances of getting out of her parents' house to live on her own were pretty remote. It was why she came to sleep at his place in West Warwick a few nights a week. He wanted to respond sympathetically, but his mind kept wandering back to his day with Maureen Donovan. He knew he should feel guilty, and probably would have if his relationship with Rachel hadn't turned from one of love to one where they acted more like old friends.

"So what're you working on at Doherty and Associates? I haven't seen any paperwork on the secretary's desk lately."

He was hesitant to tell Rachel about Johnny Briggs hiring him to find Gus, and was determined not to bring Maureen Donovan into the conversation under any circumstances. He stalled by getting up and pouring himself another cup of coffee. He asked Rachel if she wanted more. She asked for a half cup.

"You remember Gus Timilty, don't you?" he began.

"Sure. He was like your rabbi when you were a cop, right?"

"Rabbi?"

"Just an expression meaning mentor, advisor, confessor, however you want to interpret it."

Doherty was searching for the right words to explain the case so as to give Rachel the impression he was confiding in her when he really wasn't – not fully anyway. He understood it was what she needed at the moment.

"Well Gus has gone missing and his partner Johnny Briggs has hired me to find him. He gave me two hundred bucks to get started, but wants to keep the case off the books. He's afraid if anyone in his outfit finds out their best investigator is missing it would be bad for morale. And if word got out it would be even worse for business."

Rachel nodded her head. It was the first time in months she seemed interested in one of Doherty's cases. "Do you have any leads?"

"Just one so far. What I know is that Gus was on the trail of some small-time booster named Frankie DeAngelo. This guy sells hot goods out of his apartment in Cranston and apparently has another place down in South County near Bonnet Shores. Problem is no matter what I do I can't seem to pick up this guy's scent, either up here or down there. A lot of people know him, but nobody's seen him in a while." He purposely did not mention that one of those people was the girl he went to bed with the day before.

"So what're you going to do?"

Once again Doherty wasn't sure if he wanted to let Rachel in on the course of action he was contemplating. "About five years ago when Gus was still a cop he got mixed up with a Negro pimp in Providence named Jimmy Ricks. From what I've been able to piece together, he fixed something up with the Providence police for this pimp in return for getting a girl out of the skin trade. His reward for doing so was being fired from the West Warwick police force. Though technically he was asked to resign. Now it seems this DeAngelo I just mentioned has had some recent dealing with Ricks, or so I suspect. I'm thinking if I can get to Ricks then maybe I can locate DeAngelo and through him find Gus."

Rachel picked up their now empty plates and walked them over to the sink. When she returned she lit a cigarette. He joined her with one of his own.

"You don't know anything about pimps and prostitutes, so how're you going to get in touch with this guy? Are you thinking about approaching him as a customer?" There was a time when Rachel would have made such a comment in jest just to provoke him. Those days were now past.

This was the moment Doherty hadn't been looking forward to. "I was hoping that maybe that jazz musician you introduced me to up at the Café Medici, the fellow you called Tango, would be able to help me."

"Dave Tancrene? Why would Tancrene know anything about some downcity pimp? Tango's a musician, not a street hustler."

"I just thought …"

"You just thought what?" Rachel's voice had taken on an angry edge. "That because Tango and this Jimmy are both Negroes they must know each other."

"Well hell, Rachel. I know just about every Irishman here in West Warwick. If somebody wanted to talk to a person down here I could probably arrange it."

"Jesus, Doherty, you are some piece of work. Providence is not exactly West Warwick; it's a goddamn city. You think that because Tango and this other guy are dark-skinned they must naturally be acquainted. And then what? Suppose Tango does you this favor. How are you going to repay him? By getting him involved in your dangerous business. Is that how you work, Doherty? Using innocent people to do your dirty work for you."

He knew her harangue was no longer about asking Dave Tancrene to help him connect with Jimmy Ricks. It was about blaming him for what happened to her that night on Federal Hill. Despite months of Rachel reassuring him that what had occurred was not his fault, it was now clear that she really did hold him responsible. If Doherty had not purposely antagonized a group of Polish ex-Nazis, Rachel would never have been dragged into his nasty business.

Ignoring her tirade, as calmly as possible he said, "I'm going up to the Medici tomorrow night to see if I can talk with Tango. Would you like to come along? It's been a long time since we've been out and that was always one of your favorite night spots."

Rachel stood up and leaned on the table. She gave him an unpleasant look and said, "No thank you." She then turned and walked into the living room.

He followed her. "Is there anything you'd like me to tell Tango on your behalf?"

When she turned around her expression was one of pain mixed with anger. "Yeah, you can tell him what an asshole I think you are!"

Ten minutes later, dressed and with her goods under her arm, Rachel left the apartment, slamming the door loudly on her way out.

Chapter Eleven

H e could hear the strumming of a banjo long before he opened the red door at the Café Medici. It was not one of his favorite instruments. A lot of southern boys played it in the service, often not very well. Over time the clanging, bell-like sound of it got on Doherty's nerves. It was an association memory he preferred to forget.

A burly fellow met him at the café door and informed him that the cover charge for the club was now three dollars to help pay the musicians. However, since it was already after nine he dunned Doherty only two bucks for the privilege of listening to music he didn't especially like.

On the stage were two guys about college age dressed in matching blue and white striped short sleeve shirts. One was playing a guitar while the other was strumming the banjo. Between them stood a very attractive girl with long black hair in a tight fitting, rose colored dress that had some elaborate embroidery across the chest area. They finished the song they were playing by stomping their feet on the stage. The crowd gave them a hardy applause, something they hadn't done for the musicians the last time he was at the Medici. Perhaps the cover charge made the patrons more responsive to the music.

As Doherty scanned the room looking for Tango, the group on stage began a slow ballad that featured the girl as a soloist. Her voice had a lovely timbre to it and the room dropped into a quiet mood as she poured much emotion into her delivery. The song had something to do with a girl who has left her lover and is now five hundred miles away on a train. Despite his general disinterest in folk music, Doherty found himself transfixed by her delivery. It also gave him a chance to locate two Negroes sitting at a table to the right of the stage near an exit door. They were the only dark folks in the club so he was pretty sure one of them was Tancrene. When the song ended the girl's performance was greeted with shouts and whoops from the crowd. He took the opportunity to ease his way through the close-set tables to where Tango was sitting.

He grabbed a free chair and pulled it over and sat down with the two Negro men. When he did they both looked at him quizzically. He stuck his hand out in Dave Tancrene's direction, reminding him that he was a friend of Rachel Katz and they had met before. Once recognition set in the jazz musician took his hand and greeted him warmly. Tango was wearing the same black pork pie hat and goatee he had last time they met. The folk trio was about to launch into another song so Doherty very quickly asked Tango if they could speak in private. He agreed. Then everything said afterwards was drowned out by the music onstage.

The group introduced what they described as an original song about Mexico. The chorus stuck in Doherty's head for the rest of the night.

Mexico, why did I go, this I never will forget
If it hadn't been for a dancing girl, I think I'd be there yet

The folk singers finished their set on a raucous note and the audience went wild. Or at least as wild as people would allow themselves in a beatnik coffeehouse. As the members of the folk group passed through the crowd, they shook hands and hugged several people, which indicated that the boisterous audience was made up of friends or if they were still in college, fellow students.

Before Doherty could engage Tango in any conversation the bass player excused himself, saying he had to prepare for his set. He suggested that Doherty join him backstage afterwards. Doherty might have been miffed at being put off, though at least now he could enjoy the jazz set while getting his money's worth from the cover charge.

A short, perky young woman with close-cropped hair came by to ask if he'd like anything to eat or drink. Doherty ordered a café au lait and a piece of crumb cake. The jazz group was introduced as the East Side Quartet and they immediately launched into an up-tempo number that featured a long, beautiful solo by the white flute player. The coffee and cake arrived during the quartet's second number. Doherty sat back and relaxed for the first time all day. The confrontation with Rachel had put him on edge since morning. The set wound up a half hour later to tepid applause from the remaining customers. Apparently there weren't a lot of jazz enthusiasts among the college kids that made up the bulk of the crowd.

A few minutes after the group left the stage the waitress came by to say that Mr. Tancrene would like him to join them in the back room. He followed her down a narrow hallway that opened into a larger space whose four walls were festooned with posters for musical shows at the Medici as well as the Newport Jazz Festival and other Rhode Island venues. Sitting around a small table on a number of mismatched chairs were the three folksingers, the jazz musicians and two older people. Tango introduced Doherty all around. The older couple were the husband and wife owners of Café Medici.

The drummer from the jazz trio lit up a thick reefer and began passing it around among the group. The two male folksingers had taken off their striped shirts. One was wearing a white T-shirt, the other a sleeveless undershirt. The girl with the beautiful voice had her long dress hiked up above her knees showing a lot of white thigh. Doherty even caught a glimpse of her pink panties. When the reefer cigarette came his way he passed it on explaining that he had a long drive home. No one seemed to mind and thankfully no one asked him if he was a cop. Apparently any friend of Tango's was automatically a friend of theirs.

The flute player didn't partake in the smoke either. He stood in a corner away from the sitters contenting himself with an occasional hit from a hip flask. The shorthaired waitress reappeared with a tray full of coffee cups that she set down on the small table. She took a quick drag on the reefer before leaving the room. Doherty couldn't follow much of the conversation; it was mostly about music and musicians he'd never heard of. In time another reefer began to circulate. The conversation became more disjointed, punctuated by lots of silly laughter. He was afraid he wouldn't be able to engage Tango in a serious exchange before everything degenerated into the ridiculous. Meanwhile he couldn't take his eyes off the female folksinger's long, slender legs.

When he caught Tango's attention he motioned from them to step out into the hallway. The goateed Negro took one more hit from the reefer before excusing himself from the group. At this point no one seemed to notice their exit, nor care. In the dimly lit hall Tango gave Doherty his friendliest smile, one that was surely reefer enhanced.

"Tell me, man, how's Rachel doing? I haven't seen her here in months. She used to come to the Medici almost every Friday night."

Doherty didn't know where to begin in explaining Rachel's condition. "She's doing okay, under the circumstances," he said knowing that Tango probably wasn't aware that her circumstances involved rape. He figured the guy knew that they'd been brutally attacked and robbed on Federal Hill by what the newspapers identified at the time as 'unknown assailants'.

"She doesn't like to go out at night if she can help it. We're not really dating anymore, though we're still good friends," he added, not even sure if that were true after her angry outburst that morning.

"How about you? I heard you took a hard one on the head."

"I'm pretty much healed. The doctors said I was lucky. If I'd been hit a few inches to one side or the other they might've cracked my skull."

"Damn, man."

The two men stood and looked at each other for a few moments without saying anything. Tango had a sympathetic look on his face, or maybe it was just the reefer swirling around inside his head. Doherty paused, giving Rachel a chance to remove herself from the conversation.

"I need to ask a favor of you," he began. "And if you can't do it, there'll no hard feelings or anything."

Tango smiled again. "Sure, man, ask away."

"Do you happen to know a pimp here in Providence named Jimmy Ricks?"

The smile immediately left Tango's face. They were now in real time not reefer time. He nodded. "Yeah, I know that cat. Wish I dint, but I do."

"Do you mind if I ask how you know him?"

"Me and the boys do some gigs now and then at a club over on the South Side where Ricks and his *employees* hang out. It's called Club Mocambo. Our flute player Cecil won't go there with us. He says he doesn't feel comfortable when it's all black. He also doesn't like being where illegal things are going on."

"You mean like where reefer is being smoked in the back room?"

The two men laughed. "Cecil's kinda selective about what illegal things he'll tolerate and what he won't. I think 'cause he doesn't smoke himself, he can waive that objection. My guess is he doesn't feel comfortable being around all us darkies when he's the only white boy. You know how it is. When we play at the Mocambo I get this other cat to sit in with us on piano."

Doherty didn't know how it was but was hoping he would soon find out. "What can you tell me about Ricks?"

"For one, he's high yella."

"What does that mean?"

"It means he's light skinned, very light skinned. Could pass for white if he didn't have a flat nose and kinky hair. His hair is light colored too. I hear tell that his mama was from the Azores, which makes him part Portuguese. Nobody knows who his daddy was, but he surely was a colored man."

In his mind's eye Doherty visualized the Negro chauffeur opening the door of the cream colored Cadillac for a light skinned black man outside of Frankie DeAngelo's place in the Village.

"Can you arrange a meeting for me with Ricks?"

"Oowee, man, you aren't asking for much are you. Just a friendly get together for some ofay from Warwick with one of this city's most dangerous pimps."

"Actually I'm from West Warwick, not Warwick. And what the hell's an ofay?"

"An ofay is a white man." Tango shook his head. "Well shit, man, you being from West Warwick 'stead of Warwick, that makes all the difference in the world. I'm sure Jimmy Ricks would be delighted to sit down and talk with a white boy from West Warwick."

Doherty gave Tango a straight on look. "This is important. Can you arrange it?"

"Damn, boy, you don't give up do you. I'll see what I can do," Tango added without much enthusiasm. "But I'm warning you, it'll have to be on his turf. And once you're there you'll be totally on your own. Nobody gonna protect you at the Mocambo. Not me, not the police – and if you're thinking of bringing a piece with you, they'll take that offa you before you even get in the door. Ricks and his boys are dangerous cats who'll do whatever they haveta to protect their interests."

"Can you set it up?"

Tango shook his head in bewilderment at Doherty's persistence. "I'll give it a try. If it works out I'll call you."

Doherty handed Tango one of his business cards with his home number on the back. "I look forward to hearing from you."

"Yeah, man. And if you see Rachel, tell her everybody at the Medici misses her."

"Will do."

Chapter Twelve

There was a message on the answering machine when Doherty clocked into the office Saturday afternoon. It was from Dave Tancrene saying if he still wanted to meet with Jimmy Ricks he should pick him up at the Medici at 12:30 that night. Although Doherty didn't like to drive into the city late at night, aside from Frankie DeAngelo, Ricks was the only other live lead he had on finding Gus.

He pulled up in front of the Medici at 12:15 and sat in the car smoking while people began to filter out of the coffeehouse. He didn't want to pay another cover charge nor did he want to sit in the back room again while the musicians blew reefer. Twenty minutes later the folksingers emerged from the club. The two men shook hands and one of them hugged the longhaired girl and headed off by himself carrying a guitar case. Then the girl and the banjo player walked in the opposite direction arm in arm.

Doherty got out of the car to make himself visible. Pretty soon the jazz guys came up the stairs carrying their instrument cases. Tango slid his bass into the back of a station wagon that belonged to the white flute player. Before leaving, the flutist waited until Tango eyeballed Doherty standing by his Chevy.

Once he was spotted the jazzman walked slowly over to the car. "Are you sure you still want to do this, man? Saturday night at the Mocambo can be a little wild," he added when he drew within earshot.

"Let's go before I change my mind," Doherty said, trying to keep his nerves in check.

Once in the car they both lit up cigarettes and headed over to Wickenden Street and then down the hill toward the city center. At the corner of Pine, where Ballard's Restaurant is located, Tango instructed him to head south on Pine away from the downtown area. Going by Ballard's reminded Doherty of the lunch he'd taken there with Gus a little over a year ago when he was working the Wainwright case. It was at Ballard's that Timilty referred him to a science doc at Brown whose insights helped him to figure out why Wainwright was murdered.

About five blocks along Pine Doherty noticed that the complexion of the people milling around on the sidewalk had changed. This far outside of the city center everyone he saw on the street was Negro. Men in slouch hats sat on chairs outside of bars and food joints, drinking out of paper bags while women paraded by, many of them looking to him like hookers even if they weren't. There was a lot of noise and good-humored joshing going on among the groups of people on the sidewalk. Loud music played from every corner. Although the neighborhood was shabbier than the ones closer to downtown, there was a lot of good-time energy along these blocks.

When Doherty stopped at a traffic light, a few unfriendly looks were shot his way. Except for the Negro soldiers he'd consorted with in the service, he'd never been around a lot of colored people before. In the army the Negroes were kept in their own units, under the command of white officers. This was the first time he was in an environment where Negroes were in the majority. It only increased his anxiety.

Tango flashed him glances every now and then. At one point he asked how he was doing. Doherty answered that he was okay, though he wasn't sure if he was. Finally the jazz musician told him to pull over to the curb. There was a small neon sign identifying the Club Mocambo on a side street just off Pine. They parked the car and walked with their heads down in the direction of the club. A number of Negro men were standing around outside; a few mumbled incoherent words under their breath as Tango and Doherty passed by. He was glad he couldn't decipher what they were saying.

Two tall black women were standing outside of the Mocambo wearing tight fitting outfits that left little to the imagination. Their pants were skin-tight and one wore a blouse that was opened pretty far south of her breast line. Doherty saw a bright red bra in full view. The other wore a sweater that fit her like a second skin. They each had straight, processed hair and wore a lot of jewelry that jangled when they moved. Their lips were painted with bright red lipstick.

When Doherty and Tango drew closer one of them said, "Hey white boy, you lookin' for somethin' dark tonight. You know what they say, 'the darker the berry, the sweeter the juice'." The girls then laughed in unison. Tango said something to them that caused the two hookers to fall into hysterics.

Doherty turned to Tango and asked, "What did you say to them?"

The musician shook his head. "You don't wanna know, man."

Stationed at the door of the Mocambo stood a man who must have been six and a half feet tall and at least three hundred pounds. Doherty'd never seen anyone that large outside of a professional wrestling ring. Tango spoke with him while Doherty snuck sidelong glances at the two hookers. He wondered what it would be like to have sex with a black woman, especially one as experienced as these two. He was shaken out of these thoughts when Tango grabbed his arm and quickly ushered him inside.

There was loud, bluesy music coming from a jukebox somewhere; a thick haze of smoke hung over the Club Mocambo. The place was crowded and noisy. It didn't take long before Doherty realized his was the only white face in the club. Many eyes turned in their direction as Tango moved him through the crowd toward another room in the back. This one was dimly lit and more sparsely occupied. It had booths that ran along one wall and a long bar on the opposite side. As they passed by the booths Doherty noticed that most of the couples in them were kissing or doing other, more advanced things.

In one a girl was bent over with her head in a man's lap. When she looked up he saw that she was grasping his member. She shot Doherty a brief smile and then went back to work. Doherty did his best not to look directly at them. In the next booth a large man had two girls on either side of him. Both girls had their tops undone and their breasts were hanging out for the man to fondle. Doherty gulped as he and Tango made their way to the last booth.

Standing beside that booth was a man who stood no more than about five feet tall and was equally as wide. He reminded Doherty of the singer Jimmy Rushing, who performed with Count Basie's band and sang a song about himself called "Mr. Five-by-Five." He thought this must be the guy who accompanied Jimmy Ricks on his visit to Frankie DeAngelo's. Sitting on the far side of the booth facing them was a very light skinned colored man with his arm over the shoulder of an absolutely gorgeous black woman with long straight hair. She smiled at Doherty and Tango with shockingly white teeth that were set off by her ruby red lips. The man was wearing a maroon silk shirt and a black do-rag on his head. He was handsome almost to the point of being beautiful, if such a term could be used to describe a grown man. Doherty assumed this was the infamous Jimmy Ricks. He looked up as his two visitors approached and smiled. When he did two gold teeth flashed at them.

"Tango, my man," Ricks said, as if they were long lost friends. Tango held out his hand and Rick's slid his almost yellow paw across it. Then he turned his over and Tango made the same gesture in return. Doherty'd learned in the army that this gesture was called 'giving skin'. Tango introduced Doherty and Ricks looked at him closely without smiling or saying anything. In time he nudged the girl out of the booth and told her to go over by the bar and get herself a drink. He made a hand gesture that indicated Mr. Five-by-Five should pat down his two guests. After the fat man had done his job thoroughly, Ricks invited Doherty and Tango to sit across from him. The fat man stayed close at hand, momentarily pulling aside his suit jacket to show them a sizable weapon resting under his arm.

"What're you drinking my friends?"

Tango asked for a Seven and Seven and Doherty for a Jameson neat. Ricks dispatched his heavyset friend to fetch their drinks. He then pulled out a pack of Kools and offered them a smoke. Tango took one while Doherty opted for one of his Camels instead. He lit all their smokes with his Zippo.

"I guess we can cut to the chase since you boys already know who I am and what I do. So what's on your mind, white boy?"

"I'm a private investigator looking for someone who's lost. I was hoping you could help me out."

"Aren't we all lost in our own way, Mr. Doherty," Ricks said and then burst into laughter. "I'm just funnin' with you whitey." Doherty smiled back. The fat man arrived with the drinks. Doherty took a large gulp of the Jameson to help settle his nerves. Ricks was drinking something clear. It might have been water, though from the way he sipped it and grimaced afterwards, Doherty assumed it was either gin or vodka.

"I guess that makes you a regular Mike Hammer, like in those Mickey Spillane books. I like Mickey Spillane; his books always got a lot cheap women in them. Nothin' more attractive than a cheap woman, right Mr. Private Eye?" Doherty didn't bother to answer.

"The man I'm looking for is named Gus Timilty. He used to be a cop in West Warwick. I believe he did you a good turn about five years ago. A favor that ended up costing him his job."

Ricks sipped his clear liquor and for a few moments was lost in thought. He smiled, his gold teeth flashing at Doherty. "Oh, yeah. I remember him. Big Irish guy. He was tryin' to get this white girl who was workin' for me outta of the business. She was already done in so I dint mind lettin' her go. Bitch was too junked up anyways to be any use to me so I cut a deal with him. What he didn't know is I probably woulda let that skank go without anythin' in return. But, you see, I was gettin' jammed up by the Providence cops at the time on some two-bit drug charge. I could see that this Gus fella might be useful in helpin' me get out from under it."

"What exactly did he do for you?"

"I don't rightly know. I assume he talked to some cops he knew here in the city and they agreed to drop the charges. In return I gave him the bitch, for what she was worth. Now that I think back on it, you could say he saved my career."

"Career, huh," Doherty said, as if being a pimp was like being a doctor or a lawyer. "How do you figure?"

Ricks leaned back and sucked on his Kool, perhaps thinking about his early days in the skin trade. "You get a drug conviction when you startin' out, the big boys don't want any part of you. I needed to keep my record clean. One tiny little drug arrest woulda ruined all my plans."

"Who are the big boys?" Doherty asked.

Ricks let out a short laugh. "Who do you think they are, motherfucker? I'm talkin' about the Italian gentlemen from up on the hill. You don't run whores in this city 'less they say you can. The girls bring me their bread and I give a slice of it to those cats every week. I don't give them what they think they deserve they'll cut my balls off. And Mr. Private Eye, I kinda like havin' my balls in their proper place. Nowadays they rely on me because I can provide somethin' special down here," Ricks said proudly.

"Special, huh. What is it you provide that's so special?"

"Listen motherfucker. All these questions are startin' to get on my nerves. Maybe I should call Tiny over here and have him and the boys haul you out back and kick the shit out of you." The last comment caused Tango to squirm in his seat.

"Jimmy," Tango said weakly. "Mr. Doherty didn't mean no offense."

"He's right, I didn't mean no offense, Jimmy. But let's get something straight between us. I did a big favor for Mr. Frank Ganetti Jr. last year. I assume you know who he is. As a result he assured me if I ever needed something in return I should feel free to call on him at anytime. If you want to get your boy Tiny and his pals to take me out back to tune me up then you run the risk of displeasing the Ganetti family. Special or not, to them pimps are still a dime a dozen. So why don't you cool it with the threats so we can have a nice friendly conversation. Now what can you tell me that makes you so special in this business?"

Ricks retained his smugness and said, "You know what white guys want more than anythin'? They want Negro girls. I mean real dark-skinned girls, so dark they almost black. These girls open their legs and white men go ape shit, surprised to see some pink among all that black. None of them guineas can recruit girls like that, but I can. I've seen everythin' in this business and there ain't no end to the things that'll make a man's prick hard."

"Is that it?" Doherty asked.

"Not entirely. You know what else these johnnies like. They want 'em young and innocent. Of course, none of these bitches are innocent; they just have to look innocent. Ain't nobody in this business innocent on neither side. I seen men come down here they wanna fuck some young girl looks like their own daughter. Sometimes they so disgusted with themselves afterwards they knock the girl around like it's her fault they so sick. Times like that I have to send in one of my boys to straighten 'em out. I'm tellin' you, Mr. Private Eye. I seen some crazy shit in this business."

"These young girls you mentioned, are they underage?"

"I don't ask and I don't really give two shits how old they are, as long as they bring in the cash. If they get in trouble with the law, my benefactors and their lawyers take care of it."

"Has Gus Timilty been around lately, maybe in connection with that girl from the past? Or with some business about another girl?"

Ricks shook his head. "I ain't seen that man since he done me that favor, what was it … five years ago?"

"What can you tell me about a two-bit booster named Frankie DeAngelo, and don't bother playing dumb, Jimmy. I got witnesses that've seen you and Tiny at his place in Cranston on a couple of occasions."

Ricks smiled at Doherty. "You pretty sharp for cat from West Warwick. Oh don't get all shit-in-the-pants on me now. When Tango told me you wanted to meet I had you checked out. I may be a pimp but I ain't stupid. I know all about Doherty and Associates and your connections with the Ganetti family. As for my business with Frankie DeAngelo, he sells me drugs, small quantities but primo stuff – reefer and smack mostly, occasionally some coca. That shit the Italians sell me been stepped on so many times it might as well be baby aspirin. Sometimes I think junkies get high offa it just 'cause they wanna be high."

"I don't know where Frankie gets his stuff from but it's top grade. I buy a little from him now and then just for the girls or for their johnnies when one of them wants a special treat to help him get off. Mostly the gage is for them 'cause they don't know nowhere else to get it. The smack's for my special girls, like Darlene who was just sittin' here. I haveta keep a close eye on them, though. I give 'em just a little taste now and then, mostly up the nose. I don't want my best earners ending up as useless smack addicts."

Doherty wanted to tell Jimmy Ricks that was mighty generous of him, but he thought it best not to push the pimp's buttons any more than he already had. He'd played the Ganetti card and hoped that would be enough to prevent Ricks from having his boys work him over just for fun.

"Gus Timilty was chasing after Frankie DeAngelo. I thought it might have something to do with your business on account of you being seen at DeAngelo's. I was looking to put those pieces together. You know, Rhode Island is a small state where it seems like everybody knows everybody else. Apparently the pieces I was looking at don't fit. In that case, we'll be shoving off. It was nice to meet you. I'm sorry we took up so much of your time."

Ricks head snapped back and he broke into sustained laughter. "Time? Shit man, I got nothin' but time. Besides talkin' with you was a pleasure. You probably know more words than all of these motherfuckers in here put to-gether. And my man Tango here, he can play that bass of his like an angel - and sometimes like the devil when he has a mind to. All that shit you threw out about Frank Junior, I knew all that already. That's why I agreed to this here meetin'. You think I would've sat down with you except for you knowin' him. Now, gentlemen, before you go would you like to take one of my ladies next door? It'll be on the house, though you'll have to tip the princess when you're done."

Tango and Doherty graciously thanked Jimmy Ricks for his offer, begging off because of the late hour. Ricks shook his head and laughed as his two guests stood to leave. Tango skinned him again. Doherty shook his hand the old-fashioned way. They both drew a lot of smiles from the working girls on their way out.

Once in the car Tango let out a deep breath. "Man, you're one crazy motherfucker. I thought you were going to get us fucked up back in there."

Doherty smiled, more to himself than at the jazzman. "Could have happened. It's a good thing he likes your music."

"And good thing for you he knows who Frank Ganetti is."

"Yeah, especially since Mr. Ganetti and I haven't spoken to each other in over a year."

Chapter Thirteen

Although he had no real reason to think it, Doherty couldn't help but feel that Ricks had seen Gus Timilty sometime more recently than five years ago. Nothing obvious jumped out from their conversation except that when he told the pimp early on that it was five years ago that Gus had done him that big favor, Ricks remembered the girl involved as if it were yesterday. Then later in the conversation he made a big point of not remembering when it was that he traded the girl's freedom for Gus getting his drug bust kicked. Truthfully, Doherty wasn't in a frame of mind to believe anything Ricks told him. The only honest gesture the pimp made all night was when he offered to fix him and Tango up with a couple of his whores.

For the time being he'd exhausted any possibility of going further with Ricks without putting himself in danger. He understood that Jimmy Ricks was not someone to trifle with or lean on too heavily. He would only be able to go after him again if he had some leverage, or was willing to call in a favor from Frank Ganetti Jr. For the time being Doherty had no intention of cashing in that marker if he could avoid it. He would take another run at Frankie DeAngelo by going down to Bonnet Shores to see if he could flush him out there. Maybe even employ Alex Klinoff to give him a hand. He'd try to appeal to the ex-cop in Klinoff, figuring he might've lost his badge but not his instincts. There had to be some deep-seated reason besides simple curiosity why Klinoff spent his off-hours listening to a police scanner.

A third play could be through Maureen Donovan, though Doherty had no intention of betraying the trust of a girl he was sleeping with. Her suspicions were already up and he didn't want to give her any more reason to think he was just using her to gather information. She was a good girl living a hard life and there was no call for him to tighten the screws on her to get to DeAngelo.

Thinking on it now, he might've gone too far already when he told Ricks that he had eyewitnesses that saw him and his men at DeAngelo's place in Cranston. He hadn't mentioned any names, though he might have put Maureen and her son in harm's way without realizing it. It was possible that Ricks saw Maureen and Mark eyeballing him and his boys when they first visited DeAngelo's. If the mob controlled the drug trade in this state, then Ricks would be wise to keep a cover on his drug connections with Frankie DeAngelo, especially if he was purchasing larger amounts of the stuff than he let on.

Another thought that rattled around in Doherty's head that weekend was how little he actually knew about Gus Timilty's personal life. Here was a man who'd been his mentor as a cop and later his friend and advisor in setting up his own private practice. During that time Gus was always a willing backup man whenever Doherty needed him. Yet he knew virtually nothing about his personal life. The fact that he never learned the full story of why Gus was forced to leave the West Warwick police was a prime example. He did know that Gus had once been married but wasn't any longer. Aside from that he had no clue as to who the ex-wife was, where they'd lived, or if they ever had any kids.

So here he was, setting out to find a friend he knew so little about. Who the hell was he kidding. He was searching for Gus because Johnny Briggs was paying him to do so. The arrangement with Briggs was his most lucrative payday in the last three months. Prior to Briggs contracting his services, Doherty'd barely made enough money in the past year to keep his office open and pay rent on his apartment. He certainly wouldn't have been able to keep Agnes on the payroll much longer.

Nevertheless the case was now his, and as poor a friend as he was to Gus, he was determined to see things through to the end. It was what he did. If he couldn't locate Gus Timilty in what could be his hour of need then he wasn't worth a damn as a private eye or a friend.

When Tuesday rolled around he put all concerns about the case on the back burner while turning his thoughts to his day with Maureen Donovan. He might sneak in a question or two about Frankie DeAngelo, though was determined to make the girl feel that he was there because he cared about her, which he did. Doherty showered and shaved that morning and put on his best sport clothes. He cleaned old food wrappers, used cigarette packages and empty coffee cups out the Chevy. He was thinking he might take her out to dinner if the day went well. In anticipation of that, he threw his herringboned sports jacket onto the back seat.

The sky was overcast though no rain was in the forecast. They could go out or, if they chose, they could spend the better part of the day in bed. Either option appealed to Doherty. Maple Street was quiet when he pulled the Chevy up in front of #36 behind Maureen's beat-up Ford. Doherty was whistling when he approached the door. He knocked but there was no answer. After the second attempt he tried the knob and the door opened without resistance.

He knew something was wrong the minute he stepped inside. Cabinet doors in the kitchen were wide open as were drawers where silverware and other utensils were normally stored. Most of the contents of both were dumped onto the floor. The bleeding heart Jesus lay amid the shattered dishes, its glass frame a series of jagged pieces.

He checked the master bedroom. Everything there was in disarray. Drawers were thrown onto the floor and clothes from both Maureen's dresser and closet were strewn everywhere. He called for her but there was no answer. He checked the bathroom. The medicine chest had been ransacked, as had her vanity. Toiletries and beauty products lay everywhere. Some of the glass containers were broken, oozing their sticky content across the linoleum floor.

He walked slowly up the flight of stairs to the second floor, being careful not to touch anything as he did. He didn't want to leave any prints in case the apartment later became a crime scene. Once again he called Maureen's name but there was no response. He peaked into one bedroom at the top; everything in it was flung about. The mattress had been tossed from the bed and the bare spring sat on the frame like a skeleton. Large dust balls had gathered underneath it.

The door to the other bedroom, the one he assumed belonged to her son Mark, was closed. Doherty took a deep breath and then removed his handkerchief, which he used it to turn the knob. All of the young boy's goods had been tossed here and there. But what immediately caught Doherty's eye was the body of Maureen Donovan lying on her back amid the chaos. A star shaped bullet hole marked the center of her forehead. Doherty knelt down beside her and with a shaky hand reached up to check for a pulse at her throat that he already knew wouldn't be there.

Her beautiful green eyes stared up at him, but there was no life left behind them. Doherty closed his own eyes and ground his teeth. The only thing that came out of his mouth was the word, "sonofabitch." Using his handkerchief he reached up and shut the dead girl's eyes. Her body was already turning cold though it was still warm enough to tell him that she hadn't been dead all that long.

Doherty made a quick inventory of the room. He even looked deeply into the closet. Neither the boy nor his body was anywhere amidst the disorder left by her killers. He hoped this meant that her son had already left for school before the murderer, or murderers, arrived. Back in the kitchen Doherty reached into the cabinet under the sink where the door was already ajar. He extracted the rubber gloves Maureen had worn when she cleaned DeAngelo's bathroom. He then moved a chair over to the bedroom door and withdrew the key to DeAngelo's place that she kept hidden. Before exiting he took one last long look at the bedroom where he and Maureen had made love.

Once outside he carefully wiped her doorknob with his handkerchief. When that was done he jammed his hands into his pockets so no one would see the rubber gloves. It didn't matter since there was no real action on Maple Street at that time of day. He went to slide the key into DeAngelo's lock but it wasn't necessary. The door had been kicked in, leaving slivers of wood hanging by the handle where the lock had been. The destruction in DeAngelo's place was like that in Maureen's, though much worse in that many of the hot appliances he stored there were smashed in a wanton fashion. Doherty cruised quickly through the apartment surprised that whoever had beaten the door in hadn't bothered to take any of the valuable merchandise. Whatever the motive, it clearly wasn't theft.

Upstairs where the room had been padlocked, the lock and hasp had been violently torn off the door; it stood wide open, revealing the expensive goods inside. The screens on most of the TVs were smashed and the clock radios and record players had been thrown to the floor with enough force to leave them in pieces. Doherty took a few seconds to survey the expensive goods left in fragments. The intruders were obviously more intent on sending a message than on burglary. Quickly he crossed the hall to DeAngelo's bedroom. Like Maureen's it too had been ransacked and much of the smaller merchandise from his dresser, especially the jewelry, lay scattered on the floor. Some of it might have been taken though Doherty wouldn't have known if it had.

DeAngelo's closet door stood open and the myriad boxes of shoes lay strewn on the floor in front of it, as did the expensive suits that had been hanging from the metal crossbar. He carefully cleared the debris around where he'd earlier detected the loose planks in the floor. They had not been pried up. Whatever the intruder had been searching for, he apparently missed this secret hiding place. He took out his pocketknife and kneeling down cleared the space above the planks. Then using the knife he pried up two of them. This allowed Doherty enough of an opening to slip his hand underneath the floorboards. He felt around before his outstretched fingers touched something round and metallic. He couldn't get a grip on it at first.

Realizing the limitation of the space, he pried up another plank. This one came out reluctantly. Now he had enough room to extend his arm deep into the space under the floor. He could feel two round metal cases, each about a foot in diameter. After getting a good grip he gingerly removed each from its hiding place. In the light he could see that they were film canisters. He removed the top of one and as expected, there was a film inside. It was the kind people used for home movies. The second canister held a similar reel.

Still wearing the rubber gloves Doherty carefully replaced the loose flooring and piled some of the now mismatched shoes and suits on top of them. He slipped the canisters inside his windbreaker and zippered it up so the films were resting snuggly against his stomach. He then tiptoed through the chaos and down the stairs to the front door. When he got outside he quickly removed the rubber gloves and stuffed them into his pockets along with the key to DeAngelo's apartment. He sat in the Chevy long enough to bid Maureen Donovan a decent farewell while also making sure no one on Maple Street spotted him.

He drove slowly around the block and returned to Park Avenue. As he did he removed the films from under his jacket and slid them beneath the front seat. A half-mile up Park he pulled into the lot of a donut shop where a phone booth was located. Before exiting the car he checked to make sure the films were jammed snugly under the seat so they couldn't slide out. He climbed into the phone booth and dialed the emergency number for the Cranston police that was posted by the phone. His call was answered after one ring.

"I'd like to report a shooting," he said in as calm a voice as he could muster.

"Where was this shooting?" the official on the other end asked.

"It was in the Village, on Maple Street. Somewhere in the thirties," he said trying to sound vague, but not too vague. He wanted to be sure the local cops had the place covered before Maureen's son came home from school or from his grandparents.

"Could you please identify yourself sir," the voice at the other end said.

"I'm sorry, I'm just a concerned neighbor," Doherty lied. He hung up while the dispatch cop was in the middle of his next question.

Before going into the donut shop he surreptitiously shoved the rubber gloves and DeAngelo's key into a trash bin outside. He sat at the counter and ordered a black coffee and a plain cruller. Less than ten minutes later three squad cars with their sirens blaring flew down Park past where he was sitting in the direction of the Village. He finished his coffee, paid his bill and drove slowly back to West Warwick.

Chapter Fourteen

Doherty drove directly to the office. Once there he took a bottle of Jameson out of his desk drawer. It was about half full. He looked around for a glass, but all he could come up with was a dirty coffee cup. He spit in the bottom and used his handkerchief to clean it out. He poured himself four fingers of whiskey and took a healthy slug. The second gulp drained the cup so he refilled it with another four fingers. After the third swig he picked up the phone.

Agnes answered after the fourth ring.

"It's me Agnes; I need to talk to you."

"Oh hi," she said pleasantly. "How're you doin' over there at Doherty and Associates without your prize secretary?" Doherty took another swallow of Jameson.

"I need to talk to you, Agnes."

"You sound awful serious. Would you like me to come in tomorrow? I can be there by ten."

"No, I need to talk to you now."

"Jeez boss, I don't know."

"Please Agnes, it's important."

There was a long silence on the other end of the phone. "I'll be there in a half hour," she said finally.

"Thanks."

By the time Agnes made it to the office he'd polished off the remainder of the fifth of Jameson. He normally wouldn't have called his former secretary when he was troubled by a case. He'd have called Gus Timilty. Under the present circumstances that was not an option. He could hear Agnes huffing and puffing as she climbed the stairs long before she appeared in the outer office. She looked good; pregnancy obviously agreed with her. She was nearly six months along and had a healthy belly to show for it. She slumped down in the chair that was adjacent to her old desk and tried to catch her breath. While she did Doherty assumed the seat that clients usually sat in before being ushered into his space.

She gave him a concerned look. "You don't look too good, boss. It's kind of early to be hittin' the sauce, isn't it?"

"I got a problem with a case I'm working on. I didn't know who else to call."

"What about Gus? Did you try him?"

"That's just it, Agnes. Gus is part of my problem." He then spent the next half hour laying out the tale of his pursuit of Gus Timilty including his encounters with Maureen Donovan and Jimmy Ricks, as well as what he'd learned along the way about Frankie DeAngelo. The only thing he left out was that he'd slept with the Donovan girl on two occasions. When he got to the part about her murder Agnes' face blanched.

"Is there any way you can be tied to this girl's death?"

"It's possible. We went out to lunch the second time I visited with her. She took me to a local restaurant and introduced me to the guy who owned it. I'm thinking once this guy hears about her murder he'll deal me to the cops."

"What about Gus? Do you think he had anythin' to do with the girl gettin' killed?"

Doherty shook his head. "I don't know. She met Gus once when he came by her place looking for DeAngelo. According to her, they didn't converse very long. He just asked about DeAngelo and she told him he wasn't around. If you're asking me if Gus could've killed her, the answer is definitely no."

Agnes altered her position trying to find some elusive comfort in her present condition. "Jeez boss, I wasn't suggestin' that Gus killed her or nothin'. I know he wouldn't do somethin' like that. I was thinkin' if you and Gus were lookin' for this same guy, then maybe you led the bad guys to his place as well. That might've gotten the girl killed just 'cause she was his friend and neighbor."

Agnes was immediately sorry she'd pushed things this far. The last thing Doherty needed was for someone beside himself making him feel responsible for Maureen's death. He already had that one covered. Agnes did a slow perusal of the office as Doherty tried to consider where he should go next in his search for Gus. The half bottle of Jameson he'd consumed wasn't helping his reasoning process.

"I think you should go home and sleep off some of that booze," Agnes said. "In the meantime I'll come in the next few days. Maybe I can help you dope things out." What she really meant was she wanted to keep an eye on him so that he didn't slide all the way down into the bottle. Without Rachel or Gus around, Doherty agreed, knowing he could use Agnes' company.

"What about your pregnancy?" he said, not really sure what he was asking.

Agnes laughed. "I'm pregnant, not crippled. My only problem'll be climbin' those damn stairs with all this extra weight. Otherwise I can still do this job in my sleep. It's not like I'll have to do a lot of runnin' around. I'll leave that to you."

Chapter Fifteen

When Doherty woke up it felt like the middle of the night. Before he opened his eyes the first image that presented itself was of Maureen Donovan's beautiful and dead green eyes. In an effort to banish her from his mind he stumbled into the bathroom and took a long, hot shower. When he emerged he saw that it wasn't even six a.m. He seldom rose this early. It was only then that he realized he hadn't put anything in his stomach since the previous afternoon save for a half bottle of Jameson.

He warmed up a pot of coffee and scrambled some eggs that he layered onto a couple of pieces of toast. Three cups of coffee later he was ready to face the world. The walk to the office in the cool morning air helped him to feel human again. Once there he retrieved a worn briefcase he kept in the lower drawer of his filing cabinet. It was mostly used as a prop when he was out on an industrial investigation. The two film canisters had been safely locked overnight in his filing cabinet. As a precautionary measure he did not want to leave them in his office any longer. After witnessing the thoroughness with which Maureen and DeAngelo's apartments had been tossed, he figured if the searchers were onto him they'd do the same to his office, and probably his apartment as well. These films had to be stored somewhere safe.

A little after nine he passed through the doors of the Centreville Bank and approached a woman named Nina who sat at one of the desks on the other side of a low barrier. She was an attractive brunette who generally wore too much makeup for Doherty's taste. Still, she was always friendly toward him whenever he needed to do some business other than make a deposit or a withdrawal.

"Good morning, Mr. Doherty," she greeted him with a sly smile. He checked her hand and noticed that her engagement ring no longer took up space on her third finger. Another budding romance had apparently bitten the dust.

"Morning, Nina. I was wondering if I could purchase a safe deposit box?"

"Need to store some secret documents, eh," she said, more indiscreetly than she should have. Doherty responded to this remark with a fake smile.

"Sure, come this way," she added, as she rose from her desk and swung the gate open for him to pass into the bank's inner sanctum.

"What size would you like?" she asked over her shoulder as she ushered him back toward the bank's mighty vault. The large, multi-levered door stood open for the day. He followed Nina inside where she used a key to gain entrance to a room where three walls were covered from floor to ceiling with the faceplates for safe deposit boxes. The ones nearer to the top were the small, thin kind that would be useful for holding documents and small amounts of cash, and possibly jewelry for people who wanted to keep their valuables in a bank vault rather than on their bodies or at home. Below waist level were larger boxes. One of those would be necessary to hold the film canisters. He pointed at the boxes lower down and indicated to Nina that he wanted to rent one of those. She gave him a curious look, though she did not accompany it with a smart remark this time.

Instead she led him back to her desk where she produced some forms for him to fill out. Once that was done Nina informed him that the box rental would cost fifteen dollars for the year. Doherty forked over a sawbuck and a fin, which she immediately took to one of the tellers to be placed in a cash drawer. Upon her return she handed him a receipt and then led him back into the vault, carefully unlocking the gated door once again. She handed Doherty a key and kept a duplicate for herself.

"The way this works is that whenever you need to get into your box you have to see me or whoever else is sitting at the desk out front and ask if you can access it. We will require you to sign a form each time. The signature on the form must match the one you just signed. Unless you put someone else on the form, only you and you alone will have access to your box. Each time you come in you and I, or another bank employee, will enter the vault with these keys. You will put your key in first and if it turns okay then the bank employee will enter her key and the door will open. Once that's done you'll be able to retrieve your box. Then you'll be allowed to enter a small room by yourself where you can privately put in or take out whatever you wish from your box. After you've finished your business, the bank employee will accompany you back into the vault where both of you will lock up the box again. Do you have any questions?"

"When you say no one can access the box besides me, does that include legal authorities as well? You know, like the police or lawyers?"

Nina gave Doherty a suspicious smile that nevertheless had a wicked edge to it. Under some circumstances he wouldn't have minded. But today Maureen's dead body and the trashed apartments in Cranston still loomed too large in his consciousness.

"Mr. Doherty, the box cannot be accessed unless both keys, yours and the bank's are available. There is no way the bank can get into your safe deposit box without your presence and consent. It's only on rare occasions that police show up with a court order to retrieve the content of someone's box. In such situations the only way it can be entered is if the lock is drilled out. I can assure you that such a circumstance has never occurred in the seven years I've worked here at the Centreville. Even if someone were to steal your key they wouldn't be able to access your box without your signature. It doesn't get much safer than that."

He then asked Nina if he could put something into his new box. She handed him his key and then escorted him to the safe room. Once she returned to her desk Doherty carefully removed the dusty film canisters from his briefcase and placed them on the table that was the only piece of furniture in the room save for the three metal chairs arrayed around it. He lifted the lid off one of the dusty containers. There was a bit of dust inside as well, which he blew off before removing the film. He held the strip up to the light and spooled out about three feet's worth. He couldn't see very well so he moved the film closer to his eyes. The images were hard to make out on the small strip. He waited until his eyes adjusted to the miniature figures. When he finally could see what was on the film he was wasn't exactly surprised. He couldn't make out their faces, but it was clear enough that three feet into the strip there were two people, a man and a woman, about to engage in sex.

While at Quonset and in the service Doherty'd seen stag movies projected onto fold-up screens or white sheets hung on a wall. He knew such products were illegal, though just about every guy he'd ever met over the age of eighteen had seen one. Never being the procurer of such films, he didn't know how they were obtained or who ran the market on them.

He checked the second canister and the film inside held similar images. Possession of stag films was not something that usually led to murder, nor the fury with which the two apartments had been ransacked. Therefore, he had to think the wreckage must have something to do with who was in the films rather than with their mere existence. That was why he now felt better about securing them in a safe deposit box for the time being.

When he returned to the vault area a security guard summoned Nina to join him for the replacement of the box. Once the box was secured Nina accompanied Doherty out to the bank lobby. He surprised her when he reached out to shake her hand. Most men didn't shake hands with women, but Doherty'd gotten into the habit because some of his clients were women. He thought all business deals should be sealed with a handshake as well as a written contract. Nina held his hand for a few seconds longer than was necessary; he didn't mind at all.

Chapter Sixteen

Agnes stayed for a few hours on Wednesday even though no clients came in, no one called and there were no business reports to be typed up or filed. They talked of little else than her and her husband Louie's plans for the baby. Agnes' husband was a merchant marine who was at sea for long stretches at a time and then home for three weeks. Because of the nature of his work Louie often got bored when he was on dry land for too long, so he spent a lot of his shore time hanging out at the merchant marine hall in Providence with other commercial sailors. Her husband never knew she worked at Doherty and Associates. Whenever Louie was in port she had to absent herself from the office. It was a ruse that Doherty was perfectly willing to go along with considering how little he paid her.

When she left permanently because of her pregnancy Doherty realized how much he missed her and her wise counsel. On the surface she was a simple townie girl. But in time he saw that she had good common sense and understood women much better than he did. Her advice had come in handy in several of his cases. Once Agnes was absent, Rachel came down from Providence a few days a week to help out with the paperwork and to spend the night at his apartment. He knew she did this mostly to get away from her parents, who hovered over her constantly since the attack. However, their recent falling out left him with a nagging suspicion he might not be seeing Rachel for a while. Given the turn their relationship has taken since that night on Federal Hill, her absenting herself from his life might be a good thing for both of them.

Doherty was at his desk Thursday morning contemplating a trip to Bonnet Shores to see if he could scratch up something down there on Frankie DeAngelo when Agnes appeared at his door.

"You have a visitor. He looks like a potential client."

Not sure who this visitor might be, Doherty unlocked the top drawer of his desk where he kept his snub nose .38. He spun the mechanism to make sure the gun was loaded and kept the drawer partially open while remaining in his chair.

Agnes returned a moment later with his Uncle Patrick in tow.

"As I live and breathe," Doherty said rising from his chair. "Aren't you a sight for sore eyes? Agnes, this is my uncle, Patrick McSweeny, my mother's younger brother. Patrick, meet my secretary, Agnes Benvenuti."

Patrick stepped back and admired Agnes' ample belly. Then he embraced her in the kind of hug the old boy was famous for. Agnes turned beet red at the liberty Patrick had taken with her. "Ah, nothing so beautiful as a woman with child," he said once he released her.

He then turned to Doherty. "So boyo, how's my favorite dirty politician?" As long as he could remember his uncle Patrick had always greeted him by referring to him as a 'dirty politician.' It wasn't until he had dealings with Judge DeCenza's political machine that he understood what that phrase truly meant.

"Damn, Patrick," Doherty stammered. "You're looking…"

"Old," Patrick interjected. "You can say it. I am old. I turned sixty this past March. And now I have to carry this sheleighly around to help me walk," he said, brandishing a walking stick Doherty hadn't noticed. "The arthritis in me knees is just too much for this old body." Patrick was a big man but was never a terribly fit one. He carried a large stomach around that he gladly filled with good food and drink whenever it was available. His face was always flushed with enough broken blood vessels to make up a road map of the Emerald Isle.

"Still you're a sight. Where have you been keeping yourself? I haven't seen you in what, almost a year."

Patrick took the opportunity to drop himself into the client's chair on the other side of Doherty's desk. Agnes slunk out of the room, saying she would leave the relatives alone so they could catch up. While she did Doherty quietly shut the drawer holding the loaded .38.

For many years his Uncle Patrick had been the father Doherty never had. While his own father, Peter, was busy pouring whiskey down his gullet at

Paddy's Tavern or some other gin joint in town, it was his uncle that came to watch Doherty play ball, took him to the wrestling matches and the Reds games at the Providence Arena, and played catch with him until Doherty began to throw too hard for his uncle's tender hands. Patrick spent most of his adult life as a lawyer, first in West Warwick, then in Providence. But his real forte was as a fixer. Doherty didn't know exactly what his uncle fixed though he knew the old Irishman traveled among the rich and powerful in the business world as well as in politics. In fact it was Patrick who used his connections in town to get Doherty appointed to the West Warwick police force.

"So what have you been up to lately, Patrick?"

"Ah sonny boy, I've been a busy man these past few months." Doherty liked it that his uncle could add a bit of an Irish lilt to his voice whenever it suited his purposes. "Matter of fact I just came back from Wisconsin a couple of days ago. Had to get out of that god awful place before old man winter crept in."

Doherty took out his cigarettes and offered one to his uncle who gladly accepted. Each enjoyed the pleasure of the first puff. "I'd prefer one of my stogies," his uncle said, "but I don't want to smell up your office. It wouldn't do with that young lady out there carrying a child."

"Dare I ask what you were doing in Wisconsin? I thought you were working out of Boston these days."

Patrick smiled. "I was or am. To tell you the God's honest truth, I was out in dairy country spreading Joe Kennedy's money around. You see old Joe has it in his mind to run his boy Jack for president next year. He's determined that his son will be the first Irishman to sit in the White House. But before that can happen the boy needs to get the party's nomination. Right now the junior senator from Massachusetts isn't too well known outside of New England. That's why I was in Wisconsin – spreading his name around along with his old man's cash."

"But why Wisconsin?"

Patrick hit his forehead in mock exasperation. "Oh, I forgot who I was speaking with. It's my beloved nephew who's too grand for the dirty political arena. Must be on account of me calling you a *dirty politician* all these years." They both laughed at Patrick's joke. "I suspect having to deal with the likes of Martin DeCenza has put a little more skin on those bones, eh boyo?"

Without waiting for an answer his uncle continued, "Wisconsin will be holding one of the early primaries next spring. The man I work for, Kevin O'Shaughnessy, is one of Joe Kennedy's chief lieutenants – or bagmen if you prefer. So when Kevin asks me to go someplace for the Kennedy family, your Uncle Patrick answers the call by simply asking 'when do I leave?' No other questions need to be asked. They want me to go to West Virginia next month. Talk about God-awful places. I hear tell it's full of coal miners and people who marry their cousins. O'Shaughnessy says they only have five Catholic churches in the entire state and even fewer Irishmen."

"Then why are you doing all of this traipsing around, especially at your age?"

"Because we've got a good chance at electing the first Irish president of these United States. Do you know what that would mean to people like us? After everything we've been through to have one of our own as president."

"But the Kennedys are lace-curtain. They've never given a damn about shanties like us."

"Speak for yourself young fella. Those lace-curtain folks are the kind of people I consort with nowadays. And let me tell you something about this great land of ours, the country you fought and almost died for. We are never going to elect a common man president. Do you think some shanty Irishman could ever get within hailing distance of the White House? Boston City Hall maybe – but not the presidency. The bluebloods who run this country have already ceded us most of America's big cities. They knew there was nothing they could do about that since we procreate faster than them. But the White House? Not on their lives. Look what they did to Al Smith back in the twenties. They called him the candidate of 'rum, Romanism and revolution'. But the Kennedys – hell they're practically royalty. Oh, they'll try to smear us again as being storm troopers for the pope. And they'll bring up Joe's connections to gangsters and movie stars. But we've got to make sure it doesn't work this time, boyo. This is going to be a battle royal you'll be able to tell your grand-children about." Patrick paused here then added, "That is if you ever have grandchildren."

"And you think Joe Kennedy's money can get it done?"

"His and that of a lot of other well-heeled Irishmen, many of whom will remain anonymous throughout the campaign. Even the Irish who don't like the Kennedys, or the Democrats for that matter, will vote for the boy because he's one of our tribe. Blood is thicker than water, my boy. Don't you ever forget that."

Doherty and his Uncle Patrick spent the next two hours catching up on old times. He filled Patrick in on his hand-to-mouth practice and some of his more well-known cases. Despite some pointed questions, Doherty chose not to divulge any details about his most recent one. Patrick and Gus Timility went way back and he didn't see any reason to cause his uncle concern about his old pal being missing. Under other circumstances Patrick might have been able to help him. But with his uncle busy tramping about the country for Joe Kennedy, the last thing he needed to worry about was Gus' disappearance. Doherty did give the old boy some meat to chew on about his more recent run-ins with the DeCenza machine. Patrick got a kick out of Doherty besting West Warwick's boss man at his own game. As far as he knew there'd never been any love lost between him and Martin DeCenza.

His uncle spent a fair amount of time reminiscing about his sister, Doherty's mother. Most of his stories had to do with the way she treated him so badly when he was a young boy. He related how what his sister Mary Ann resented more than anything was having to take him along when she went to the Palace Theatre with her girlfriends.

"Mind you, she tried her best to lose me every time we went. I constantly had to remind her of the whipping she faced from our da if she ever came home without her little brother."

Patrick got a great laugh out of that. Doherty wished he hadn't finished the bottle of Jameson the day before so he could offer his uncle a nip. However, when he suggested that they walk up to Paddy's for a quick drink, Patrick begged off complaining that he had to drive back to Boston before nightfall. When they ran out of things to talk about, with much effort Patrick rose to take his leave.

Doherty walked him down to his car and they embraced warmly before he left. He asked Patrick what brought him back to West Warwick. His reply was that he just wanted to see the old town again and see how his favorite nephew was getting on. His response should have made Doherty feel good, but there was something hollow about it. A hollowness that nagged at him long after his uncle drove away in his vintage Cadillac sedan.

Chapter Seventeen

In the morning Doherty drove to the Centreville Bank to retrieve the two films from their place in his safe deposit box. Nina was at her desk and flashed the same sly smile she usually reserved for him – exclusively he hoped, though probably not. She said she was surprised to see him back so soon. He offered no explanation. Once he had the films in hand he stuffed them into his briefcase. He then headed north toward Cranston. This time he did not take the left down Park toward the Village. Instead he turned right off Reservoir and headed east on Park toward the intersection with Elmwood Avenue. St. Mathew's large Catholic Church stood on the corner of the cross-roads. In front of the church was a large marble statue of Jesus with his arms outstretched welcoming visitors. Doherty hoped J.C. had welcomed the late Maureen Donovan to his bosom.

He cruised north up Elmwood toward the capital city. Just past the entrance to Roger Williams Park, Cranston turned into Providence. Further along Elmwood merged with Reservoir Avenue and they both turned into Broad Street going toward downtown. That's when he began looking on his right for the camera store he'd searched out in the yellow pages. It was called United Camera and advertised itself as the largest store of its kind in Providence. It would have been pretty hard for him to miss it since the place stretched nearly a city block amidst a series of smaller mom and pop stores.

Once inside Doherty perused the largest collection of photographic supplies he'd ever seen. He strolled along aisles of film paper, chemicals, and photo accessories whose purpose he had no clue. There were enlargers of enormous size as well as smaller replicas for the same purpose. Glass counters lined two sides of the store. Inside one were cameras of every size, shape and price range from simple Brownie Hawkeyes to the expensive models imported from Europe and Japan like Leicas, Nikons and Minoltas. One locked case contained the very expensive Hasselblad and Bronica cameras used by professional photographers and amateurs with pretensions and thick billfolds.

On the racks behind the counters were shelves full of films of many different sizes and kinds. Since Doherty knew little about photography, he had no idea what the differences were between these many variations of films. The glass display cases on the left wall contained movie cameras of different styles and types, from small ones used primarily for home movies to larger ones that took the kind of high quality films that were shown on commercial projectors. On the shelves behind that counter were projectors of various sizes, including ones Doherty recognized as the kind that were used to show instructional films to kids in schools. He never learned how these machines actually worked. While at school he and his buddies used to make fun of the kids on the AV squad who set them up for his classes. For all he knew some of those AV nerds might now be cinematographers in Hollywood.

He moved uncertainly over to that counter and peered at the projectors as if he knew what he was looking for. Finally a tall gentleman approached him. He was wearing a short sleeve white shirt and a paisley tie. The pocket of his shirt contained a plastic pocket protector with several pens inside. He had thinning hair that was neatly combed over his white scalp and glasses on a thick lace hanging around his neck. Doherty was certain this fellow must have been on the AV squad while in school.

"May I help you?" he said in a soft voice.

Doherty cleared his throat, trying to remember what he'd rehearsed on the car ride over. "I recently came into possession of some old home movies of our family. I'd like to take a look at them. But to be honest with you I don't really know anything about photography."

The clerk's look added a dash of disdain as he took in his new customer. "What size are they?"

"That's just it, I don't know that either. I brought them with me so I was hoping you could help me out." Now came the hard part. He had to show the films to the sales clerk without letting him see what was on them. By being evasive he was certain this fellow would suspect that Doherty was in possession of stag movies, which in fact he was.

He slid one of the canisters out of his briefcase and placed it on the counter, being careful not to remove his hand from the case. The clerk looked at it and back at Doherty. The blank look on the man's face betrayed nothing.

"Could you open the canister so I can take a look at the film, please?" More disdain leaked into the last word. Doherty carefully opened the still dusty case and held the film up without letting it leave his hand.

The man put on his glasses and looked at it closely as Doherty rotated the film to give him a full view. He was sure the salesman suspected what it contained.

"So what exactly do you need from United Camera?"

Doherty hesitated for a few beats. "I would like to rent a projector so that I can take a look at these *home* movies."

"I'll bet you would," the clerk said, no longer bothering to mask his suspicions. "We can rent you a sixteen-millimeter Bell and Howell, which would be sufficient for viewing this film. Renting a simple sixteen-millimeter will cost you $10 for the week plus a $30 deposit to insure that the projector is returned. I will also need to see some form of identification."

Doherty wondered if United Camera was required to report to the police if they suspected someone was in possession of smut films. He knew they were compelled to if a customer asked to have sexy still photos developed. Nevertheless, Doherty stood his ground, mostly because he had no other choice. He'd come to United in the first place because it was some distance from West Warwick where he was well known. Besides he wasn't sure if there were any stores in his hometown that rented projectors like this. For now he wanted to keep his business strictly to himself.

"That'll be fine," he said, peeling two twenties out of his wallet as well as his driver's license. To allay some of the clerk's qualms he also flashed him his PI license. He didn't know if that made a difference. Nevertheless, the guy bent down and unlocked a cabinet below the showcase without making any more snide remarks. When he straightened up he placed a solid case with a molded handle on the counter. He then unsnapped four clips and removed the top of the case to reveal a good-sized projector sitting on the base.

He turned the mechanical part of the projector so that it faced Doherty and began to explain how a user should loop a film through it. There were white arrows along the way to indicate the path the film should take. At that moment Doherty wished he'd spent some time on the AV squad.

"What's most important is that you provide a loop here," the clerk said, pointing to a spot above where the film would pass in front of the projector's lamp. "If you thread it too tightly here you could easily break the film, especially if it's cheaply made or old as yours seems to be." This last remark was accompanied by a look that amounted to a leer. "When you wish to rewind the film you can do so simply by turning the on/off knob all the way to the left where it says 'rewind'. That will allow you to rewind it slowly through the projector if you wish to watch a scene over again. Otherwise, once the film has run all the way through you can move the take-up reel to this position," he said, as he raised a lower arm where an empty reel rested, "and run the film straight back up onto your original reel. Just make sure to tuck the film's end into this small slit in each reel or else the film will come loose and fly all over the place." This was turning out to be a little more complicated than Doherty'd anticipated.

"Do your films have sound on them?"

Once again he was caught off guard. "I'm not sure. This is the first time I've taken one out of its case since my sister gave them to me," he stammered.

"Well, whether they do or not, be sure that the perforations on the film fit over the sprockets on this first grip point," the clerk said, pointing to a spot where the film would be initially looped. "Once that's done the sprockets inside will grab it and take it through all the way to end. Then you just pass it under and onto the take-up reel and you're in business. This knob here," he said, pointing to one on the outside of the projector's mechanism, "adjusts the sound. Then if you need to sharpen the focus all you have to do is turn this lens," he added, while twisting the lens through which the bulb would project its light. "Whatever you do, do not run the projector for long periods of time without turning this off. The bulb is relatively new, but they tend to burn out if they stay lit for too long a time. Now Mr. Doherty, do you have any questions about how the projector operates?"

Even if he did he wasn't about to give this guy any more time to look down his nose at him. "No, I think you've about covered it."

"In that case, if you wouldn't mind filling out this card, I'll get your machine ready. There is an instructional manual tucked into the cover if you run into any other problems." He placed a registration form in front of Doherty that asked for the usual information like address, phone number, etc.

While he did so the clerk replaced the cover on the projector and attached a tag to the handle. Afterwards he ripped a receipt form from the bottom of the card Doherty had filled out and handed it to him. He would have extended his hand for the clerk to shake but he was afraid the man might reject it. Instead he carefully replaced the films in his briefcase, grabbed the projector and headed for the door. He let out a sigh of relief once he hit the street.

Chapter Eighteen

He locked the rented projector in the trunk of the Chevy while keeping the film canisters tucked safely in the briefcase on the floor by his feet on the ride back to town. When he arrived at the office Agnes was sitting at her desk working over her nails with an emery board. It was a ritual that used to irritate Doherty to no end. Now that she was there to give him some moral support, he found the familiarity of the act almost endearing. She looked up and handed him a copy of that morning's *Providence Journal*.

"I think you oughta take a look at this, boss."

Doherty glanced at the front page and then withdrew into his office. He shut the door, which he seldom did unless he had a special client in with him. Before taking up the paper he lifted the canisters out of his briefcase and put them in the bottom drawer of his filing cabinet and locked it. Only then did he remove his coat and hang it on the antler rack. It was important for him to keep Agnes in the dark about the films. He thought he'd be protecting her by doing so – though after the wreckage at Maureen Donovan and Frankie DeAngelo's apartments, he wasn't sure he could even protect himself from the people searching for them.

He knocked out a Camel from a fresh pack and sat down in his chair, placing his heels in their usual worn spot on the flat desktop. When he spread the paper out in front of him his eyes immediately gravitated to the front-page story below the fold entitled "Cranston woman slain in home"

Cranston police have reported that twenty-nine year old Maureen Donovan was found dead in her home yesterday from a single gunshot wound to the head. Mrs. Donovan, who worked as a nurse at Rhode Island Hospital, appears to have been the victim of a home invasion and robbery. Officer Ronald Anderson, first on the scene, described Donovan's apartment as having been "ransacked and left in total shambles."

According to police, Donovan had no criminal record and there was no reason to believe that the single mother of a nine-year old boy was involved in any illegal activities. At present the son is in the custody of the deceased's parents who also live in Cranston. Indications are that Mrs. Donovan's son was at school when the slaying occurred. Her ex-husband, George Donovan, currently resides in the Scottsdale, Arizona area and could not be reached for comment. The two were divorced three years ago.

Donovan resided at 36 Maple Street in the Knightsville section of Cranston. Her apartment is located in an area referred to by locals as the Village, as it was once a neighborhood of company housing for employees of the Cranston Print Works.

Cranston Police Chief Anthony Lamorello told the *Journal* that in canvassing the neighborhood, police discovered that the adjacent unit at 34 Maple Street had also been broken into and ransacked. He described that unit as containing a great deal of what he termed "possible stolen merchandise." "There were a number of televisions, clock radios, kitchen appliances, expensive suits, shoes and jewelry inside. Many of them had been seriously damaged by whoever had broken into the apartment," Lamorello said.

There is strong evidence that the person residing at 34 Maple Street was involved in a number of criminal enterprises. Police speculated that Mrs. Donovan's home may have been broken into by mistake by whomever was looking for the man in #34. One officer on the scene suggested Mrs. Donovan could have been shot by the intruder, or intruders, to protect their identities.

There was no sign of a struggle at #34 and police refused to divulge who the current resident is. However, the *Journal* has learned that the tenant of record at 34 Maple Street in Cranston is Francis DeAngelo, a person with a long record of petty crimes. At this point the Cranston police have been unable to provide a motive as to why Mrs. Donovan was shot other than that she may have been the victim of a burglary gone awry. They did announce later in the day that they would be using State Police resources to help with the investigation. As of this writing law enforcement officials have not been able to locate Mr. DeAngelo. The *Journal* was informed that an anonymous person called the police about the shooting on Maple Street that morning.

Doherty found it interesting that the Cranston police had waited an extra day before publicly announcing the shooting. He wondered if they chose to take this time to see if the murder of Maureen Donovan would flush out Frankie DeAngelo. Based on what he could gather about the events from that morning, whoever was looking for DeAngelo did not find him at home. It's possible that the killer suspected Maureen was somehow connected to DeAngelo's criminal activities. From what Doherty had gleaned from his brief search of DeAngelo's place, this was no ordinary robbery. In fact, it didn't appear to be a robbery at all. He was convinced that the intruder was after the well-hidden films; the very same films that were now locked in his filing cabinet.

He walked into to the outer office and handed the *Journal* back to Agnes. She looked up expecting some kind of response to the article. Doherty said nothing except that he would be sequestered in his office for a while and did not wish to be disturbed. She looked at him skeptically, but knew enough not to ask any questions.

After closing the door he removed the films from the locked drawer and took out a magnifying glass he kept for cases where he had to read some fine print on a document. With it in hand he felt like Sherlock Holmes. Unspooling one of the films he examined it closely through the glass. Eventually he would have to run them on the rented projector, but thought it best to do that at his apartment rather than here at the office. He didn't want to pique Agnes' curiosity any more than he already had. Besides, he thought it best that his secretary not catch him looking at stag films, even if it was in the service of a case.

The first film started out with a teenage girl dressed in an outfit that was intended to make her to look much younger – perhaps no older than about nine or ten. She wore heavy lipstick and had two rouge marks on her cheeks that caused her to resemble a silent film star. Her light colored hair was wound up in pigtails that stuck out from either side of her head. Doherty tried to get a closer look at her face but the image, even under the magnifying glass, was too indistinct. She skipped around a non-descript bedroom like a child.

He unspooled the reel until another figure appeared on the scene. It was a man, an older man in a suit. He was quite corpulent and was very animated as if he were scolding the young girl. On closer look Doherty took the girl to be in her mid to late teens and was only playing out some little girl fantasy for the man. He could not see him well enough to recognize the person who was chastising the young girl.

Soon the girl pressed her hands to her face as if she were crying. The scene reminded Doherty of silent movies where the actors always overemphasized their gestures in the absence of words. Next the man took a seat and grabbed the girl by her wrist and laid her across his knees. This was your classic spanking pose. At that point the girl looked directly at the camera and smiled in its direction. Doherty'd be able to better analyze this look when he ran the film through the projector. The man then raised the girl's skirt and pulled down her panties and began to slap her bare bottom. Once again the girl looked directly at the camera no longer bothering to hide her pleasure at what was happening.

After a few minutes the man rose and bent the girl over the chair with her buttocks to the camera. The camera zoomed in and dwelled for a few seconds on her bare bottom and spread cheeks. The fat man then dropped his pants and his boxer shorts and released his member. Even with the magnifying glass Doherty could not get a good look at his face from such a small image. With his back and shirttail filling the camera's view, he mounted the girl from behind and began to thrust at her with great vigor.

The rest of the film simply played out this scene without Doherty getting a good look at either character or the act itself. In Doherty's somewhat limited experience in watching stag movies, he was aware that the role of the camera was to zero in on the sex act being performed as closely as possible. Male viewers wanted to see fornication up close and personal or oral sex in a graphic fashion. They did not want to see the back of some fat man's shirt as he rutted away at his barely visible female partner. That coupled with the two leering glances the girl threw at the camera convinced Doherty the man in the picture did not know he was being filmed. He was thinking that this film was not made for commercial purposes, but rather was part of a possible shakedown being perpetrated against an unwitting participant. He stopped the film and wound it back on its reel. After carefully removing it from the projector he replaced it in the briefcase.

Doherty did not bother to look at the second film through the magnifying glass. He would save that for a full projected viewing at home. It was barely three o'clock when he told Agnes he was checking out for the day. She looked surprised though not unhappy to be relieved of duty, especially given that Doherty and Associates had no business to speak of. She tried to ask him some questions about the *Journal* article, but he put her off by saying he would have to think about it overnight and that they would talk in the morning. She seemed pleased that he wanted her to return for another day. Before she left he slipped her a five-dollar bill for her time. She tried to refuse the payment but he insisted and stuffed it into her purse.

Chapter Nineteen

Once Agnes had descended the stairs, Doherty tucked the films back into the briefcase and drove to his apartment. He put up some coffee and then tacked a spare white sheet onto his living room wall. He closed all the blinds to block out the sunlight, and more importantly so that no one in the neighborhood would see him watching smut films. He set up the projector and looped the film on its path as the clerk at United Camera had shown him. He ran into a problem when he attached the end of the film to the take-up reel from the wrong direction. As a result when he turned the projector on the film began to bunch up in a loose tangle. He turned the machine off and retraced his steps, winding the film back through the projector and then attaching it to the take-up reel correctly this time.

Pouring himself a cup of coffee he sat down on the couch and began to run the same film he'd examined at the office. The girl appeared on the screen looking even more ridiculous than she had under the magnifying glass. She must have been at least sixteen, not at all convincing as a prepubescent child. When she looked directly at the camera Doherty stopped the film to get a good look at her face. Despite her absurd make-up there was nothing familiar about her. Nonetheless, he clocked her face for future reference.

After she minced around the bedroom for a few minutes the fat man appeared. Doherty watched him closely. At no point did he look directly at the camera or appear to be aware of its presence. There was no snide grin or leering gesture, which in Doherty's experience, was usually part and parcel for *actors* performing in stag films. They were supposed to give viewers the impression that they were up to no good, and in doing so, help those watching feel like they were participants in the lurid acts on the screen. Whenever he'd watched stag films with a group of men they often made smart-ass or off-color comments to hide their own discomfort with what they were viewing.

At the point where the fat man dropped his pants and removed his undershorts Doherty once again stopped the film. He noticed that he had to manipulate his penis to get it hard enough for the act. Apparently the anticipation of screwing a young girl wasn't enough enticement. In looking closer at the man Doherty could see that he was at least in his fifties. That might explain why his erection did not come as easily as it would've had he been a younger man – or a man who made a profession of performing in stag movies. Such men were usually hired for their sexual prowess. This was evidently not the case with the fat man. On top of that he wasn't very attractive physically.

Doherty drank his coffee accompanied by a cigarette while watching the broad back of the man's shirt as he mounted the young girl from behind. On the screen he could tell when the man was nearing climax as his back began to shudder as he got closer to the end. Once satisfied the fellow wiped his member with a handkerchief, retrieved his clothes and quickly dressed. He then handed the girl something that looked like a wad of bills before leaving the scene. The fellow looked like he was embarrassed at what he'd just done. Once the fat man was gone the girl did something Doherty hadn't been able to detect under the magnifying glass. She looked directly at the camera and gave it a quick wink before the screen went blank.

While the film was rewinding Doherty poured himself another cup of coffee. He then unpacked the second film, wiped some dust off it and looped it through the projector. Within seconds the same girl appeared on screen, this time dressed in the traditional parochial schoolgirl outfit of plaid skirt, white blouse, dark button-up sweater over the blouse and knee socks. Doherty couldn't see her feet but was sure she was wearing a pair of patent leather Mary Janes. This time she sat at a table reading a book, a pamphlet that on closer inspection looked like a catechism text. Doherty was more than familiar with the standard Catholic catechism tract from his school days at St. James.

Within minutes the same overweight man appeared on screen. As in the previous film he was dressed in a suit and tie. The girl looked happy to see him. She rose quickly and ran to kiss him on the cheek. No punishment this time – not yet anyway. He was all smiles as he handed her a box in elaborate wrapping. She quickly unpacked the gift. Inside was an ornately dressed doll that she hugged to her chest as she mugged for the camera. While she did this, the big man removed his jacket and loosened his tie. Next the girl was kneeling on the floor pretending to play with the doll. Every so often she stole glances at the camera. For his part the man never made eye contact with it at all.

While she knelt on the floor he stole up behind her and began to rub her shoulders. She looked up him and smiled. When she did this the man averted his eyes. She quickly returned to playing with her new doll. In due course he slowly removed her sweater and then her white blouse. She did not resist or even seem to notice. Doherty found this part of the scene very peculiar. The fat man then unhooked her bra, revealing breasts that were far too substantial for a girl of the age she was pretending to be.

The man stood behind her and gently rubbed her breasts and squeezed her nipples. As he did she never once looked up from the doll, as if she wasn't at all aware of what he was doing. This part of the film gave Doherty the chance to get a good look at the guy. He didn't recognize him, yet knew he wouldn't forget his face. The man had a double chin and dark hair going to gray. Although clean-shaven, a late afternoon shadow circled his jaw. His eyes betrayed nothing but lust as did his full lipped mouth.

The girl then pressed the doll to her breast and feigned nursing it, which was not hard given the size of her breasts. In time the man turned back to the table and picked up the catechism book and handed it to the girl. He tried to give it to her in exchange for the doll. When she resisted he tugged at the doll more forcefully. She would not give it up until he slapped her across the face. By her reaction it was apparent it was a real slap not a staged one.

After he did this she looked at the camera with a long, nasty stare, as if to say, 'I didn't bargain on this'. She soon relented and gave the fat man the doll, replacing it with the catechism book. Next she leaned forward and placed her palms together and closed her eyes as if in prayer. It was a strange picture: the young girl topless in repose, lost in some pretended deep reverie.

Meanwhile the man lowered his fly and removed his now swollen member from his pants. He worked it slowly with his hand to keep it stiff. The girl glanced at him and then positioned herself so the camera would be able to clearly view the next act. This time whoever was filming the scene did not want footage solely of the fat man's back. He slid his penis into her mouth and she purposely turned to the camera as he did. Over the next few minutes she worked his member like a pro. Her costar didn't seem to mind that she was no longer playing the young, innocent schoolgirl. As he got near to the end he began to increase his thrust into her mouth. Finally she removed his member and he ejaculated all over her breasts and plaid skirt. She held onto him for a couple of seconds, giving him a final lick while the camera got a good view of the participants.

As he had in the other film, the man quickly wiped himself off and returned his member inside his pants. After he zipped up he handed the girl some money before picking up his suit jacket and hastily leaving the scene. When he was gone from the picture she gathered up the discarded sweater and white blouse, using the latter to wipe his semen off her chest. Once that was done she carefully removed the stained skirt. Before walking off the set in just her underpants and knee socks, she gave the cameraman a broad knowing smile. The film then turned as white as the hanging sheet.

Doherty was so disgusted by what he'd just witnessed he substituted a couple of fingers of Jameson for his coffee. He spent the next half hour trying to dope out what these films meant. First of all, in each of them the girl was trying to play a young girl, though she didn't seem all that old herself. He would be surprised if she were any more than sixteen or seventeen. As Doherty suspected from the earlier viewing, the man was clearly much older, at least in his fifties if not more. And judging from his clothes, was a man of substance. In each film he entered the scene wearing a nice suit, a white dress shirt and tie. Why else would someone be setting him up for blackmail if he weren't a man of means with a reputation to protect.

It was obvious from the outfits the girl wore that this guy had a fetish for very young girls. Doherty remembered Jimmy Ricks bragging about how one of his specialties was providing young, often-underage girls for men with perverse tastes. Because the man always dressed quickly, paid the girl and hurriedly left the scene just seconds after ejaculating, Doherty took this to mean he was ashamed of what he'd just done. If he were really taken with the experience he might have hung around for some expert clean up. And what did Doherty make of each fantasy? Well, from the second film he could only deduce that the fat man was Catholic, possibly a practicing one, who harbored fantasies of having sex with Catholic schoolgirls – especially when they were kneeling in prayer.

And what of the doll as a gift? That could be his attempt to say, 'I am a benevolent man despite what I'm about to do to you'. It was also interesting that he never made direct eye contact with the girl in either film, even when she looked straight at him. While engaged in each sex act the man made it a point not to look at the girl's face. In the first one he mounted her from behind; in the second he gave the girl the doll by handing the box to her over her shoulder. After that he massaged her shoulders from behind, and when she fellated him he looked everywhere but at her face.

Evidently this was a man who bore some shame for these sexual desires. But the questions that lingered were, who the hell was he and why did Maureen Donovan have to die so that he or someone else could get ahold of the films? Doherty's supposed there were at least four people who could answer these questions: obviously the girl and the man in the films, Frankie DeAngelo - and Jimmy Ricks. There was no obvious reason to suspect Ricks, but Doherty felt strongly that he was part of this shakedown operation; most likely as the person who supplied the young girl for the films.

Chapter Twenty

Doherty woke the next morning still shaken by what he'd seen on the two films. The nuns and brothers at St. James had done everything in their power to make the kids under their tutelage feel guilty about their sexual desires and actions. Despite their constant efforts in this regard, Doherty was able to get beyond those regressive preachings. His recent short relationship with Rachel had helped him become more comfortable having sex with a woman.

He was not exactly a prude, but what he found on those films was deeply disturbing. The fact that grown men used young girls in the way they did and fantasized about having sex with even younger ones was pretty disgusting. Jimmy Ricks was right - some men will do almost anything to satisfy themselves sexually. Ricks ought to know, he made his living fulfilling those perversions.

These thoughts were roaming around in Doherty's head as he walked from his apartment to the office. He planned to lock one of the films in his filing cabinet and the other one back in the safe deposit box. That way if anyone accosted him or tossed his office they would find only one of the films. By having the other one safely locked away at the bank, he'd have some protection against whoever was after them. He suspected the man in the films already knew that two stag movies of him existed. By putting one in the vault at the Centreville Bank Doherty would have some bargaining power if, or when, he needed it. Having the other film more accessible could be a way of luring the person searching for them out into the open. For now he would keep that film out where it would serve as bait in his effort to catch a murdering rat.

Fortunately Agnes wasn't in yet so he didn't have to answer any awkward questions during his brief stop at the office. When he got to the bank there was no sign of Nina at her desk behind the low barrier. That meant he wouldn't have to deal with any queries as to why he was coming in to check his safe deposit box so often. She might not've said anything, though he was sure she would have given him her usual eye tease. He liked Nina and certainly didn't mind flirting with her whenever he was at the bank. However, right now it was better not to arouse any more suspicions than were necessary. The new girl at the desk spoke with him in an officious manner while saying little else than what was required for him to access the safe deposit vault.

With one film tucked safely away at the bank, Doherty stopped at the Donut Kettle for a brown sugared cruller and a cup of joe. When he finished the coffee he asked for a refill in a cardboard cup to take with him back to the office. The five-block walk gave him a chance to think about his next move. So far his search for Frankie DeAngelo had come up empty. Given what happened to Maureen Donovan it was conceivable that DeAngelo was in hiding, or worse, was already dead. For now Jimmy Ricks was his only path to DeAngelo.

When Doherty turned off Washington onto Brookside he was immediately confronted by two men in suits. He would've been frightened if they both didn't have cops written all over them.

"Are you Doherty?" the bigger of the two asked.

He didn't answer right away, purposely taking his time to finish his take-out coffee. The speaker was large in a blocky sort of way, which caused him to wear his dark gray suit in an ill-fitting manner. He had a strong jaw and piercing brown eyes. He also sported a brown fedora with a little feather in the hatband. Not too many cops wore fedoras anymore now that the plainclothes guys on TV were often bareheaded. Without hesitating the big guy flashed his badge while introducing himself as Lt. Walter Bonnano of the state police.

The other cop hung back, letting Bonnano take the lead. Once Doherty agreed that he was who they thought he was, the second cop showed his shield, identifying himself as Sgt. Mike Sullivan of the Cranston PD. He was younger and wore an equally ill-fitting brown suit. His tie was some kind of scarlet design and his white shirt had a noticeable yellow ring around the collar. For some reason Sullivan would only look at Doherty sideways.

He nodded a greeting at the two men but offered no handshakes. "What can I do for you gents?"

"We'd like to have a little chat if you're not too busy." The two cops exchanged smirks as if this line actually had some humor in it.

"Should we go up to my office? We can talk there."

"How's about if we get in the car," Sullivan said. His voice made a little whistle when he pronounced the ess.

"Are we going for a ride somewhere?"

"No. We just want to ask you a few questions," Bonnano said as he placed a hand on Doherty's arm. Doherty looked down at the state cop's grip. Bonnano slowly removed it, though not before an unpleasant smile creased his face.

Doherty crossed the street with the two men to an unmarked sedan that may as well have been a black and white. Bonnano opened the rear door and suggested that Doherty get into the back seat. Sullivan joined him while the big man took the passenger seat in the front. Without asking for their permission Doherty immediately torched a Camel and rolled down his window to let the smoke out.

"Could you identify yourself, please? For the record," Bonnano began, his arm rested on the seat back as he looked directly at Doherty.

"My name is Hugh Michael Doherty and I live at 26 Crossen Street, here in West Warwick. My profession is that of a private investigator." To support this last piece of information Doherty took out his wallet and flashed his PI license for the two cops to look at. He didn't give them the courtesy of removing it from behind its plastic window. Sullivan studied his card carefully then handed it over to Bonnano who gave it a cursory glance before tossing the wallet back to its owner.

"Are you familiar with a woman named Maureen Donovan?" Sullivan asked. From the look Bonnano shot the Cranston cop Doherty was sure that the statie's style of interrogation was usually along subtler lines.

"Yes, I am. I met her a few weeks ago while working a case. I understand she was recently murdered. I'm assuming that's why you're here."

"You say you met her a few weeks ago. Could you be more specific about the date when you first made her acquaintance?" Sullivan asked, once again whistling through his esses.

"I'm not very good with dates," Doherty said as he blew smoke out the window. "I'd have to check my calendar to be more exact as to the day."

"How did you meet Miss Donovan?" Bonnano pitched in.

"Actually I believe she was Mrs. Donovan. I met her while trying to locate a guy who by coincidence lived next door to her. The person I was looking for wasn't at home, but Mrs. Donovan was and we got to shooting the breeze."

"I don't understand," Sullivan said, a look of confusion taking up residence on his face.

"It's simple. I walked around to the back of her neighbor's side of their duplex and knocked on the rear door. While I was knocking Mrs. Donovan was taking in some sun in the next yard. She informed me that the man I was looking for wasn't at home. We then got to talking about one thing or another." If he could help it, this was about as far as Doherty was going to take his relationship with Maureen for these two.

Bonnano broke in here, "Who was the guy you were looking for when you went to Maple Street?"

"Some mook named Frankie DeAngelo." The two cops traded knowing glances.

"What was your interest in this DeAngelo?" Bonnano asked, now taking over the interrogation.

"I'm a PI. My specialty is finding people who are missing. I was hired by a guy whose business partner had gone missing. He was paying me to find him. The only lead he could give me was that the missing man was looking for someone named Frankie DeAngelo. When I looked into the DeAngelos in this part of the state the only one who came up dirty was the guy who lived next door to Mrs. Donovan."

"I'm a little confused here," Sullivan said. Doherty could have told him that beforehand but stayed mum. "Why did you think this DeAngelo was the one your missing guy was searching for? There are a lot of DeAngelos in Rhode Island."

Doherty looked at Bonnano while he answered Sullivan's question. "Yeah, there are. But not too many of them are small time boosters who wholesale hot goods."

"How did you come by this information, Mr. Doherty?"

"I got a tip – and after I met Mrs. Donovan she filled in some of the details about DeAngelo's business practices."

"Are you telling us that the dead woman was in business with this DeAngelo?" Sullivan asked.

"No, I don't believe she was. Though she was well aware of what he was up to. I mean he did live right next door to her and she saw a lot of shady characters going in and out of his place. According to her it was hard not to notice. She confided to me that DeAngelo gave her some stuff every now and then. Small things like jewelry for herself or sports equipment for her son. Nothing big or expensive. DeAngelo was her friend and neighbor, but he wasn't that generous with her." Doherty had no intention of adding that the dead girl occasionally slept with DeAngelo in return.

"Do you have any idea where this Frankie DeAngelo is now?"

"Not a clue. I never laid eyes on the guy or even looked at a picture of him. So far my search for him has been like shooting in the dark."

"Any idea who might've killed the Donovan woman?" Bonnano asked, still taking the lead.

"From what I read in the papers it sounds like whoever did it was looking for DeAngelo and either hit the wrong apartment, or shot her because he thought she was in cahoots with him. My best guess is that the killer figured she was somehow connected to the guy he was after."

"We need to know who you're working for and who this lost person is you were hired to find," Sullivan said. Doherty looked at Bonnano. The big man turned away letting the Cranston cop run this part of the show.

"I'm afraid I can't do that. It would be bad for business if I revealed my clientele to the police. As far as I can tell neither person has committed a crime so…"

At this point Sullivan roughly grabbed Doherty's arm and said, "You know we have ways of getting this information out of you."

Doherty didn't know what the Cranston detective meant by this nor did he want to find out. Instead he just calmly looked Sullivan in the eye. The cop quickly averted his gaze.

"C'mon, Mike. We don't have to resort to threats," Bonnano broke in. "I think Mr. Doherty has been more than forthcoming with us." Sullivan grumbled yet let go of Doherty's arm.

"I have one final question for you, Mr. Doherty. Did you have a sexual relationship with the Donovan woman?" the state cop asked.

"I think I'll take the Fifth on that one."

"Jesus Christ, Doherty," Sullivan exploded. "A woman is dead – and you don't seem all that broke up about it."

Doherty turned toward Sullivan and said, "I tend to keep my emotions under wraps. You ought to try it sometime."

"Why you sonofabitch!" When he saw Sullivan ball up his right fist Doherty opened the car door and stepped out before anything unpleasant happened. Once he was on the sidewalk Bonnano got out of the car and came up next to him. Some men would have been intimidated by the state cop's size. Doherty wasn't. In his time he'd been around enough big men who thought their size alone gave them an advantage. It was often a phony bluff.

"If you can think of anything more that might help us in our investigation we would appreciate you getting in touch." With that the big guy handed Doherty one of his contact cards.

"Will do. By the way, how did you connect me to Mrs. Donovan?"

"It was the meatball subs at Marcello's. People tell me they're worth the visit."

Chapter Twenty-One

Frank Ganetti Sr. was the well-known boss of one of Rhode Island's most notorious crime families. For years he headed a crew called the Manton Avenue gang, which acted as an important subcontractor to the real mob powers that operated out of a small vending machine company on Federal Hill. Fortunately for law enforcement, Ganetti was now in his third year of the 10-20 stretch at the state prison in Cranston. It was called the ACI, which stood for Adult Correctional Institution, a nice antiseptic term for a place where some of Rhode Island's most hardened criminals were housed.

After the elder Ganetti went to the can, a power struggle ensued among the family's underlings. The main players were Sal Patrullo, one of Ganetti's most trusted lieutenants, and the boss' son, Frank Ganetti Jr., referred to simply as 'Junior' by just about everyone in the state, though never to his face.

Young Ganetti originally had been brought into the family's business primarily to move its ill-gotten gains into legitimate interests. With an MBA from Harvard and the smarts to go with it, he was the perfect man for the job. Apparently his old man's initial intent was to keep him out of the rougher side of his operations while using him to find creative ways to launder money. However, when an anti-crime task force was able to convict Frank Senior on several racketeering charges, Junior was pressed into service running the whole operation. The precipitating event for his rise to power was when Sal "The Snake" Patrullo tried to have Junior eliminated. Despite, or perhaps because of his Ivy League education, Junior was smart enough to strike first, eliminating Patrullo via the law and many of his followers by harsher means.

From what Doherty could glean from the papers, Junior now ran the whole Manton Avenue enterprise. About a year ago Doherty'd had some unexpected dealings with Frank Ganetti Jr. thanks to a missing person's case he was working. He was initially hired by Judge DeCenza to find a Warwick real estate developer and Republican County Chairman named Spencer Wainwright, who had gone missing right before an important statewide election. The man returned to Warwick, but then went missing again. This time Doherty was hired by a woman named Annette Patrullo, who worked for Wainwright and was doubling as his mistress. It turned out she was Sal Patrullo's daughter, though Doherty didn't know it at the time. After Wainwright turned up dead – murdered by a slug to the head, young Ganetti hired Doherty to find out who killed Wainwright and why. The connection between the Ganetti and Wainwright revolved around some common interests they had in commercial real estate development. For Wainwright his plan was to use this connection to make some big financial scores; for Ganetti it was in finding new ways to clean the family's money.

Doherty had been reluctant to involve himself in that aspect of the Wainwright case, but Frank Junior gave him little choice in the matter. It turned out that one of Ganetti's own men had thrown in with Patrullo's people and murdered Wainwright in hopes of queering Junior's business deals by having him blamed for pissing away a large amount of mob money. However, the plan to discredit Junior backfired. In the end Patrullo wound up joining Ganetti's father in prison, thanks to a law enforcement crackdown. In the meantime Doherty was able to unwind the mystery of Wainwright's death to Ganetti's satisfaction and was generously remunerated for his efforts. That, coupled with the fact that Ganetti probably saved Doherty's life in the process, left the two men somewhat beholden to each other.

Doherty had hoped to leave that chapter in his life permanently behind him by returning to more mundane cases that required him to find lost mates that ran off with persons not their spouses. And that was what he'd been doing more or less successfully for the past year. However, he now realized that the only way he could get back at Jimmy Ricks was to play the Ganetti card.

For that reason he'd called Junior's office the day before and arranged for an appointment at ten the next morning.

Frank Ganetti Jr. had a practice as a certified public accountant in the center of Providence's small but thriving financial district. His building was located on Weybosset Street across from the Arcade, one of city's more attractive old buildings.

A good-looking, red haired girl with long limbs, red lips and a sly smile had replaced the pixyish secretary who'd sat at the front desk in Ganetti's office a year ago. Doherty wondered if Ganetti had changed his secretary to go along with his increased activities on the other side of the law. The girl welcomed him warmly and told Doherty he could go right in, that Mr. Ganetti was expecting him.

Frank Junior was sitting behind his oversized desk with a pair of reading glasses resting on the end of his nose. When he saw Doherty he rose quickly from his chair and greeted him with a warm smile and a firm handshake. As always, Ganetti was impeccably dressed in a starched dress shirt set off by gold cufflinks and a thin, muted tie held in place by a gold tie clasp that matched the links. He still wore his hair brushed across his scalp in an Ivy League style, though some strands of gray were now mixed in with the black. A tailored suit jacket matching his neatly creased slacks hung on a hanger not too far from the desk.

Doherty was offered a chair while his host reassumed his seat behind the desk.

Ganetti offered a genial smile and said, "How're tricks, Mr. Doherty? I don't hear from you in over a year, and then out of the blue you call to make an appointment. I suppose I should ask what's on your mind?" No need for false pleasantries or introductory chitchat from the crime boss; no reason to ask polite questions about Doherty's non-existent family or the success of his threadbare PI practice.

"My apologies for not keeping in touch. I guess you could say there haven't been any reasons for our paths to cross since the Wainwright ... case." He was going to say *murder* but decided that might dredge up unpleasant memories for both of them. "Have you heard anything about Annette Patrullo?" he asked.

Ganetti was quiet for an uncomfortable amount of time – no doubt considering whether to tell Doherty he'd had her murdered or that her whereabouts was none of his business. Sal Patrullo's daughter Annette had played a key role in Spencer Wainwright's death and Ganetti's men as well as the Providence police have been on her trail ever since. He'd bet on Ganetti's crew finding the girl first since they had a much longer reach and greater motivation than the PPD. The last Doherty knew the girl was on the lam in Miami. This was knowledge he purposely hadn't shared with either party.

"Have you come all the way up here from West Warwick to ask about Annette Patrullo?"

"Not really. I was just making conversation. After all, she was a person of interest to both of us."

Ganetti smiled again. Then he pulled out his gold cigarette case and offered Doherty a smoke. Instead he popped out one of his Camels and lit both of them with his Zippo. It was a routine they'd adopted during their earlier dealings.

"Last I heard Annette was in Vegas trying to work out a deal with some of my father's old associates. They tell me she'd like to return to her family here in Rhode Island. Frankly, I'd prefer that she stay out there. If she comes back home we might have to dispose of her." This last remark came out so matter-of-factly that it was more frightening than if it had come dressed up with grisly details.

"I'm not really here to talk about Annette Patrullo or any of that Spencer Wainwright business. I'm here on another matter altogether." Doherty waited a few seconds then jumped back in. "I was wondering if you know a pimp who works out of the South Side named Jimmy Ricks?"

Ganetti's face screwed up into an unpleasant expression. "Jimmy Ricks is a bottom feeding slug that, much to my dismay, our associates up on the Hill insist plays an important role in their operations. If it were up to me I would've cut that lowlife scum loose a long time ago. But you see, Mr. Doherty, prostitution is still a very lucrative enterprise here in Rhode Island. I've been informed that some of our state's finest citizens periodically indulge in that kind of consumerism."

Doherty had to hand it to Frank Junior, he sure had a way with words. As the certificates on his walls attest, his BA from Brown and his MBA from

Harvard were money well spent. They provided him with the best vocabulary of any gangster Doherty'd ever encountered.

"May I ask what your interest is in the half-breed Ricks?"

Doherty pulled on his smoke while considering how much he was willing to share with Ganetti. "I've been hired to find a missing person. This person had some important dealings with Ricks several years ago. From what I've been able to piece together, they were not dealings of a sexual nature per se. I have a hunch this man has been in touch with Ricks again more recently. When I met with Ricks a few days ago he denied having seen my guy since their earlier interaction. I didn't believe him, but you see someone like me hardly has the leverage to force Ricks into truth telling. That's about all I can tell you at this point, either about the person I'm looking for or the one who hired me. For now I have to protect their identities."

"And you thought I might be able to help you get this pimp to be more forthcoming," Ganetti said with a sly grin.

"Well, that's not all of it. When I tried to push Ricks a little harder on this issue he threatened to have some of his boys take me out behind the Club Mocambo to work me over. I happened to mention my past connection with you in order to save my ass. At the time I didn't see any other way."

Ganetti chuckled and shook his head knowingly. "I must say, Doherty, you seem to have a knack for putting your nose in all the wrong places. Despite that, I do not mind you using my name to avoid any unpleasantness with the likes of Jimmy Ricks. Nevertheless, you still haven't explained why you drove all the way up here to see me." He probably wanted to say have this *audience*, but that would've made him sound too much like the pope.

"I need to take another run at Ricks. I knew he was holding out on me at the Club Mocambo, but I could only push him so far on his own turf in front of his people. I was there without any backup except for a jazz musician friend who set up the meeting. My options were obviously limited."

Ganetti stubbed out his filtered cigarette and said, "I suspect you found the environment at the Mocambo a little too dark for your taste. Ricks is a small time minnow who thinks he's a hammerhead shark. He preys on the weaknesses of women. He likes to act the big daddy role though most of his girls are virtual captives - if not to the money he gives them, then to the drugs he feeds them so they'll keep whoring. There is nothing classy about his operation.

But he's important to some people because of his ability to recruit desirable Negresses that no other pimp in the city would be able to get within sniffing distance of."

The conversation had reached an awkward point where Ganetti was trying to dope out what he could or should do on Doherty's behalf. Meanwhile Doherty had no idea if the crime boss still felt he owed him anything for his work on the Wainwright case.

"This is what I can do," Ganetti said in a controlled voice. "I will set up a meeting between you and Ricks at a neutral site – not some place that has a lot of black whores and thugs hanging around. And I will make sure Ricks attends as you wish. In addition, I will have Gio accompany you for support. I would ask your old friend Angelo to do so, but Angelo harbors strong negative feelings about Negroes that could lead to trouble. Ricks will no doubt want to bring one of his henchmen, so I will insist that it be only one. You can meet and talk as you wish. But I must warn you, I cannot and will not do anything to make this pimp bastard tell you whatever he doesn't have a mind to. What you extract from him will be entirely dependent on your powers of persuasion."

Doherty stood, sensing that his audience with Frank Junior was just about over. "Thank you, Mr. Ganetti. I'll owe you one for this."

"Please call me Frank. And yes, you will owe me."

Chapter Twenty-Two

Ganetti's man Gio picked up Doherty at six the next evening. Unlike the taciturn Angelo, Gio was practically loquacious by comparison. His big black Pontiac Catalina provided a swell ride as they sped toward Providence. Gio was shaped like a fireplug with a neck as wide as his head. His black hair was greased down and quite thick. He had a genial smile that regularly spread across his face, revealing a large array of very white teeth that didn't look like they were his originals.

Gio started the conversation by complaining about his wife and three kids. He told Doherty how he stopped at Solitro's Bakery in Knightsville every other day to pick up pastries and when he brought them home to his family they always complained about his selection. His mention of the Knightsville section of Cranston reminded Doherty of Maureen Donovan and her stone cold murder.

He was surprised to hear that Gio had a family given his line of work. Then he realized all he knew about the man was that he drove a car for Frank Ganetti Jr. - and tonight he was driving one for him. That plus Gio's expertise in frisking people was the full extent of the man's skills as far as Doherty knew. He hoped Ganetti's man had other abilities that could be called upon if things with Ricks got dicey.

Their conversation soon veered into a discussion about Italian restaurants around Rhode Island. Doherty knew that many Italians in the state were partial to their native cuisine. His own knowledge was limited by the

fact that there were few such places in West Warwick. His driver insisted
that the best Italian eateries were on Federal Hill. He enumerated several of
them including the Old Canteen where Doherty and Rachel had dined the
night they were attacked by Stanislaw Krykowski and his cohorts. That event
prompted Doherty to later shoot the big Pole. He wondered how well versed
his companion Gio was in the art of killing. Enough he hoped to put a fright
into Jimmy Ricks.

They drove north on Broad Street toward Providence but soon took a right
and headed toward an industrial area along the waterfront near the old shipyards. It was not a section of the city Doherty was familiar with. They'd seen
a number of Negroes as they drove through South Providence, though hardly
any over the last mile or so. Eventually Gio pulled up in front of a small, run-
down looking place called George's Tavern in an industrial section of the city.
A darkened Narragansett beer sign hung above the front door, its neon bulbs
looked like they had given up the ghost a long time ago. There was no evidence
of a vehicle that would have belonged to a pimp like Ricks or one of his dark
skinned crew. They didn't linger in the car as Gio urged Doherty to follow him
inside.

George's was your standard issue tavern with a bar that ran the length of
one wall while several booths lined the facing one. It looked like every taproom Doherty'd ever frequented in his hometown where men went to drink
and sometimes fight. The walls at George's were covered with photographs of
prizefighters, some of whom Doherty recognized, others he didn't. Two men
sat at the bar nursing glasses of beer. They gave Doherty and Gio a cursory
glance then went back to their mumbled conversation. The place smelled of
stale beer and urine. It made the Club Mocambo seem like the Copacabana.

They took seats in a booth where the plastic cushions were cracked in a
few places. Soon a stocky guy wearing a dirty white T-shirt and dark slacks
held up by suspenders came over to greet them. A tweed snap-brimmed cap
completed his ensemble. His face was a mass of scar tissue and his nose took
so many detours it made Doherty's bumped one look aquiline by comparison.
Gio spoke to the guy in Italian and their host replied in kind. Then Gio introduced the man to Doherty as George DiMucci.

Doherty stuck out his paw and George enwrapped it in a grip that would
have crushed the hand of a smaller man.

"George used to be a boxer," Gio said to Doherty. "His ring name was Tiger DiMucci. He once fought Kid Gavilan at the Arena."

"Nice to meet you, George," Doherty said. "I guess this is your place, huh?"

"Yeah. It was my fadder's before me. George Sr. He's dead now. I took it over after I quit fightin'. It ain't much but I make a livin' here," the former boxer said, his words filtered through gravel. Doherty took another look around and wondered how Tiger DiMucci made any money off this dump.

During this perusal his eye caught a large picture of a fighter on the wall near their booth. It was of a younger, less damaged version of George DiMucci, posing with his dukes up. Time and left hooks had taken a toll on their host.

"Hey, Gio when's this spook suppose to show?" DiMucci asked. Doherty assumed *spook* was how DiMucci affectionately referred to Negroes.

Gio looked at his watch and said, "He's suppose to've been here by now. Probably thinks if he shows up late he'll be sendin' us a message. You know how them niggers are – always late for everythin'."

George asked if the two men wanted a drink. Gio ordered scotch rocks while Doherty opted for his usual Jameson neat.

When the owner was out of earshot Doherty leaned across the table and said in a quiet voice. "I think you two should go easy on the *spook* and *nigger* stuff. This Ricks may be a first class asshole, but I'm not going to get anywhere with him if you guys start throwing around insults like that. You don't have to make him feel welcome. But it would be better for me if he didn't feel hostility."

Gio smiled at Doherty. "You'll have to excuse me. Most of the niggers, I mean Negroes, I come into contact with are involved in some kinda illegal stuff. They ain't exactly your chamber of commerce types."

"I understand. It's just that I need to get some information out of this guy who's going to be reluctant to give it to me. If he feels threatened by you two, things could end up very bad all the way around."

"Frank Junior told me to follow your lead, so I'll do what I gotta to help you out. But if this jungle bunny cracks wise I may have to teach him some manners."

"There you go again, Gio."

Fortunately their drinks arrived to break up the conversation. George lingered near the table without saying anything until Gio gave him a wrist flick to indicate that the owner should return to his place behind the bar.

"I was just teasin' you, pal. Me and George'll be on our best behavior I promise. But if you feel things are going south just give me the high sign and we'll take over from there."

They drank while making small talk for another ten minutes until they heard a loud motor outside. The three of them wandered over to the window and split the blinds just as Ricks' cream-colored Cadillac convertible eased to the curb. A dark skinned guy with processed hair so shiny it looked like it had been painted on his head sat at the wheel. Beside him was the fat man Ricks called Tiny. The pimp slouched across the back seat in a casual pose. He was wearing dark wraparound sunglasses and a lime green suit over a black silk shirt that shimmered in the fading daylight. His conked hair looked almost blond.

The driver got out first and opened the rear door for his boss. Then all three slowly sashayed to the entrance of George's. On the way Ricks craned his head around checking out the bar and its shabby surroundings. His mouth twisted up in a look of disapproval. Gio and Doherty returned to their seats in the booth waiting for the pimp's grand entrance. Meanwhile George stood by the door holding a large baseball bat by his side.

Ricks passed into the tavern first, followed by Tiny. The driver with the processed hair tried to enter as well but the former boxer held his bat across the entrance.

"I was tolt only two of yous would be comin' in. I think you should go wait in the car," George said to the driver. Everyone froze for a few seconds as the guy gave the owner a menacing look. It was a look the ex-prizefighter had probably seen dozens of times in the ring; it didn't seem to faze him one bit. Doherty was concerned that the meeting was about to go off the rails before it even started.

Ricks then turned to the processed hair guy and said, "Harold, why don't you go sit in the car. And while you're at it, put the top up. I heard it might rain."

There was no rain in the forecast, but Ricks wisely didn't want his dark skinned driver sitting in an open convertible on a street in a seedy neighborhood that had few Negroes in it. Ricks made some disparaging comments about George's while Tiny approached Doherty and asked him to stand. Reluctantly he did so and Ricks' wide-bodied accomplice gave him another professional patting down like he'd done at the Mocambo.

Gio did the same to Ricks while their mulatto guest looked down at him with a condescending grin on his yellow skinned face. The fat man then ambled up to the bar and ordered drinks for himself and his boss. The two fellows down the bar still nursing their beers swiveled their heads around, befuddled by everything that was going on. Apparently George's Tavern didn't attract too many Negroes among its clientele.

DiMucci went over to where the men were sitting and said, "Why don't yous two blow for a while. Consider your drinks on the house." He looked at Gio who nodded his approval at the gesture. After the men left, Gio and the guy Ricks called Tiny assumed seats at the bar out of earshot. They both placed large pistols on its top next to their drinks.

At the table Ricks used his index finger to swirl the clear liquid over the ice cubes in his glass. He tried to stare Doherty down, but the PI was used to this game and refused to blink.

"So Mr. Detective, what can I do for you - and *Mr. Ganetti*?" He added just to let Doherty know he was only there because Frank Junior had requested that he be. Doherty lit a smoke and waited. With no response forthcoming Ricks slid a pack of Kools out of his jacket pocket and torched one with a gold lighter.

"Last time we talked you said you hadn't seen Gus Timilty in five years or so. I don't think you were being honest with me. I believe you've seen him more recently and I need to know why. I'm assuming he approached you, and it wasn't to have sex with one of your girls. What did he want?"

Ricks removed his sunglasses and placed them on the table beside his drink. The glass was empty so he held it up and clicked the cubes in Tiny's direction. His bodyguard fetched him a new drink while Doherty waited patiently.

"He was lookin' for a girl," Ricks said without prompting. Nothing else was volunteered.

"Was she a girl involved in your operation?"

"You might say that."

"What do you say? Was she a whore or wasn't she?"

Ricks smiled. "I like to think of my girls as pleasure women, not whores."

"Really. I saw a lot of pictures of Filipino and Chinese *pleasure women* the Japs used during the war. They didn't seem to be getting much pleasure out of what they were doing. But I'm not here to argue about semantics," he added knowing that Ricks probably didn't know what that word meant. "Why was Gus so hot to find one of your girls? He didn't want her for sex, did he?"

"No, *he* dint, but a lot of other johnnies do. She's one of my best earners. I told your boy that but he wouldn't listen. He offered me money to give her up. Fool dint understand how valuable she is to what I've got goin' on."

"And what exactly is it you've got going on?"

Ricks sucked on his Kool and smiled. "Movies, man. We're in the movie business."

"By *we* are you referring to yourself and the girl, or you and Frankie DeAngelo?"

Ricks shook his head and smiled his leering grin again. The gold teeth in his mouth sparkled under the harsh lighting in George's Tavern. "Frankie DeAngelo, huh? You're a pretty smart motherfucker for a small-time private dick."

"I still don't get what Timilty's interest is in this girl."

Ricks leaned back and said in a voice just above a whisper. "She's his daughter. Her mother was the bitch I threw out of my harem five years ago. She was too fucked up on H at the time to be any good to me. Timilty did me a favor by takin' her off my hands. But the daughter, now she's a different story. You might say she's my little princess. Not only can she fuck and suck like a pro, she can act like one too. Girl oughta be in Hollywood."

Doherty was trying hard not to let his anger at Ricks' callousness get the better of him. He needed information and didn't want to put the pimp off until he got it. He figured his next step should be to focus on the movie angle while putting Gus aside for the moment. "Tell me about these movies you and DeAngelo are making. Are they just your standard stag films or is something else going on?"

Ricks held up his glass and his boy Tiny refreshed his drink for a third time. "At first they was just the usual fuck movies. You probably seen them when you was in the army. We rent or sell 'em to all kindsa people: college fraternities, the Lion's Club, guys who play poker together. You know, cats who wanna see girls do stuff their wives or girlfriends wouldn't never do. Course we always gotta be careful of the law. But shit man, even the cops like to watch fuck movies."

"What happened between you and DeAngelo that changed things?"

Ricks maintained a casual demeanor, slowly smoking his Kool. He didn't want to give Doherty any indication he was willingly passing on information.

"It all started when Frankie began sellin' me some of his primo gage. I'd give it to my girls for when they was with some of our high-class customers; you know, business guys, politicians, cats with money to burn. Once we saw how much they liked the reefer and the girls together, Frankie came up with this idea for shakin' some real cash outta them."

"Is that how the movie making came into it?"

"Yeah. You see I'd been tellin' these cats all along that bein' high on reefer makes the sex all the more better. Then after a while I could tell these johnnies were way too high to pay attention to anythin' else than what they were doin' with the girls. So me and Frankie rigged up a couple of rooms in a flop I own near the Mocambo. In one of the rooms we had a nice bedroom set-up and in the other a camera shootin' movies through a hole in the wall. We always had the girls put some music so the johnnies wouldn't never hear the camera in the next room."

"At first we just filmed them sexin' it up. But here's the thing, some of these cats wanted to put on little plays. You know, different kindsa fantasy shit. Most times they just wanted the girls to put on some costume. A couple wanted the bitches to spank them; others wanted my girls to dress like little girls who they could spank. One customer asked if he could have a girl dress up like a nun and paddle him like they done when he was back in school. Another johnnie wanted my girl to put a diaper on him. Whatever they wanted we'd do it for an extra fifty bucks. These cats dint complain on account of they all had lotsa money. But sometimes we had to be careful like when a customer would get rough with one of our girls. You know, hit her or tie her up too tight – shit like that."

"And you and DeAngelo made movies of these shows so you could blackmail the johns afterwards?"

Ricks smiled, pleased with the scam he and Frankie DeAngelo had cooked up. "I don't like that word. It's not like we forced 'em to pay. We just tolt 'em what we had on film and aksed if they'd be interested in buyin' them. You know, we called 'em home movies that they could take home and watch whenever they wanted. These johnnies weren't stupid. They knew what we was sayin' and how it wouldn't work out too good for them if the movies got sent to their wives or to people they did business with. And if they were some kinda big deal politicians, they sure as hell dint want their movie gettin' out to the public. Most times they'd gladly pay. And we was smart; we never aksed for too much or more than these cats woulda been able to come up with. That girl Timilty claimed was his daughter, she turned out to be our best actress. Little bitch knew how to play to the camera. She dint need no promptin' neither – she knew zactly how to get our mark on film without him ever knowin' it."

"Why are you telling me all this?"

"Maybe you should aks your Italian gumba over there?"

Doherty turned his head toward Gio. His back-up man was engaged in a heated discussion with George and Tiny about great boxers and fights. He heard the names of Johnny Saxon, Sugar Ray Robinson, Carmen Basillio and Rocky Marciano being thrown around.

When he looked back at Ricks; the smile was no longer creasing the pimp's handsome face. "Yesterday word was passed on to me from Ganetti that if I dint cooperate with you he would put me out of business. I knew the Federal Hill crew wouldn'ta let that happen, but you know in my world accidents happen sometimes. I dint want one to happen all over me."

"So what's the status of your little film business now?"

"Well first your friend Timilty showed up makin' a big deal about our little star. I assumed it would only been a matter of time 'fore he got to her. I mean I couldn't keep the little bitch locked up all the time. And I still needed her to do her reg'lar customers. Then Frankie up and disappeared. I dint know how to work the movie thing without him. He's the one that set up the camera and shit and helped me choose our new marks. When I couldn't find him I figured it was a good time to close up shop. Next thing I hear some girl in Cranston who was Frankie's next-door neighbor been shot. After that I began to think one of the customers we was shakin' down was tryin' to get back at us. I got concerned 'cause some of these cats got more contacts with the mob than me. Way I seen it, we had a good run and it was time to close things down 'fore anybody else got hurt."

"Except for one thing."

"Yeah, what's that?"

"An innocent girl in Cranston got killed. And Frankie DeAngelo might not be far behind. By the way, where's your starlet now?"

All the smugness drained from Jimmy Ricks' face. For a moment Doherty thought he saw a flash of fear, though the pimp quickly recovered.

"That's just it. I don't know where she's at. I ain't seen her in over a week. First I thought she was just doin' an overnight with some johnnie. But when she didn't come back I figured maybe she was with Frankie, or Timilty'd gotten to her. Then I couldn't raise Frankie, so I tried calling your boy. He'd been leavin' messages for me, but I dint have no reason to talk to him till my princess disappeared."

"She could be dead. If she is, then that would be on you."

Chapter Twenty-Three

It was after nine when Gio dropped Doherty back at his apartment in West Warwick. All the way home he couldn't get the images of the young girl in the movies out of his head. And to think she was, or at least could be, Gus Timilty's daughter. The films he watched were too grainy for him to detect any clear resemblance to his old friend; for now he'd have to take Ricks' word for it.

Doherty was so consumed by these thoughts that he didn't notice things weren't right in the apartment until he flicked on the lights. His place had been tossed, but not in the way Maureen Donovan's or Frankie DeAngelo's had. Although his possessions and furniture were strewn about, nothing was needlessly destroyed. After doing a careful inventory, he couldn't identify anything that'd been stolen either, though he'd be the first to admit he didn't have much of value in the first place.

Whoever'd been through his place was in search of something and not there for purposes of theft, or vengeful destruction as with the two apartments in Cranston. The intruder must've been looking for the films. Doherty was in the midst of straightening things up when he realized that his burglar's next stop would probably be his office, if he hadn't been there already. The Chevy was locked up in Belanger's garage so he hotfooted it into town as quickly as his feet would carry him. Although the office was only a few blocks up Brookside, the urgency of the trip made it feel like it was miles away.

Once there, Doherty stood on the sidewalk carefully scanning the building. Everything seemed to be dark as it should be. His inner office had the only window that faced onto the street. As always he'd left the blinds turned down. He eyeballed the window very closely. At first he saw nothing. Then he thought he detected some muted light inside, possibly from a flashlight.

He pulled out his .38 from his waistband and chambered a bullet. With revolver in hand he quietly opened the building's front door and entered as stealthily as he could. Before mounting the stairs he undid his shoes and left them resting in the foyer inside the front door. On stocking feet he slowly ascended, trying as best he could to remember which steps were the ones that creaked. He'd climbed these stairs hundreds of times, but for the life of him he couldn't recall which made noise when trod upon.

To avoid making any undue sounds he elected to inch his way up on the outer edge of each riser. Moving very slowly he reached the landing outside of Doherty and Associates without being heard. The office door had been forced open and was ajar enough for him to hear some rustling inside. He slowly eased his way into Agnes' space. Someone was in his office rattling around in his filing cabinet. He shuffled across the distance between his secretary's desk and the inner office. He could see the flashlight beam before he saw its holder. Someone was squatting on the floor leaning over the bottom drawer of the cabinet.

When he had an angle where he could get off a clean shot, Doherty said very loudly, "Stay right where you are. I have a gun. If you pull out a weapon or point the beam from your flashlight in my direction I will shoot you. Now slowly stand up and put the light under your chin so I can see your face."

A large person unfolded himself into a standing position. He turned around and held the flashlight as directed. Doherty recognized the intruder immediately.

"Jesus Christ, Gus. What the hell are you doing tossing my office?" Timilty lowered the light and Doherty lowered his pistol. He then walked over to the desk and turned on the green shaded desk lamp. Gus looked embarrassed as well he should.

"I need to find those movies. For some reason I thought you had them." The two old friends stared at each other for a moment without saying anything. "And I was right," he said as he held up the film canister Doherty'd locked in his filing cabinet. When he glanced down at the drawer he saw that Gus had crudely jimmied it open.

"Maybe you should sit down, Gus, so we can talk."

"Where's the other film?" his friend said anxiously. "I have to find that film."

"First you're going to tell me what this is all about."

Gus slumped down into Doherty's swivel chair and let out a long sigh. "I'm in trouble, pally. And those films are the only way I can get out of it."

"Why don't you start at the beginning?"

"Damnit, Doherty. I could use a drink. Do you have anything here?"

He thought about the bottle of Jameson he usually kept in his desk. Then remembered he'd killed it the day Maureen was murdered.

"Let's go up to Paddy's; we can talk there and get something to drink. I'll let you cover the first two rounds for damaging my filing cabinet."

The two friends said little as they walked the two blocks into the center where Arctic's best-known Irish taproom would be serving booze until midnight. Before they left Doherty returned the film to its place in the bottom of his filing cabinet. At Paddy's he greeted Mickey Flannery, who was working the taps alone tonight. Mickey had taken over running the place when his father Pat, the Paddy for whom the place was named, became too old and debilitated from drink to do it anymore. Timilty gave the men leaning on the bar a good going over before he took a seat in one of Paddy's booths. He wanted to make sure no old acquaintances from his cop days were there.

Doherty went to the bar to get a Jameson for himself and a Bushmills on ice for Gus.

"Hey, Doherty," Mickey said as he came down the bar to deliver the drinks. "Your Uncle Patrick was in here the other night. I ain't seen him in a coon's age. What's a fancy-pants lawyer like him doin' in a dump like this?" he added with a self-deprecating laugh.

"Patrick was here? When?"

Mickey Flannery wrestled with the question for a few beats. "I think it was Monday night. Yeah, it was Monday night 'cause that was the same night the cops had to come in to break up a fight. Don't worry, your uncle was long gone by then."

"What did the great Patrick McSweeny want?"

"He was askin' 'bout you among other things. Started out by sayin' how proud he was of you for shootin' that Nazi bastard up in Pawtucket. Then he wanted to know if I knew what you was workin' on now."

"What did you tell him?"

Mickey Flannery shrugged his shoulders. "Nothin' really. Told him I only knew about you killin' that Nazi fella last spring 'cause it was all over the news. Said you didn't come in here too much no more. I didn't say nothin' I wasn't 'spose to, did I?"

Doherty shook his head. "No, Mickey. No reason not to talk about that case in Pawtucket. It was on the news even up in Boston so I'm sure my uncle read about it. That's all he wanted to know, what I was up to?"

Mickey began to wipe down the bar as he talked. "Yeah, but you know how he is. He stayed long enough to throw some blarney around. Told everybody who'd listen that the Kennedy guy from Massachusetts was gonna be the next president. Then he bought a round for the house and got all the regulars to toast to Jack Kennedy. Nobody minded him talkin' politics. Fellas in here'll toast damn near anythin' long as somebody else is buyin'."

"Thanks, Mickey. Listen, I'm going to be sitting over there with a friend. Could you keep the rounds coming every ten minutes or so? And make sure nobody bothers us."

"Sure, Doherty. No problem."

He returned to the booth still wondering why his uncle had been in Paddy's asking about him just two days after visiting the office – and later telling him he couldn't go to Paddy's for a drink because he had to be sober enough to drive back to Boston.

Gus' face was glum as Doherty slipped into the booth with the two glasses in hand. His best pal looked old and tired, and embarrassed for breaking into the office. When he sat down he gave Gus a look that was not his friendliest.

"You want to tell me about the girl?"

Gus tried to put a surprised look on his face, but it didn't wear too well. Instead he took a good slug of the Bushmills. "She's my daughter. Not by marriage or anything. She's my daughter from this hooker I used to frequent back in the day. I never told you this, but long before you came onto the force I was married for a short time. The marriage didn't last too long and it ended pretty bad for both of us. In those days I was mostly married to the job and well, eventually my wife found another man to keep her company. When she told me about him we had a terrible fight. I'd been drinking so I'm pretty sure I hit her. That didn't help matters."

"What happened after that?"

"She left me for this other guy and moved to Connecticut. We didn't have any kids so it was a clean break. I haven't seen her since I signed the divorce papers. Must be over twenty-five years now. We were just kids ourselves who shouldn't gotten married in the first place. After that it was just booze and the job for me. Sometimes I'd drink so much I'd black out. Funny thing was I could always get up in the morning and put on the uniform. At work I was all business; off the job I was a mess."

"Are you going to tell me about the mother of your daughter?"

"I'm getting to that. After the wife left I started going to whores. Sometimes they were girls I met while on duty. When they found out I was a cop they'd do me for free. Professional courtesy I suppose. Or else they figured I could help them out if they got into a jam. I was partial to this one girl, so I started going to her regular. I could sit here and tell you she was the proverbial hooker with a heart of gold, but that would be a lie. I went to her mostly when I was in the tank and needed to get my ashes hauled. She was already using junk so she didn't mind if I was soused. We made a fine pair: a drunk cop and a junkie whore."

Mickey came over and set down two more doubles. Timilty slipped him a ten and told him to keep them coming. Doherty urged Gus to continue his story.

"Then one night she told me she was pregnant. Must've been about sixteen, seventeen years ago. I can't remember now. I didn't know what to think. I always figured when that happened to whores their pimps got them fixed up. But she didn't tell her pimp she was knocked up till it was too late. Said the baby was mine and I believed her. I think I wanted it to be mine so I'd have one decent thing in my life."

"After the baby was born she kept working. Left our daughter with her mother most nights. After a while she started working for Jimmy Ricks. A few years down the line Ricks told her he was thinking of cutting her loose 'cause she was too junked up. Trouble was she knew she couldn't take care of our daughter without the money she made whoring. One day she called me and asked if I'd speak to Ricks on her behalf. Thought because I was a cop I could convince him to keep her on, or maybe get some money out him. I guess you could say she was looking for some severance pay. She wanted me to use my badge to lean on him."

"I told her I would take care of her so she wouldn't have to turn tricks anymore. That's how Ricks was able to play me. He agreed to let her get out of the game if I fixed up some trouble he'd gotten into with the Providence police. Most pimps just pay off the cops with dough or free tricks. Ricks was an independent operator back then so he didn't know how the game was played or who to play it with. He wanted to move up the line and knew an early bust would ruin his plans. This was before he was doing business for the mob. When I think about it now, I should've let that prick go down for the bust."

Gus drained his Bushmills though it didn't seem to ease his pain any. "Instead I called some people I knew in the Providence PD and fixed it so he didn't take the fall. I did it because he was threatening to do something bad to Loretta; that was her name, Loretta Russo – a nice Italian girl who fucked strangers for a living. In the end my intervention with the Providence cops cost me my job in West Warwick. Somebody who had it in for me leaked what I'd done to the chief and he had to let me go. I think Judge DeCenza had his hand in getting me fired but I could never prove it. The Judge never liked me because I was reluctant to be a toady for his machine."

There was a break in the conversation as both men were served more drinks. Doherty lit up a Camel to keep his company. The jukebox was playing some Clancy Brothers song about a guy named Brennan. It was so loud that it made conversation difficult. When Bing Crosby replaced it crooning about things in Glocca Morra Timilty resumed his story.

"After Loretta left the trade I put her and our daughter Christina up in an apartment in East Providence. Even though she wasn't whoring anymore, she was still on the needle. She tried to kick a few times; would stay clean for a couple of months, but without a job she had too much time on her hands. I guess being a mother wasn't enough to fill up her life. I couldn't give her much dough 'cause I was only making a sergeant's salary. Then I got canned from the force, which made things worse. After a while we were barely speaking to each other. The daughter was a spitting image of me, or at least I wanted to believe she was. For all I know she could've been the product of anyone of Loretta's johns. Christina never looked anything like her mother. Loretta was dark haired and dark eyed while her daughter was fair like me with blue eyes. Loretta used to say if she hadn't hatched her she wouldn't've believed Christina was hers."

"Things were okay for a few years. I gave them money as best I could while they continued to live in East Providence. I saw them now and then. She would always introduce me to Christina as an old friend. Wouldn't ever let on that I was her father. When I began to make more dough working for Briggs it became less of a financial burden to help them out. Meanwhile Loretta had a series of boyfriends along the way. I think they were just guys she would score from in exchange for sex. It didn't take long for me to realize that a lot of the money I was giving her ended up in her arm."

"When things got really bad, Christina was passed around among Loretta's relatives - most of whom froze me out. Loretta told them I'd been one of her johns so that put me on their shit list right from the jump. Aside from the money I was feeding them I had no way to prove I was the girl's father. As far as they were concerned I had no right to see Christina unless Loretta said I could. Then just like that," Gus said snapping his fingers, "the two of them disappeared."

"Jesus. What did you do?"

"I tried calling Loretta's sister, her cousins, anyone connected to her family. By then I wasn't a cop anymore and thanks to Briggs & Co. I had a lot of connections I could use to track them down. But I came up with a lot of nothing. I began to think maybe they were dead. That Loretta'd been driving junked up and drove off a bridge or something. I checked the obits and police reports all over the state and even in Massachusetts and Connecticut for accidents involving a mother and daughter. I was going crazy looking for them. I kept on searching, even using some of our people at Briggs to help me out. But I couldn't find out anything."

Mickey Flannery dropped two more drinks on the table and told them that he'd be closing in half an hour. Appropriately, Sinatra was singing a song on the jukebox about the wee small hours of the morning.

"Then one day a few months ago I get a tip from one of my snitches that a girl named Christina was working for Jimmy Ricks. Jimmy Fucking Ricks of all people. I shoulda put that sonofabitch down when I had the chance. Now I hear he does a big time hustle for the mob. Around Providence Ricks is known as the purveyor of all things indecent. A regular Svengali of whoredom. He has a clientele so top-shelf he's practically untouchable. I staked out Ricks' zone a couple of times and eventually caught sight of the girl I thought was Christina.

I wanted to believe she was my daughter; I just didn't want to believe she was whoring for Ricks."

"What happened to her mother?"

"Dead. A year ago this winter. They found her with the needle still in her arm in some fleabag motel in Attleboro. Cops up there told me she was turning tricks for five bucks a pop. Five fucking bucks! Making just enough money to keep herself high. And my little girl is now in Jimmy Ricks's stable. Or at least she was until a couple of weeks ago."

"What happened then?"

"I get a call from Ricks. I'd been trying to get ahold of that prick ever since I got the tip about Christina, but he wouldn't return my calls. I left messages offering him big money to let her out of his operation. Then out of the blue he rings me up at the office to tell me Christina's missing and wants to know if I have her. He was trying to be all threatening and shit. I told him I hadn't seen or spoken to her in years. Then he wants to know if *I* can get her back. Wants to hire me as a PI. I told him I'd think about it."

"A few days later he calls me again to inform me that the people who have Christina contacted him. They say they won't let her go until they have possession of some sex films she made for Ricks and some scumbag named Frankie DeAngelo. If they don't get the films they tell him they're gonna kill Christina – but not before they do some awful things to her first. That's why I went looking for DeAngelo. At that point I figured Ricks didn't have the films because he wouldn't be so stupid as to jeopardize his whole operation over them. And while I'm looking for DeAngelo and the films your name pops up."

"I don't understand. How did my name play into this?"

"One of my sources told me you were seen visiting that Donovan broad in Cranston who got shot. The one that lived next door to DeAngelo in that side-by-side duplex. So I start putting two and two together and what it added up to is that it's no coincidence that you're making time with some honey who just happens to live next door to the same guy I'm looking for. A guy who's directly connected to Jimmy Ricks."

"I shouldn't tell you this, but I was looking for *you* because your partner Johnny Briggs hired me to. Said it had to be on the QT because it would be bad for business if anyone found out you were missing. The only lead he could give me was that you were on the trail of some guy named Frankie DeAngelo. I made the acquaintance of Maureen Donovan while looking for him. According to her I was only a day or two behind you in my search."

Gus looked puzzled at first but after rolling these facts around in his head for a while was able to put things together. "That doesn't help us get any closer to Christina."

"No it doesn't. Do you have any idea who these people are who snatched her?"

"Not really. At first I thought they were mob guys, but this doesn't sound like their kind of play. If they needed to they would've just whacked Christina."

Doherty trusted Frank Ganetti enough to believe that if any known mob people were involved in this girl's abduction he would've known about it. Killing or kidnapping a minor is bad business, even in their world.

"Obviously this all has to do with the films. And most likely with the guy who's in them with her."

"You've seen them?"

"Yeah, I've seen both of them. Same older guy, same young girl each time. I'm thinking DeAngelo and Ricks were trying to use them to shake down this guy. According to Ricks, it was a racket they'd been running on respectable customers for a while now. They'd secretly film them having sex with under-age girls or with women in embarrassing situations. Then they'd blackmail these men for some serious cash."

Gus took a moment to consider where things had gone wrong. "It looks like somebody's turned the tables on Ricks and DeAngelo and their little extortion racket."

"And on your daughter as well, given that she was the star in the movies I saw."

"That doesn't explain why the Donovan girl got killed."

"They must've thought she was in on it. Or they killed her because she wasn't able to give them DeAngelo." Doherty came up short here, not sure himself if Maureen Donovan knew more about DeAngelo's operation than she'd let on. Not that it mattered now that she was dead.

"It's a shame though; she was a nice girl with an nine-year old kid of her own. Whoever's behind killing her and taking your daughter is clearly desperate to get ahold of those films."

"Where are the films now?"

"Well, I think it's pretty obvious that one of them is at my office."

"Where the hell is the other one, pally?"

"I can't tell you that. Not for the time being anyway. Right now those films are the only bargaining chips we have. We give them up there's no guarantee you'll ever see your daughter alive."

At that point Mickey Flannery flashed the lights in Paddy's to indicate it was closing time. Timilty and Doherty were well into their cups so he invited his old friend to spend the night on his couch. On the way home Doherty mentioned that the flop would give Gus an opportunity to help clean up the mess he'd made at the apartment.

Chapter Twenty-Four

In the morning Doherty rose to the smell of something cooking. When he ventured out to the kitchen Gus was standing barefoot at the stove in a sleeveless undershirt and boxer shorts.

"What're you frying up there?" Doherty mumbled, still half asleep.

"Pancakes. You like pancakes, don't you?"

Doherty scratched his head. "Yeah, I guess so. How did you do that?"

Gus looked over his shoulder and smiled. "It's easy. All you need is flour, eggs, sugar and butter. You had all of those things, though not much else in your cupboard. You don't have any maple syrup, do you?"

Doherty hadn't bought any maple syrup in about three years. "I'll get dressed and run down to Belanger's for some." It was the least he could do. When he passed back toward his bedroom he noticed that Gus had cleared up most of the mess he'd made the night before in his search for the movie reels. Some things weren't exactly where Doherty normally kept them, but the place was neat enough given its usual disarray.

Denny's wife Gladys was working the register at Belanger's. They exchanged the usual stale morning greetings; the kind of things people say to each other early in the day when they don't expect any kind of response. He picked up some Aunt Jemima's maple syrup along with a package of sausage links before walking back to Gus' pancakes.

The big man pulled a stack of cakes out of the oven where he'd put them to warm. While he laid them out on the folding card table, Doherty retrieved some silverware and a couple of plates. He poured some coffee for the two of them. In the meantime Gus fried up a half dozen sausage links.

"I didn't know you could cook," he said, as his guest, still in his skivvies, lowered himself into a chair across the small table. Except for his occasional meals with Rachel, Doherty seldom ate sitting at this table. Usually he took his meals sitting on the couch in the living room with his plate on the crowded coffee table or standing at the kitchen counter. Gus, who took pride in always being well-groomed, looked out of sorts this morning with stubble growing on his chin like unwanted crab grass on a usually well-manicured lawn.

"When you live alone as much as I have you pick up some domestic skills. Cooking is one of them; house cleaning isn't." They each laughed at their slovenly ways. They ate greedily while throwing down a couple of cups of black coffee. Neither man wanted to initiate conversation about what had transpired the night before. The deal with the films and the fate of Gus' daughter sat with them at the tiny table like an uninvited guest.

Gus finally broke the silence that had only been chewing noises up to that point. "What do we do now, pally?"

Doherty took some time to consider the question. The truth was he wasn't exactly sure where they could go from here, though he had a few ideas left they could try.

"I'm going out to talk to some people. In the meantime I suggest you try taking another run at Jimmy Ricks. To be honest with you, I think I've burned all my bridges with him. From what you said last night, it sounds like he thinks you're available for hire in helping him get Christina back. I recommend you continue to let him think that. He trusts you in a way that he may not trust anyone else right now. But whatever you say to him keep me out of it. I had a hard time being civil with that piece of shit the last time we talked."

"I can do that, or at least try to for Christina's sake. What're you going to do in the meantime?"

Doherty wanted to be honest with his old friend, but Gus' violation of his apartment and office caused him to hold back. "Why don't you leave that to me. You work on Ricks while I try to scare up something more on DeAngelo. How can I get in touch with you if something important shakes loose?"

"You gonna take a look-see down at Bonnet Shores?"

"I'm not sure yet. Let me handle the DeAngelo end of this investigation my way for now. Trust me, Gus. I won't do anything to put your daughter at risk. One girl's already dead because of this business. Neither of us wants to see anyone else get hurt on account of those films."

They finished breakfast and dressed quickly. It was only then that Doherty decided he was going to give the film resting in his filing cabinet to Gus. He figured if each of them had one of the films it would give them some flexibility in negotiating with whomever had Christina. He also thought this would be a wise strategy in case something unexpected happened to one of them.

They parted with a handshake outside of the office on Brookside. Before leaving Gus gave Doherty two phone numbers where he could be reached. He asked Gus if he could tell Johnny Briggs that his search for his missing partner was over.

"Tell him you located me and I'm okay. That's all. I'm not going back to the job until I make sure Christina's safe. Don't give him any other details about what we're doing. I'll fix things up with Briggs after we wrap this case."

When Doherty arrived at the office Agnes was already inside surveying the damage from the night before.

"Jeez, boss, what happened here?" was the first thing out of her mouth.

Doherty looked over the disorder inside Doherty and Associates and pretended it was the first he'd seen it. He walked into the inner office. Once he'd scanned the mess he began to pick up the files that were strewn across the floor. Agnes followed, frowning at what had been thrown about. He placed the loose file folders on his desk and then carefully examined the drawer of the filing cabinet Gus had jimmied open. Agnes stood in the doorway waiting for Doherty to answer her.

Eventually he turned in her direction and said, "Why don't you call over to Majestic Hardware. See if they can send a locksmith up here to fix the lock on the outside door and maybe this one on the file cabinet. After that, can you see about putting these files back in order?"

"Are you gonna tell me what this is all about?" Agnes said, not at all pleased with Doherty's evasive demeanor. She couldn't understand why he wasn't more upset about the burglary. She even suggested that he call the police.

"I would but for now I think it'd be better if you and they didn't know what whoever broke in here was looking for. I can tell you it has something to do with my search for Gus. I'm afraid we may be dealing with people who are more dangerous than I suspected. My hunch is that the people who did this are the same ones who killed that girl up in Cranston. If that's the case you might want to stay home for the next few days."

His secretary looked more scared than he'd ever seen her. She rubbed her expanding belly as if to indicate that her safety was no longer just about herself. She now had the baby to think about.

"I'm going down the street to talk to the Judge for a while. You can make yourself scarce once the locksmith shows up. Doherty then slipped a five spot out of his ever-diminishing bankroll and handed it to Agnes. "This is for you. If the guy from Majestic comes by tell him to leave me a bill for the work he does."

Chapter Twenty-Five

T hings were much quieter at Democratic Party headquarters than last fall when Doherty was hired by Judge Martin DeCenza to find the now deceased Spencer Wainwright. At that time a statewide election campaign was on and the Judge and his minions were working full tilt. Today there were few workers in the large space that had once been the ballroom on the second floor of the Plaza Hotel. DeCenza was alone in his glassed-in private office. His number one gofer, Angel Touhy, was nowhere to be seen, nor was his muscle boy, Rene Desjardins. It was just as well as Doherty'd already had three unpleasant run-ins with Desjardins and had no desire to go for a fourth.

He knocked on the Judge's office door and the town's political boss quickly raised his head. This unexpected visit took him by surprise. DeCenza stared at Doherty for a short while before rising from behind his oversized desk to let him into his space. They shook hands but not in a friendly fashion, which was understandable given how their past business dealings had ended. The Judge resented the fact that Doherty had some information about one of his shady business deals that he could hang over his head. He was the kind of man who was used to having the upper hand in all his business. Neither man had any desire to cross paths again, yet here they were. The Judge was the political power in this part of the state, at least on the Democratic side. If Doherty wanted some insight into the political world, DeCenza was the man to see.

"Hugh Michael Doherty. I would say this is a pleasant surprise, but to be candid with you, it really isn't. I thought when we last met it would be the end of our business with one another. Yet here you are, at my door with hat in hand."

Doherty smiled. "Actually I left my hat at the office today. Besides they tell me hats are going out of style."

The Judge was a small man whose once reddish hair was now almost entirely consumed by gray. Doherty figured he must be over sixty now as the lines on his face betrayed all of that. But Judge DeCenza still ran things in West Warwick and exuded the confidence of a man that did.

"You don't look too busy up here where the *people's business* is done," Doherty said, repeating a line the Judge had used on him last fall.

"Well, we're over a year away from the next election so most of our attention these days is toward providing constituent services."

"Constituent services huh. I like the sound of that. So do I count as a constituent?"

"Yes, of course you do. Though right now I'm consumed with helping the party find a viable candidate to fill Green's senate seat now that Theodore Francis has finally decided to retire at the ripe old age of 92. I believe Rhode Island needs a Democrat with stature to hold onto the seat Green has occupied for the past twenty-three years."

"Really, so who's the party thinking of supporting in that horse race?"

The Judge demurred. "Well we had expected Johnny Fogarty to step up from the House, but apparently he doesn't want to give up his seat for one in the Senate. It's unfortunate; he would've been a shoo-in if he chose to run."

Doherty knew that John Fogarty was the U.S. rep from this side of the state. He wasn't sure if a jump to the senate was a promotion or not. "Why's he so reluctant to run for Green's seat? Being a senator seems like a pretty cushy job."

The Judge shrugged as he took his chair behind the mammoth desk that only served to reduce his physical stature. He offered Doherty a seat on the opposite side. "Apparently Mr. Fogarty doesn't want to give up his seniority in the House only to become a junior senator. You see, he chairs a couple of powerful committees and with over four hundred members in that body, having seniority gives him a lot of clout. Committee chairmen in the House have their own little fiefdoms. If he went over to the Senate he'd have to start at the bottom again. Besides, he hardly ever has a serious opponent when he runs for re-election. Means he doesn't have to do the obligatory fund raising. Running for the Senate would require him to raise a substantial amount of money. Right now he can keep his house seat for however long he wishes to serve."

"So what's the party going to do instead?"

"At this point the jury is still out. Roberts wants to make a comeback after losing the governorship last year, and he will probably get the state committee's endorsement. He certainly has name recognition after being mayor of Providence and then governor for so long. Unfortunately, it's not exactly the right kind of name recognition given his behavior in the last two elections. I hear tell that Howard McGrath is thinking of jumping into the race. You might remember him. He was one of our senators before Truman appointed him to be his attorney general. I'm not sure how many supporters he has left here in Rhode Island after spending so much of the last decade in Washington cashing in on his connections. To many people he seems like a relic from the past. These days he only has his summer home down in Narragansett to use as his legal residence."

"Doesn't leave you Democrats too much to work with. Maybe we'll elect a Republican senator this time."

DeCenza leaned back in his chair; a smug look crossed his face. "Oh, I doubt that. It looks like they're going to run West Warwick's own Raoul Archambault Jr., another guy who's been living high off the hog in DC while holding down various government jobs. I doubt he'd have a chance even with the Democratic field so thin right now. Politically he stands just to the right of Mussolini. We're still a liberal Democratic state, young man, despite Del Sesto's victory last fall. Pastore is busy talking up this guy from Newport named Claiborne Pell. Apparently Pell is considering the race unless he chooses to challenge Foran for the other rep seat. He has a lot of government service and a clean record. Most importantly, he and his good-looking wife are extremely wealthy. That means the party would be able to use its resources elsewhere."

"What are his negatives?"

DeCenza rocked forward and looked Doherty straight in the eye. "Well the main problem is this Pell is something of a kook. Despite being richer than

Croesus, he wears threadbare suits, drives an old car and talks every now and then about UFOs and other paranormal activities. If he sticks to the issues he'll be fine; if he goes off the record the press boys'll have a field day with him."

"I'd like to ask you about another campaign if you can spare the time."

DeCenza looked at his watch. "I have a wake to attend later this afternoon. Otherwise there is always plenty of time to talk politics with a war hero who, by his own admission, once told me he had no use for politics. Has that notion changed for you, Mr. Doherty?"

"Not really. I thought I'd stop by to pick your brain because politics is what you're all about. I couldn't think of anyone better to get some inside dope from." The Judge smiled, acknowledging how transparent Doherty's attempts at flattery were. They were two men who did not like each other yet understood one another implicitly.

"What can you tell me about the Kennedy campaign for president?"

"Oh my, aren't we getting up in the world. For someone who once barely showed any interest in local politics you now want to ask me about John Kennedy's bid for the White House. I think your Uncle Patrick would be able to tell you more about the workings of young Jack's campaign than I. Rumor has it that your uncle and a number of other wealthy Irishmen have been scouring the country spreading money around like grain seed on behalf of the Kennedy family. Personally I was hoping Stevenson would run again, but that doesn't seem to be in the cards."

"It's partially because of my Uncle Patrick that I've come to you. It also helps that you appear to be impartial about the race at this point."

"Indeed, that I am. I'm sorry to say, despite all of Joe Kennedy's cash, I don't think the American people are ready to elect a Catholic president. Here in Rhode Island we elect nothing but Catholics. The rest of the country is different from us. In fact, the Catholic thing is a can of worms I was hoping the national party wouldn't open up in this election cycle. I'm old enough to remember when we Catholic were seen as interlopers, even here in Rhode Island. My father often told stories about how we were characterized as the storm troopers for the pope bent on 'Romanizing' America. There was even a time when the Irish couldn't even get work or a place to live in Boston. Now they run the whole damn town."

"What do you know about a man named Kevin O'Shaughnessy? He's the person my uncle is hauling coal for these days."

"This could take a while, Hugh. Would you like a cup of coffee? I would offer you something stronger but technically it's still morning." DeCenza then left the office and called to a girl named Donna to fetch them some coffee. He stuck his head back in and asked, "How do you like it?"

"Black would be fine," Doherty said.

The girl brought their coffees forthwith and both men lit up their own cigarettes as an accompaniment.

DeCenza then launched into one of his history lectures. "Kevin O'Shaughnessy started out as a barrow boy working the docks in Boston. By most accounts he was a pretty tough customer. His dad died when he was quite young and his mum raised him and six siblings on her own. Kevin was the oldest and took the father's place as the man of the house at a very early age. You might say he was the kind of fellow who was old before his time. He was only in his teens when he came to the attention of Martin Lomasney, the boss of Boston's notorious Ward Eight. Everyone referred to Lomasney as 'The Mahatma' – you know, like that Gandhi fellow in India. Only Lomasney was the polar opposite of the Indian Gandhi. Whereas the Hindu was a man of peace and non-violence, Lomasney was not above busting a few heads to get things done. You see Lomasney had been the leader of a street gang in his younger years. That was before he discovered that politics were an easier means of getting your way."

"At some point while the Mahatma was head of the city's board of health someone tried to assassinate him. The poor fellow only hit Lomasney in the leg, which left him with a limp and a bad case of nerves about anyone who opposed him. I'm sure, my boy, you can imagine the amount of graft one could rake in as chief of the board of health in a city like Boston."

The reference reminded Doherty of all the dubious appointments DeCenza had made over the years to various boards in and around West Warwick. Most particularly that of Angel Touhy as commissioner at the water department.

"Anyway, as Lomasney rose through the ranks from city alderman to state rep, young O'Shaughnessy rose with him. It was well known that no matter what position Lomasney held, he was the real power in Boston politics. Mayors came and went but the Mahatma stayed on. He died right as the Depression was coming on. But not before bequeathing much of his legacy to Kevin O'Shaughnessy, who was barely out of his twenties at the time."

"The difference between Lomasney and O'Shaughnessy is that unlike his master, Kevin has chosen to operate entirely in the shadows. He has never held any political office and few people outside of Boston politics have ever heard of him. In fact, it wasn't until about ten years ago that he came to my attention. I knew all about Lomasney. My God, anyone who entered into the political arena had to learn about the Mahatma. He was a legend, even here in Rhode Island."

"Once I became acquainted with O'Shaughnessy I put some of my people on him to see what they could dig up. That's how I learned so much about his background. What I can tell you is that for the last two decades he has been raising and distributing large amounts of money for his chosen candidates, all of whom have been Democrats and Irish. His people don't always win because occasionally the voters like to have a say in who serves them in public office."

Doherty wondered if voters in West Warwick ever had the same thoughts about the DeCenza machine and its control over local politics.

"Things up in the Bay State have changed enormously since Lomasney's days. His interests only covered the city of Boston. He let the Cabots, the Saltonstalls and the Lodges continue to run the rest of the state. That was true until James Michael Curley came along. Curley had greater ambitions beyond Boston City Hall, which may have contributed to his ultimate downfall. By the time the war came along many Irish, and to a lesser degree the Italians, had begun moving out to other parts of the Commonwealth. Later their children went on to college, many on the GI Bill. Eventually some of those young men ran for office as what we call 'goo-goos'. That's short for good government types. The old bullyboy tactics might still work in places like Worcester or Springfield, and even here in Providence, but they don't work in the suburbs, nor so much in Boston anymore. People want services now and clean government, not just a job for their cousin Liam or a union card for their nephew Tony."

"What does that mean for someone like you?" Doherty asked just to break DeCenza's rhythm.

The Judge threw him a knowing smile. "I don't have to tell you that West Warwick is a dying town. Most of the mills are closed. And if you walk through

Arctic, you see another store being emptied out every week. Once that new highway is finished people will think nothing about driving right past us into Providence to shop, eat or go to the movies. There are even plans afoot to build a large shopping plaza just over the town line in Warwick."

"I'm sixty-two years old and I'd like to keep doing what I'm doing for perhaps another ten years. My wife is already talking about us moving to Florida. Florida: God's new waiting room," he said dismissively. "I ask her what I would do down there. I don't like the beach and I don't play golf. So, in the meantime I'll keep at this job until there aren't any more constituents who need my help."

"Can we get back to O'Shaughnessy? What's exactly is he up to these days?"

The Judge slowly sipped his coffee. "Like your Uncle Patrick, he's raising money for the Kennedy campaign. Much of it comes directly from Joe Kennedy and other Irishmen with deep pockets. They are convinced this is their best chance to put a bona fide Catholic in the White House, and an Irish one at that. Who knows, maybe they're right. I mean the boy is quite handsome and I hear that wife of his is a real beauty. They'd make a nice contrast to old Ike and Mamie. But I'm not convinced all that money can buy enough votes."

"Is that all O'Shaughnessy does, raise money?"

"That's all he's doing right now. I've been told he has other kinds of connections – unsavory ones, with people who are in the same business as your friend Frank Ganetti Jr."

"Are we talking about mob guys?"

"Yes, but mostly of the Irish stripe. The ones that run their own neighborhoods in Boston and work in collaboration with the Italian organization up there. O'Shaughnessy is the kind of man who can walk on both sides of the street at the same time. I don't know this for sure, but I'd hazard to guess that he has his fingers in some illegal activities. More as a sideline I would think. His real métier is politics. I can assure you, however, that some of these criminal types that I just mentioned will be out in force on behalf of the Kennedys come election time - and I do mean force. Old Joe has contacts with people like that all over the country. I hear tell that the boy himself is on friendly terms with Frank Sinatra and you know what kind of people he consorts with."

"What about my Uncle Patrick?"

"I believe your uncle serves in much the same role for the campaign that Angel Touhy does for my organization. He's kind of a jack of all trades."

"That reminds me, rumor has it you may be putting up Touhy for state rep next year."

The Judge flashed his Cheshire cat grin. "Rumors, merely rumors at this point. Though I do think Angel would do an admirable job representing our interests in the state legislature."

By *our,* the Judge of course meant the interests of his machine. Realizing their conversation had all but run its course, and not wanting to hear any more lectures about politics, Doherty thanked the Judge for his time and rose to leave. He did have to admit, if nothing else, Martin DeCenza was a bottomless well of political knowledge. They shook hands and Doherty left party headquarters a little wiser than when he came in.

Chapter Twenty-Six

He picked up Route One in Warwick at Apponaug Corners and drove south down through East Greenwich center past the Greenwich and Kent movie theaters on the familiar path he used to drive every day to Quonset. Nobody called it Route One except for the mapmakers; to most Rhode Islanders it was still the Post Road. Doherty passed Old Forge Road, which was the turnoff for Goddard Park, where he and his fellow workers at Quonset spent many a Sunday afternoon playing baseball, drinking beer and eating burnt hot dogs. He never missed working at the Point, though he often thought about the fellas he'd worked with. He hardly ever saw or spoke to any of them since he quit.

Being a PI was a lot more interesting than working at Quonset though the income wasn't as steady. On the other hand it meant that he had a much more private life, which he preferred. Except for the infrequent advice he sought from Gus or Agnes, his cases usually required him to sort things out on his own.

He passed by Quonset and Davisville, not bothering to slow down, even for nostalgic purposes. With the Korean War and World War II now in its tail-lights, the government no longer needed such large CB bases anymore. There was talk of dividing up these large landmasses that had served the country so well during wartime and transforming them into housing and commercial use. Knowing Rhode Island, a lot of graft would pass through many hands before such projects got off the ground. A fair number of people stood to make a lot of money if these developments ever took place. He suspected Judge DeCenza would find a way to get a finger into that pie.

Doherty continued on, soon passing by the Hilltop Drive-In movie theater. In the past few years such venues had become very popular during the summer months with families - and teenagers looking for a safe place to make out. The Hilltop was closed for the season with a message on its oversized marquee informing the public that it would be reopening in May. He was surprised that an operation of that size did well enough to stay in business for only five months of the year. He'd never seen a movie at one of these and didn't know if he ever would. He thought it would be too distracting to watch a movie from his car.

A Howard Johnson's restaurant with its bright orange and blue décor sat on the left hand side of the Post Road. It was the landmark telling him where to turn off for Wickford. He passed by several streets with names of colors that were lined with identical single-family houses built by the government during the war for married servicemen. A large sign abutting the main road now pitched these houses as affordable 'starter homes'. Having never lived anywhere but in his parents' house and the apartment on Crossen Street, Doherty was unfamiliar with the concept of a *starter home.*

Wickford was quiet this late in October now that the tourist season had passed. The village was often referred to as an art center, though the only art Doherty saw were watercolor seascapes destined to end up on the walls in dentist offices. He was no expert on fine art, but he'd seen enough of the real thing in Europe during the war to know that what was for sale in Wickford was mostly waiting room art.

At the major intersection where Main Street continues on to a dead end at the harbor, he turned right down Brown Street and drove through the commercial center of the village. It was near noon and he thought of again stopping for lunch at one of the small restaurants still slinging food for the locals. Instead he decided to get his business covered first.

A movie house was tucked into a brick building at the end of Brown. "Operation Petticoat" and "The Nun's Story" were advertised on the small marquee above the front entrance. He hadn't seen either picture and didn't know if he ever would. He turned left onto Boston Neck Road and maneuvered the Chevy over the narrow bridge that crossed the inland waterway. From the looks of the water around the boats moored in the cove it was apparent that the tide was out. The low tide gave off that odoriferous smell of salt water barely covering mud flats.

Once over the bridge he took a sharp left onto the service road that ran to the town's commercial boatyard. Rich people who owned boats stored their precious floaters here during the off-season. He was here to touch base again with Alex Klinoff.

Doherty parked on the edge of the work area and moseyed into the yard. It was lunchtime and most of the workers were sitting around eating sandwiches and shooting the bull. The men wore dungarees or overalls that were covered in dust and paint. Blue work shirts or flannel ones completed their outfits. He spotted Klinoff parked on an overturned rowboat with a cigarette in one hand and a red thermos top in the other.

Klinoff eyeballed Doherty before any of his fellow workers did. He stood up and punctuated his exit from the group with a hearty laugh. While walking in Doherty's direction he dropped his smoke on the ground and stubbed it out with a work boot.

"What're you doin' here?" was all he gave by way of a greeting.

Doherty flashed his former colleague a half friendly smile. "I'm still looking for that DeAngelo guy. I thought you might have heard something since the last time we spoke."

Klinoff ignored Doherty's query and said, "Did you ever catch up with your buddy Timilty?"

The way he spat out Gus's name reminded Doherty that Klinoff and Gus hadn't gotten along too well while they were on the force. As his superior Gus never thought much of Klinoff as a cop and often told him so. Back then whenever he could Klinoff would brag about the summer cottage he and his wife had purchased down on Great Island. The house was the product of the off-the-books money he'd made doing work for the DeCenza machine. Now the wife was gone and his prized cottage was a hovel that was the ex-cop's permanent home.

"Yeah, I found him. We're now working together on a case. That's why I'm looking for Frankie DeAngelo. I thought maybe you'd heard something about him on your scanner."

"Still hasn't come up. Though I'm not so sure I would've called you if it did. I mean, what's in it for me?" The ex-cop's tone had changed since their last conversation in the lot at Twin Willows.

"If you're talking about money, I don't have any to spare right now. I've already spent too much of my own scratch looking for Timilty. I thought I'd appeal to you as one former cop to another."

Klinoff's head sunk down so that his jaw was resting on his chest. "Sorry, man, I've had a really bad-ass day. See that big house up there on the hill," he said pointing at a good size Greek revival mansion that overlooked the harbor. Doherty nodded. "Some greaseballs from Providence, you know, connected guys, are up there all the time havin' these loud parties with a bunch of big-titted broads. I hear them all the time makin' lotsa noise, havin' a good time while I'm down here doin' this grunt work. Anyway one of these hoods came down this morning to check on his boat. When it wasn't ready he decided to give me a ton of shit like it was my fault. This guinea bastard got all up in my face about it. I woulda said somethin' back but I could see he was packin' so I kept my mouth shut and told him I'd take care of it. Times like that I wished I still had my badge."

Doherty didn't know what, if anything, he could say to improve Klinoff's day. The poor guy had lost his job with the police on account of screwing up while guarding a poker game, something he shouldn't've been doing in the first place. Now he was scraping paint off the hulls of boats owned by men who looked right through him, except for when they gave him grief for not doing the job to their liking.

The conversation had hit an uncomfortable pause as the two men tried to size up where to go next. Doherty changed the subject by asking, "What can you tell me about Bonnet Shores? I hear tell that this DeAngelo may have a house down there. It's possible he only uses it to store stolen goods."

Klinoff rubbed his hand over his thinning scalp, still not sure how much he was in the mood to help. Doherty considered telling Klinoff about the missing girl and the trouble she might be in, but quickly rejected that idea, suspecting Klinoff wouldn't offer up the proper amount of sympathy. He didn't want to think less of this ex-cop than he already did.

"It's a lot like Great Island. Snooty but not fancy as the people who live there think it is. A lot of them live at Bonnet full-time now, which means some of the houses are winterized. I get the impression they're kind of a close-knit bunch. They got a beach club there that does its best to keep out undesirables. You know, people like you and me. The public part of the beach is pretty nice. The whole area is in a little cove so it don't have no surf like at the Pier or Scarborough. That's pretty much all I can tell you about the place. There ain't much action that calls for the cops to go to Bonnet Shores. Not like at Narragansett or North Kingston. When somethin' does come up it's usually a house break-in. The way you described this DeAngelo, he'd stand out like a sore thumb down there. Any idea where his place is?"

Doherty shook his head. "Not a clue. In fact I don't even know if it's in his name. He could be renting it from somebody."

Klinoff laughed. "Well, unless he shows up on my police scanner, tryin' to track him down given what you already don't know would be like lookin' for a needle in a haystack. I suppose you could go down there and start knockin' on doors and askin' if anybody knows him. If nothin' else that would get *you* on the scanner." Klinoff laughed at his own joke.

"Well, if you hear anything could you give me a holler," Doherty said handing Klinoff one of his business cards.

"You already gave me one of them last time we talked."

"I figured you probably threw it away."

"You figured right," Klinoff said as he palmed Doherty's card and slid it into his pant's pocket.

Chapter Twenty-Seven

The next day was unseasonably mild so Doherty decided to use the fair weather as an opportunity to drive down to Bonnet Shores. The map he picked up at the Esso station just outside of Arctic gave him a pretty good idea of how to get to the beach community. Locating Frankie DeAngelo would be another story. He drove down the Post Road yet again until it turned into Tower Hill Road. The most famous landmark on that route was the forty-foot high Hannah Robinson Tower, built in 1938 as a Civilian Conservation Corps project ostensibly to spot forest fires. More likely it was one of those make-work government construction efforts undertaken during the Depression to give jobs to unemployed men.

In any case he stopped and spent ten minutes climbing the tower to take in the view. It provided a nice panorama of the surrounding area and the bay off in the distance. Back in the car he swung a left down 138 and crossed the Pettaquamscutt River to get to Rt. 1A, the shore road that trailed south all the way to Narragansett. Just before the Twin Willows restaurant, where he'd eaten dinner with Klinoff, he saw the small black and white sign indicating the turnoff for Bonnet Shores.

There was only one road down to the shore so it wasn't hard to locate the beach club or the community that abutted it. On his first pass Doherty drove by the club's large pavilion and continued on to the end of the cove where the beach turned from sand to rock and the water broke up against some steep

outcroppings. There were a few people walking on the beach and a man standing by the shore as his dog paddled in the shallow water.

Bonnet Shores was in a cove at the lower end of Narragansett Bay, along a
part of the coast well protected from the real Atlantic where actual waves hit
the shore. When he reached the outermost point Doherty hooked a U-turn
and retraced his route back along the water. Near the center of the beach he
turned off the main road and headed into the development area. Many of the
small to midsize homes there were set close beside one another.

While cruising through a number of the streets he noticed that some
houses were boarded up for the winter while others appeared to be fully in-
habited. Since he didn't exactly know what he was looking for, after driving
around the streets of the Bonnet Shores community for twenty minutes, he
gave up his aimless search. Instead he made his way back to the shoreline and
parked in a nearly empty lot by the public beach.

Now on foot, Doherty crossed over to the sand and walked toward the pavilion. He was cautious about not getting too close to the water's edge for fear
that his cordovans would pick up some unwanted salt water. When he reached
the pavilion he walked up the steps to the boardwalk. Everything in the area,
which included a snack bar, two bathhouses and some cabanas was boarded
up - closed for the season. Although the main gate that led to the pavilion from
the parking lot was wide open, everything else was locked up tighter than a
drum. He guessed that being a member of the Bonnet Shores Beach Club had
its privileges only during the summer months. A lot of the beaches in southern
Rhode Island closed down their facilities after Labor Day. Of course, the water
itself was always accessible.

To get a sense of the place Doherty walked leisurely around the pavilion,
or at least the part that wasn't chained shut. He could see some large cabanas
at one end that were as big as cottages at other holiday resorts along the Rhode
Island coast. The main bathhouse had signs designating the women's and the
men's side. In the center of the bathhouse area was a large concrete open space
that, from the marking at its base, apparently was used for children's games
and other wind sheltered activities. As he wandered around he was impressed
with how large a complex the club was.

While retracing his steps back along the boardwalk, he was confronted by a
stout fellow coming from the opposite direction. The man was somewhere in his

sixties and despite the cool fall air was wearing Bermuda shorts with knee high socks and a pith helmet like the one Dr. Reynolds wore in the TV show *Ramar of the Jungle*. He didn't look kindly on Doherty's presence at the Beach Club.

"Can I help you, sir?" he said when he got within earshot. The *sir* came out as more of a challenge than a politeness.

Doherty plastered on his best smile and said, "Perhaps you can. My name is Doherty and I was thinking about joining the beach club."

The eyes under the jungle helmet gave him a thorough going over, no doubt looking to see if he measured up to the club's stringent standards. In his khakis, sport shirt and windbreaker Doherty wasn't sure if he projected the proper image.

Apparently he didn't as the fellow said, "I'm afraid we're running a waiting list of about six months right now."

Doherty tilted his head and looked at the man quizzically. "I don't understand. It looks like this place is going to be closed for at least six months."

His host was now at a loss for a further explanation. "Are you from around here?" was all he could come up with.

"I live up in West Warwick, but my wife and kids are partial to the seashore in the summer. I was hoping to take a look at some real estate while I was down here as well. I'm sorry I didn't catch your name," he added, knowing full well that the man had never pitched it.

"I'm Ronald Clemens," the fellow said in as snooty a manner as he could muster. It wasn't snooty enough to put Doherty off. In his work he'd met a lot snootier. "I'm retired now, but I work as caretaker of the property in the off-season and overseer of the Beach Club in the summer months. My family was one of the earliest members of this community," he added proudly.

Doherty tried to put on a look that indicated he was impressed. Clemens apparently bought it.

"Why don't I show you around, Mr. Doherty." Something had changed and now his host was all politeness and bonhomie. Maybe the fellow was just lonely and bored without any miscreants to usher off the property. The two men reversed course and headed back toward the main bathhouse. On the way Clemens pointed out where the snack bar and eating hall were located.

"There used to be quite a nice restaurant here at one time. Very formal you know. The men were required to wear jackets and ties at dinner and the ladies dresses. Unfortunately, as times have changed so have styles. And if I do say so, the clientele at the club has changed as well. This area is currently used as an eating space for the snack bar. People sit in here in their swimwear, if you can believe that. It's called *the spa*." Clemens was obviously not pleased with the more informal lifestyle that had taken over in the years since the war.

Doherty's guide continued with his history of the Beach Club. "We took a terrible beating during Hurricanes Carol and Edna and had to do major reconstruction on some of the buildings here. Luckily one of our members and a lead voice at the Narragansett Development Corporation was Governor, and later Senator, McGrath. You might remember him; I believe he served in Truman's cabinet for a time."

"Yes, he was the attorney-general under the former president," Doherty said, putting his lecture from Judge DeCenza to good use. "I hear McGrath is thinking of running for the senate again to replace Senator Green."

Ignoring this last remark Clemens continued with his Cook's tour of the Bonnet Shores Beach Club. "The Development Corporation that bought the Beach Club complex back in '45 took care of all the renovation work after the hurricanes. Harry Bodwell served as the Beach Club manager during that time. He'd been in politics as well. Served in the state legislature for a number of years if I'm not mistaken. In fact, it was Mr. Bodwell who originally got this whole operation off the ground in 1928. The first club was located at the end of the beach near the rocks. That's the section down there," Clemens said pointing in the direction where Doherty'd parked his Chevy.

"The big hurricane in 1938 eroded the sand at that end leaving the beach very rocky. Back then everyone called that space Clubhouse Beach; that is until the club moved up here. Now we refer to it as Little Beach. These days it's open to the public. One of my jobs in the summer is to make sure those kind of people don't find their way onto the club's property." Clemens was clearly proud of his role of protecting the Beach Club from incursions by the riffraff.

As they walked along the boardwalk Clemens pointed out how the bath-houses are segregated for men and women. "Some of our members prefer a less expensive way of belonging to the club. It's something you and your family might consider. Instead of having your own cabana you could simply arrive fully dressed and report to the business counter here," he said patting a large boarded up window. "They give you what we call a *tray*. It's really a wooden tub to hold your clothing and other belongings once you've changed into your beachwear. Armed with your tray you can use any of the unassigned changing rooms just behind here."

"The baskets have always been called *trays*; you might say it's a Bonnet Shores tradition. You then return with your clothing and valuables to this counter where the boys will store them inside for safe keeping while you spend the day at the beach. When you return they give you your goods and you can then use the bathhouse to shower and dress for the outside world. In addition to assigned bathhouse, some of our more prominent members have their own cabanas. These are much bigger and can house whole families for the day or even overnight."

"Are they the ones located down there?" Doherty asked indicating the larger structures beyond the bathhouse.

"Those are the larger cabanas some of our members rent for the season. Many of them have been in their families for quite some time. They may be entirely out of your price range," Clemens added just to put Doherty back in his place. "Besides most of the cabanas are already rented for next season. You see, not all of the Bonnet Shores Beach Club members live in the community. Some simply stay in these cabanas or come down for the day or the weekend. The cabanas obviously don't have all the amenities of a cottage in the village, though they serve the needs of those who don't have time to spend in the area, or frankly the money to buy a second home."

Once again Doherty could have taken Clemens' last remark as a put-down, and might have been offended if he really wanted to rent one of these structures or had a family to put in it. What he really was interested in was pumping this supercilious windbag for more information.

"I was wondering about this large open area in the center of the bathhouse and cabanas. What goes on here?"

Clemens folded his arms across his chest and said proudly, "That's generally a recreation area for the children during the season. The little ones play children's games in there and then later in the day the older boys and girls use a section of it for their volleyball matches. We employ a lot of high school and college aged boys here as lifeguards, at the snack bar and as pin boys at the bowling alley."

"You have a bowling alley at the club?"

"Yes, it only has five lanes but it's very popular with the children and adults alike. We have quite a large tournament at the end of each season. Many of the boys who work here live in the cabanas in the back that are currently locked up. It helps with supervision to have them live right here on the premises. You know how young boys can be if left to their own devices." Doherty knew quite well having been one of those boys while at Quonset and in the army.

"We used to have a shuffleboard court down there as well, but it was closed when the board decided to dedicate The Pit to the younger crowd. That's what we call this area: *The Pit.*"

"Do you have much crime here at Bonnet Shores?" Doherty asked trying to steer the conversation in the direction of Frankie DeAngelo.

"I could tell you that we don't but that would be untruthful. Like a lot of seasonal communities we have our share of troubles. I'm speaking mostly of the village, not here at the Beach Club. There are some young hooligans who like to come down to the beach at night to light bonfires and drink alcohol. Often they are underage so the North Kingston police have to be summoned on occasion to quell disturbances. Otherwise, the only real crime at Bonnet Shores are home break-ins. Sometimes seasonal dwellers don't do a very good job of securing their property during the fall and winter months." Again Clemens let his superior attitude find its way into his explanation.

"Are there any known undesirables who have been spotted down here on a regular basis?"

"I don't think so. I suppose you would have to speak to the police about such things. I am only responsible for the security of the Beach Club. I can assure you I am very conscientious about my responsibilities. We've had no serious vandalism at the Club since I assumed this position."

Doherty looked out at the water. "This is a nice little cove. Do many boats come in and park in the water here? Perhaps even beach at the Club?"

"We would never allow such a thing. Why do you ask? Do you have a boat, Mr. Doherty?"

"No, but I was thinking I might get one if we decide to join your club," he lied.

"I should warn you that the water here is very shallow for a long way out. That's one of the reasons the Beach Club is so attractive as a family resort. Parents don't have to worry about their children getting in over their heads or caught in an undertow from the surf. If boaters wished to dock their craft here in the cove they would have to park it quite a ways out. The only way to get to shore would be by wading or in a rowboat or a dingy."

"Have you ever seen anyone do that?"

Clemens thought about the question a little longer than he should have. Finally he spoke. "In the summer, yes quite often, but seldom this time of year. Though recently I saw some people coming ashore from a boat parked quite a ways offshore. The odd thing is that it was at night. I didn't think anything of it at first. I just assumed they were fishermen out night fishing. I'm not an angler myself though I've been told that some of the best fishing in this part of the bay happens at night. The peculiar thing is that whoever brought the dingy to shore did not offload any fish as far as I could tell. I was quite far away on each occasion so I couldn't be entirely sure. I could say I thought what they were doing looked a little fishy, but that would be a very bad pun." Clemens chuckled at what he considered a very amusing remark. Doherty humored him by laughing along.

"Did you ever think of calling the police?"

"Oh, God, no. They were not on Beach Club property so they weren't really my responsibility. I saw them a couple of times, maybe even three, but what they were doing was none of my business. You see I'm not the kind of person who wishes to call undue attention to himself." Doherty had a hard time believing this last comment.

He didn't say anything though he suspected that the boat business might've had something to do with Frankie DeAngelo. He figured he'd gotten about all he could out of the Beach Club caretaker. To keep up the pretense, he asked Clemens to recommend some realtors in the area who could help him locate an affordable cottage. The two men then shook hands and Doherty thanked Clemens for the tour of the club.

Chapter Twenty-Eight

Doherty was trying to slug his way through the first chapter of a book called *The Sound and the Fury* when the phone rang. It saved him the struggle since he couldn't figure out what this Faulkner fellow was trying to get at. He checked his watch; it was just after ten. He seldom received calls at home, let alone ones this late at night. When he did it was usually bad news.

"I think you better come down here as soon as you can," an unfamiliar voice said.

"Down where?" Doherty answered. "Who the hell is this?"

The voice was gruffer this time. "Hey, it's no skin off my nose, but you was the one who said I should call you if somethin' happened down here in South County. Well, somethin's happened and I might not be able to convince the local cops to let me inside their ropes again."

"Is this Klinoff?"

"Who the hell do you think it is, shitheel?"

"Where are you that I've got to come out at this time of the night?"

Klinoff let out a sound that was somewhere between a laugh and a cough. "Down at Bonnet Shores - at the part near the rocks they call Little Beach. If I was you I'd get down here as soon as you can." With that his informer hung up.

Doherty dressed quickly, slipping on a pair of khakis, a sweatshirt and his old Quonset baseball jacket. This time he put on some work shoes instead of his cordovans, just in case he had to get near the water.

He sped out of Belanger's garage and headed south as fast as the Chevy would take him. He made good time given that there weren't many cars on the road at that hour on a weeknight. Once past East Greenwich center there were hardly any lights along the highway either. Without moonlight, the only real light came from his headlights. He made it to the Bonnet Shores turnoff in about a half hour. It wasn't hard to see where to stop by the beach, as there were already three North Kingston police cruisers in the parking lot along with a small crowd of gawkers. Spinning red bubbles on the top of cop cars have a way of attracting people like flies to nightlights.

A burly officer stopped Doherty as he approached the police line. "I'm here to see a guy named Klinoff," was all he said to the cop. The uniform turned his head and yelled for Alex Klinoff. Within seconds the former policeman ambled over to the line and told the large officer that it was okay for Doherty to pass under the ropes surrounding the scene. The cop wasn't so sure, but he reluctantly let the PI through.

Klinoff took his arm and escorted him to where the police had set up a couple of floodlights connected to a small, noisy generator. A large lump rested on the sand inside a loose circle of cops.

Klinoff tapped one of them on the shoulder and said, "Hey Joe, is it okay if my buddy here has a look? He's the private eye I told you about who's been prowlin' around the state lookin' for this guy."

The cop gave Doherty a blank stare and then said to Klinoff. "You're sure he's not some news reporter, right? We don't wanna see nothing in the papers about this before the chief releases a statement."

"Naw, he's legit. He ain't no reporter. Like I told you, he's a private dick who's been lookin' for this dead guy. You let him have a gander at the body and maybe afterwards he'll fill you in on what he knows. Right, Doherty?" Klinoff said turning in his direction.

Doherty wasn't sure how much he would share with the North Kingston police, yet agreed anyway just so he could see what he assumed was the body of Frankie DeAngelo. The uniform named Joe escorted the two of them over to the lump lying under the lights. He knelt down and very carefully drew back the tarp that had been placed over the body. A wet face framed by scraggly black hair stared up at them. The eyes were still wide open though they were no longer seeing anything in this world. It was not a face Doherty recognized, though it fit the description Maureen had given him of Frankie DeAngelo. The body smelled of salt water and early putrefaction, an odor Doherty was familiar with from the war. Something that looked like the dead man's swollen tongue protruded grotesquely from his mouth. Doherty squatted down alongside the cop to get a better look.

"Is that his tongue hanging out of his mouth?" he asked in a low voice.

The cop turned his head and said with a small grin, "It looks more like his prick. Apparently whoever killed this guy cut it off and stuffed it into his mouth. Have you ever seen anything like that? I sure haven't."

Doherty had seen such death tableaux several times during the war. Occasionally an enemy would desecrate a body in a similar fashion as a statement about death and humiliation. It was also a way of sending a message to other enemy soldiers. He'd seen men on both sides do such things. Each time he found these acts revolting. Some men also cut off the ears or tongues of the enemy as souvenirs. Like it wasn't enough to just kill them or to blow their bodies to pieces. They had to add personal insult to the injury.

He stood up and let out a deep breath. He lit a cigarette to get the smell of death out of his lungs. The cop rose beside him. "Any idea who might've done the poor bastard like this?"

Doherty looked at Klinoff and then back to the cop. "I never met Frankie DeAngelo before. I'm aware that he was a well-known dealer of hot goods. He had places where he stored his stuff down here and up in Cranston. Given the state of his body I'd say he made some mean-ass enemies along the way. Anything else about his condition you can tell me?"

The cop looked at his watch and said quickly, "The chief and the coroner will be here any minute now. You two'll have to step back behind the ropes. He catches me with civilians inside the perimeter my ass'll be grass."

"I hear you. Tell you what, I'll give you what I know if you give me some more particulars about the body."

The cop put a firm hand on Doherty's back and began to move him away from the scene. Klinoff followed close behind. They ducked under the ropes and crossed near to where the gawkers were gathered. The three of them kept walking away from the crowd toward the police vehicles. Some of the onlookers gave them strange glances as they passed by. Proximity to a murder scene has a way of bringing out the worst in people. Doherty saw Ronald Clemens among the onlookers. He quickly averted his face so the beach club overseer wouldn't see him.

When they got to the police cars the cop knocked out a cigarette and offered one to Klinoff. Doherty still had his Camel going. The three men didn't say anything; they just stood there smoking while trying to make sense of the horrific scene they'd just witnessed.

Doherty broke the silence. "What I can tell you is that this dead guy was making a lot of dough selling hot goods *and* drugs; primarily reefer and some smack. His main customers were some pimps up in Providence and their whores. The drug business might've been what got him into trouble with the wrong people."

"Do you think this was the work of the mob?" the cop asked excitedly.

"Could be. It's my understanding that they insist upon controlling the drug trade here in Rhode Island. From the condition of his body someone was either trying to get information out of him by torturing him - or was using the manner of his death to send a message to some other parties. That's all I can figure based on what I know right now." For the time being Doherty was determined to keep the stag films and Jimmy Ricks to himself. He didn't want to provide the cop with anything that would link this murder to the abduction of Gus' daughter.

The cop nodded his head. He pulled hard on his cigarette trying to get as much smoke into his lungs as he could.

"So what can you tell us about the body?" he asked, including Klinoff in the *us* as a courtesy.

"I can't give you all the particulars until the coroner is done with it. I can tell you he was pretty badly cut up and had what looked like cigarette burns all over his arms and chest. And you saw what they did with his other body part," the cop said, not wanting to put the dismembered penis into actual words. "Judging from the amount of water that came out of his lungs when they dragged him up on the beach, I'd say he died from drowning. If that's the case then this dead guy was seriously tortured before he was dumped in the water."

Doherty considered what the cop had just told them. It appeared that whatever the killers wanted from DeAngelo that might've saved him from such sadistic treatment he didn't have it. Most likely it was the missing films. Given what had been done to Maureen Donovan and now Frankie

DeAngelo, it was clear that whoever was after those films would stop at nothing to get them.

In light of these recent events it was time for Doherty to turn his full attention to rescuing Gus' daughter before something equally heinous happened to her. He gave the cop one of his business cards and told him to get in touch if he needed any help or if something else about DeAngelo's murder turned up.

Doherty walked slowly back toward his car almost unaware of Klinoff following at his heels. "What do you know about this killin' you ain't tellin' me or my cop friends?"

"Nothing really. Only that DeAngelo's death could be connected to a missing girl who was making smut films for him and her pimp. But you've got to keep that under your hat. The cops start poking around it could mean a death sentence for the girl in question."

Klinoff smiled as if DeAngelo's murder somehow put him back in the crime fighting game. "You don't think this was a mob hit even though this punk was sellin' hot goods and junk right under their noses?"

"It could've been, though this doesn't look like their style. It's too messy. They would've just whacked him and been done with it. Meanwhile, how is it that you're so chummy with the local police?"

Klinoff offered up his gapped tooth grin. "Like I told you, I listen to the police scanner most nights. When somethin' comes on about a break-in or a fracas down at the pier I hop in my car and drive over to the scene. A coupla times I got there before they did and was able to apprehend the perps. At first they was suspicious of me till I told them I used to be on the job up in West Warwick. I didn't let on that I got shitcanned or nothin'. Maybe I sorta let them think I left the force on account of an injury. After a while some of them began to treat me like an honorary cop. So far everythin' been jake with them as long as the chief don't find out."

Chapter Twenty-Nine

T he next morning Doherty dropped over to Lambert's Drug to buy a copy of the morning *Journal* and a pack of smokes before heading into the office. Once there, he carefully perused the local news section looking for a story about Frankie DeAngelo's murder, but there was nothing there. After reading the paper he spread most of it across the top of his desk and extracted his Smith and Wesson snubnose .38 from its resting place in the newly repaired file drawer.

With both Maureen Donovan and Frankie DeAngelo dead, he was of the mind that whoever was after the films might soon be coming in his direction. Gus' daughter Christina was the weak link, even if for the moment she could only be tied to Timilty. Just in case he thought it would be a good idea to make sure his pistol was clean and in good working order. He wasn't about to be caught out without a piece knowing there were killers roaming the state looking for those films.

Even in the service he'd always preferred having a sidearm in addition to his standard issue M1 rifle. It was easier and more efficient for close quarter fighting. On two occasions he plugged some Krauts from so close that he could see the last expression on their faces before they died. Each time it would've been too cumbersome to do it with his rifle; he might've ended up dead himself if not for his sidearm. Doherty never wanted to have to run somebody through with a bayonet, though he'd been well trained in that kind of fighting.

He extracted some cleaning and lubricating oil, a couple of rags and some bristle brushes from the bottom of his filing cabinet. He kept these materials there for just such a task. He flipped open the cylinder that was empty of any live slugs and then ran the brush through the barrel with some cleaning oil. Once he was satisfied that the barrel was sufficiently clean and lubricated, he set to work on each of the five chambers. There was something about the methodical nature of this task that took his mind off the gruesome image of Frankie DeAngelo's mutilated body lying on the sand at Bonnet Shores. After everything was well lubricated he went to work with some small scraps of rag, pushing them through the barrel and the cylinders to mop up any trace oil. He then flipped back the hammer and applied some oil to its pivot and the trigger pin.

When everything seemed well prepared, he cleaned and dried the gun all over with a larger rag, again being sure to remove any excess oil. This was the first time he thought he might have to use the .38 since the night he shot Stanislaw Krykowski. After that shooting the Pawtucket police confiscated his weapon and it took him a good two weeks to get it back. The recent murders left him no choice than to be on high alert.

Once the cleaning was finished he flipped the cylinder casing back into the main housing, pulled back on the trigger and spun the cylinder to make sure it moved smoothly. The final test was to close everything up and pull off five quick shots. Without any bullets the cylinder advanced as it should and each chamber clicked in rapid succession. The trigger mechanism was fluid and smooth but not overly sensitive to the pull. If he had to shoot at someone, each shot would require a singular decision. No shots would be fired accidentally. When finished he returned he pistol and the cleaning materials to the locked drawer and disposed of the messy newspaper.

With Agnes at home today he took a leisurely lunch at the Arctic News' downstairs counter. Instead of the usual ham or baloney sandwich he opted for their lunch special of tomato soup and a tuna fish salad sandwich. While waiting for his food he busied himself by carefully studying the sports section of the *Journal*, the only part of the paper he hadn't used to protect his desk while cleaning the .38.

The baseball season had ended in a most peculiar fashion. The Yankees didn't make it to the World Series for the first time in four years. Instead the so-called "Go-go White Sox" represented the American League while the Dodgers, now playing in Los Angeles, were the National League champs. All the LA games were played in that city's Memorial Coliseum, an edifice ill designed for baseball. It was built in the 1920s and came to prominence as the centerpiece of the 1932 Olympics. Otherwise, the Coliseum was used almost exclusively for football. The three series games played there each drew over ninety thousand people; a record that would probably stand for a good long time once the Dodgers moved into their more conventional ballpark currently under construction.

The Chisox, a historically good-pitching, weak-hitting team, won the opener by the surprising score of 11-0. They then reverted to form by scoring only twelve runs over the next five games. The Dodgers took the series in six games and a relief pitcher named Larry Sherry, who no one back in Brooklyn ever heard of, won the MVP award. A few of the old Dodgers like Snider, Hodges, Gilliam and Podres had made the transition to the West Coast, but for the most part these were a new, sunny California version of the once beloved Bums from Flatbush. Gone were Jackie Robinson, who had been traded to the Giants the year before but elected to retire instead, and Roy Campanella, who was the victim of a terrible car accident that left his once powerful body permanently consigned to a wheelchair. Baseball had moved to California and the old game would never be the same again, at least not in New York.

Back at the office Doherty was trying to scope out what his and Gus' next move would be when he was jolted out of his thoughts by a ringing telephone. Without Agnes there he picked up the receiver and barked "Doherty and Associates." He was hoping the call would be from Gus. A vaguely familiar voice asked for "Doherty," and he answered simply by saying, "speaking."

"This is Joe Marenga of the North Kingston police. We were introduced by Alex Klinoff at the murder scene last night."

"Yeah sure, how could I forget."

"I just thought I'd give you a heads-up what the coroner discovered in his preliminary exam. In return I was hoping you might be able to give me something more from your side since you'd been chasing the deceased around Rhode Island for a while." Deceased. Doherty liked the formality with which the cop referred to the mutilated body of Frankie DeAngelo.

"Okay. How's about you go first?"

"Well just as we suspected, the dead man was tortured pretty bad before he was dumped into the bay. I guess his killer, or killers, didn't realize how shallow the water is at Bonnet. Cause of death was definitely suffocation from drowning. According to what I've been able to squeeze out of some people in that department, DeAngelo'd been dead for at least an hour, maybe more, before he washed into the shallows near the beach. Strange thing is whoever did this didn't bother to take the victim's wallet. That's how we got such a quick ID on him."

"Sounds like this wasn't a case of theft given that the killers didn't try to hide who he was. Maybe they wanted to send a message to somebody else."

"That was our thought too. Since we got word, thanks partially to you and your pal Klinoff, that DeAngelo was involved in selling hot goods and drugs, the chief is working on the assumption that this was either a mob hit or one carried out by a business competitor. Do you have any other thoughts, Doherty?"

There was no way he was going to give the North Kingston cops anything about DeAngelo's role in the making of the smut films until Gus' daughter was safe. "It's always a good premise to look at the wise guys when someone is trying to cut into their drug business, though this murder seems a little untidy for their kind of work. Still, you never know. I can give you a couple of leads that might help. Last week I had a long conversation with the fellow who's in charge of keeping an eye on the Bonnet Shores Beach Club in the off-season. Do you know him?"

The cop laughed. "You mean Ronald Clemens? Yeah, I know him. Kind of an odd duck if you ask me. He's always struck me as being more interested in protecting the reputation of the beach club than in helping us apprehend any lawbreakers around Bonnet Shores."

"Yeah, that's the guy I spoke to. Anyway, when I was talking with him he told me that he'd seen some people off-loading boats at night on a couple of occasions over by the Little Beach. He thought they were fishermen until he noticed they weren't unloading any fish. I'm thinking it could've been DeAngelo picking up some drug shipments."

"That's a good lead. We'll look into it. Anything else of interest you can throw my way?"

Doherty thought for a minute. He could give the North Kingston cops Jimmy Ricks but elected to keep him on ice for the time being. Last night he told the cop about DeAngelo being hooked in with some pimps in Providence without attaching any names to them. He'd leave it at that for the time being and let them do their own digging.

"You might want to contact the Cranston police and ask about the recent murder of a Maureen Donovan. She was DeAngelo's next-door neighbor and according to the newspaper reports both their apartments were burglarized the day she was killed. Stands to reason the two murders are connected."

"Thanks for the info. I'm sure that connection would've turned up soon enough though your tip should cut down on the lag time. Anything else you can tell me?"

"Not really. If something else pops up I'll give you a call."

"Good. One other thing I might mention: a house in the Bonnet Shores community burned down the day before yesterday. Apparently the fire was of suspicious origins and the fire chief is keeping a lid on his investigation for the time being. Can't say if there's any connection to the murder of DeAngelo until more facts come out. Let me give you my home number as well as the one here at the station. Anything I can do to help solve this case will put me on the fast track to a promotion. Oh, and Doherty, as far as we're concerned, this conversation never took place, okay?"

"Sure. Whatever you say."

Doherty was convinced that the house fire was connected to DeAngelo and that it was probably the place where he stashed his *wholesale* goods down there. It must've been set by the same people who trashed Frankie and Maureen's apartments in Cranston. He wasn't surprised that the North Kingston authorities were keeping that investigation under wraps for now. If they were any good at their jobs, the fire and police chiefs would eventually put two and two together.

As far as Marenga was concerned, it was evident that he was on the make just like everyone else. No doubt hoping he could use his role in the DeAngelo murder investigation to graduate from a uniform to plain clothes. It was fine by Doherty as long as his name wasn't connected to the murder, at least until he and Gus could secure the safety of his daughter without interference from the police. His more suspicious self, however, wondered if Marenga was somehow connected to DeAngelo's death. He quickly discarded this notion, giving the North Kingston cop the benefit of only being guilty of blind ambition.

Chapter Thirty

The more Doherty thought about the brutality of Frankie DeAngelo's murder, the more he had to believe whoever wanted those films was willing to do damn near anything to get them. First he, or they, had murdered Maureen Donovan, an innocent player in this game. Then they'd done full body damage to DeAngelo before dispatching him to the great beyond. What was in those films was obviously of great embarrassment to the man DeAngelo and Jimmy Ricks were trying to shake down. Whoever he was, he obviously had a great deal to lose if the films ever saw the light of day.

He rang up Gus planning to fill him in on the previous night's events before they hit the news. He got no answer. This case was giving Doherty some sympathy for Benjy, the idiot son in *The Sound and Fury*. Maybe Faulkner, and Shakespeare from whom Faulkner borrowed the title, had it right. Maybe life really was full of 'sound and fury signifying nothing'. For Maureen Donovan and her neighbor Frankie DeAngelo, it was now just full of nothing.

His work, along with his experiences in the war, often left Doherty with a jaundiced view of humanity. It still amazed him how a person's life and all that possibly lay before him could be snuffed out in a moment. Maureen would never get to see her boy grow up; would never see him play baseball, graduate from high school and someday get married. She would never have grandkids of her own. As for DeAngelo, he was already living life on a razor's edge. He'd been tortured and killed protecting a small time con game he and Ricks had cooked up.

"Tell me, Frankie," Doherty said out loud, "Was it all worth it? And was it necessary to bring Maureen down with you?" Who else would end up dead because of those damn sex films? Gus' daughter, Jimmy Ricks, Gus, or even Doherty himself. Whatever happened next, he had to find out who the stooge was in the movies. Finding out his identity was the key to the whole case.

That evening he tried calling Gus at his apartment and once again got nothing but a ringing phone. Apparently his old buddy had gone to ground in search of the girl. It would helped if he could find out what, if anything, he'd been able to shake out of Jimmy Ricks.

In the morning, after downing two cups of coffee along with some stale toast with butter and jam, he headed to the office. A half block up Brookside he changed his mind and turned in the opposite direction. He decided to leave the case alone for a few hours. Instead he would visit Willy Legere down at the water department.

Doherty had made Willy's acquaintance when the injured naval gunner was parked outside the Arctic News selling pencils each day as a disabled war vet. Willy's destroyer had been hit by some Japanese bombers in the Pacific and most of his crewmates had lost their lives. Willy was blinded in the attack but otherwise was uninjured. For his efforts he was given a couple of medals and a license to beg for handouts in the center of town. Doherty tried to stop by as often as possible to talk baseball with Willy. In time he couldn't help seeing him as nothing more than a sorry panhandler wasting away on a street corner.

Legere was a smart boy with a real head for numbers. He could tell you the daily batting average of just about every player in the majors. A year ago Doherty had struck a bargain with Judge DeCenza to get Willy put on the town's payroll. The last time he'd seen Willy it sounded like the deal had worked out well as he'd been hired on full-time at the water department.

The same secretary, an older woman named Elaine, greeted him with a big smile when he pushed through the door at the water department office next to the old Centreville Mill. Willy heard his voice from inside his office and quickly emerged to shake hands with his old friend. Legere was smartly dressed in a starched oxford shirt and a neatly knotted striped tie that stopped about four inches from his belt line. His hair was closely cut and well oiled. As always Willy's eyes were hidden behind dark glasses.

"Why, Mr. D, This sure is a nice surprise. You're not here to pay your water bill, are you?"

Doherty laughed. "No, I let my landlord take care of that. How the hell are you, Willy? You look like a million bucks."

Legere's mouth smiled broadly under his glasses. "I been up to Harry's. You aren't the only one who gets regular haircuts these days. Mr. Tuohy told me I hadda start lookin' *smart*."

"Yeah, why's that?"

"Well, 'cause it sounds like Mr. Tuohy's gonna run for state rep next year. And if he's elected the Judge says I might be movin' up to his position here at the water department. Isn't that right, Elaine?" he said addressing the secretary.

The women who handled the paper work for the department gave the two men a big smile. "I certainly hope so, Mr. Legere. If that's what the Judge wants."

Doherty knew that whatever Judge Martin DeCenza wanted to happen in town, that's what would happen. As boss of the Democratic Party DeCenza pretty much chose who held every public payroll job in West Warwick as well as in other parts of the county he controlled. Since it was mostly voters from their town that elected the state rep from this district, Angel Tuohy would be a shoo-in if DeCenza decided on him as the Democratic nominee. What surprised Doherty was that the Judge was considering moving Willy Legere up in the party's hierarchy. It wouldn't be long before he'd have the blind vet running around town doing scut work for the machine like Tuohy did. That was not something Doherty'd bargained on when he helped Willy get this job. What the heck, it was Willy's life and who was he to interfere with him getting up in the world.

"Elaine, could you..."

"Get you two some coffee? Sure, Mr. Legere. Why don't you men go into your office and I'll bring it along right away. How do you like yours, Mr. Doherty?"

"Black'll be fine. And thank you." The woman waved him off and turned her attention to the electric percolator that sat on a shelf behind her desk.

Willy Legere's office was much more neatly appointed than the last time Doherty'd been in to visit. There were pictures on the wall of Willy standing side by side with Judge DeCenza, with Angel Touhy and even with his mother. She looked much better groomed than the dowdy woman he'd met a year ago. Another showed Legere sitting behind his desk with his hands resting on his Braille adding machine. Willy wore his dark sunglasses in each of the pictures.

"Look at this, Mr. D." he said pointing at another machine resting to the side of his large desk. "It's a Braille typewriter. It has two settings on it. One types out holes like in the Braille alphabet and another types letters out in regular type. Ain't that somethin'? Oh, excuse my language. Mr. Tuohy says I gotta stop sayin' *ain't* if I wanna get ahead. I don't do much typin' – least not for the water department. Sometimes the Judge asks me to type out stuff for the politics. He says I got a way with words."

"I can believe that, Willy. I always thought you were a smart guy. You just had to find your place."

"Yeah, and to think of all them, I mean *those* years I spent out in front of the News, practically beggin' for cash. All that time I was feelin' sorry for myself. Don't get me wrong, Mr. D, I made a lot of friends up there in Arctic. Hey, I woulda never met you and had all those good conversations about baseball. But things are different now."

Doherty took another gander around the office. "I can see that, Willy. Just a word of warning about the Judge and his people: they'll be good to you as long as it serves their purposes. But if you cross them, there's no telling what misery they can bring to your life."

Willy gave him a crooked grin. "I know what you mean. I may be blind but I can hear better than most people. I listen to what the Judge and Mr. Tuohy are sayin' when they think nobody can hear them. It don't take a genius to figure how things are run in this town - and who runs them."

"So what did you think of the World Series?" Doherty asked, purposely trying to change the subject.

Willy sat down behind his big desk and shook his head. "It sure was strange havin' a World Series without the Yankees in it."

"Well at least the Dodgers were."

"Yeah but it ain't the same with them bein' out in Los Angeles and playing in a football stadium. I mean that left field screen there was shorter than the wall at Fenway. I bet Snider wished he batted right-handed. I was rootin' for the White Sox on account of what they done to the Yankees. I thought they were gonna sweep the Dodgers after that slaughter in the first game. It kinda went downhill for them after that. I dunno, Mr. D, it just doesn't seem right that there aren't any National League teams in New York any more."

Doherty smirked. "How do you think New Yorkers feel who were Giant and Dodger fans. Those people hated the Yankees more than Sox fans up here do. Now the Yanks are all they got left. At least by the time the Braves left Boston most New Englanders had already moved over to the Red Sox. But in New York, those National League fans were always at war with Yankee fans. Losing all those World Series to them didn't help either. I met guys in the service from New York who wouldn't talk to other guys from there on account of the teams they rooted for."

"To tell you the truth, Mr. D, I was pretty disappointed in the White Sox. I know they didn't have much hittin' to back up all that good pitchin', but when they got Kluszewski late in the season I figured he would give 'em enough sock to get through the Series."

"You know what they say, Willy. Good pitching will always beat good hitting. The Dodgers just had better pitching this time around."

"I dunno, that kid Sherry who saved all them games. I never even heard of him before the Series. The only Dodger pitcher I recognized was Podres, mostly 'cause he was the guy that beat the Yanks back in '55."

At that point Elaine came in carrying two steaming cups of coffee and set them down on Willie's desk. She gave Doherty another one of her pleasant smiles. It was her way of letting him know how much she and Willy appreciated his visit.

"It looks like it's a whole new world of baseball my friend. First the A's moved to Kansas City, then the Braves to Milwaukee and now the Dodgers and Giants to California. I read recently that there's talk of adding some new teams to the leagues in a year or two. That'll be a challenge for you trying to keep up with all the batting averages."

Willy dismissed his comment with a wave. "I gave up on that once I left the News. I got more important numbers to keep track of down here. I used to memorize battin' averages 'cause I didn't have nothin' else to think about. Things are different now," he said, his voice heavy with meaning.

The two friends discussed baseball for another half hour, mostly dissecting the deplorable state of the Red Sox now that Ted Williams was talking about retiring and Jensen might follow him because of his fear of flying. With teams spread all over the map there was no way major league teams could travel from city to city by train anymore. The days of players riding the rails together, gambling, drinking and fighting were coming to an end. He wondered what Babe Ruth would make of traveling by airplane. Hell, the big guy probably would've ended up banging all the stewardesses.

Doherty then asked Willy what he thought of the candidates' prospects for next year's election. Like his boss Willy wasn't sure who the Democrats would choose to run for Green's senate seat. He did think the Democratic lieutenant governor John Notte would challenge the Republican governor Del Sesto and probably win. At least that's what the Judge said. As far as the presidential race was concerned, Willy assumed the Republicans would nominate Vice President Nixon even though nobody really liked him. At this point Willy was lukewarm about Kennedy. Still, he said, it would be nice to have a New Englander in the White House, and an Irishman to boot.

When Doherty left the water department he was glad that he'd made the U-turn on his way to the office. Visiting Willy Legere had diverted his thoughts from the case and had, at least temporarily, purged his mind of the disfigured body he'd seen the night before.

Chapter Thirty-One

Back at the office Doherty tried calling Gus a few more times. All he got was incessant ringing until he hung up. At six he packed up for the day and decided to stop at Paddy's rather than head home to his empty apartment and the Faulkner book he could barely decipher. The bar was about half full, mostly with Irish mill workers blowing off steam before heading home to do battle with their wives. It was a ritual his father had indulged in most of his working life.

Doherty slid onto a vacant stool at the far end, away from the noisy crowd. After he got Mickey Flannery's attention he ordered a shot of Jameson and a beer. He recognized a few of the guys among the crowd at the other end of the bar. Some of them were fellas he'd gone to high school with; others were guys he'd collared for one thing or another when he was a cop.

They spent their hard-earned money carelessly in Paddy's, all the while knowing that their days in the mills were numbered. It wouldn't be long before most of them would receive notices that their operations were closing down. Most of the mills had already moved down South where the owners could pay workers less for more work. Few if any of these guys would get in the years at the mills in West Warwick that their fathers had. Maybe that was a blessing in disguise since the work itself was back-breaking and mind-numbing. But like everyone else in town Doherty wondered what the locals would do for work once the last mills closed.

The closures were already having a domino effect on the other businesses in Arctic. Clothing stores, eateries, barber shops and hardware stores, even the big ones like Majestic and Benny's, were all seeing a drop off in business. It wouldn't be long before the once vibrant textile mills all across New England were nothing but a memory. He wondered if the loss of business in town would eventually affect his own hand-to-mouth operation.

Flannery pulled a few final drafts before most of the mill guys staggered on home. This gave him a chance to amble down the bar to engage Doherty in some conversation.

"Seen my Uncle Patrick lately?" Doherty asked when Mickey was within earshot.

Flannery leaned across the wooden deck. "No, I haven't. But there was two guys in here last night askin' about your buddy Timilty. Wanted to know if I'd seen him around lately."

"What did you tell them?"

"I didn't tell 'em nuthin'. Said I hadn't seen Gus since he left the cops goin' on five years now."

"Is that all they wanted to know?"

Flannery looked nervously down the length of the bar. "They asked about you too," he said in a quieter voice. "Wanted to know if you come into Paddy's a lot."

"What did you tell them?"

Flannery tried to smile but it didn't fully register on his face. "I told them you come in now and then but that you wasn't a regular like them guys," he said, nodding at the remaining mill workers at the other end. "Then they ask me where you lived. I told 'em I didn't know 'cause I really don't. I know where your office is, but I didn't tell them nuthin' about that neither."

Doherty was trying to figure out who these guys were. He suspected they were either doing some scouting work for his Uncle Patrick or for whoever was behind the two murders. "What else can you tell me about those two?"

"They wasn't from 'round here that was for sure. They had them Boston accents. You know, like them Micks from Southie have. They were askin' things like what kinda *cahr* you drive and where your *apahrtment* is. If you ask me, they look like a coupla hitters, which was why I wasn't gonna give 'em nuthin' to chew on."

Doherty had more questions but Mickey Flannery was being summoned by the last mill boys to set them up another round. It was some time before he came back. Doherty decided to have some dinner while he waited for the crowd to thin out.

"What've you got in the kitchen tonight, Mickey?"

"We got some Irish stew and fish and chips. I think Little Paddy might be able to cook you up a hamburger if you wanted."

"I'll have the stew with some bread on the side. And could you bring me another 'Gansett next time you're down this way?"

The talk among the mill guys had grown increasingly louder. Doherty fully expected a fight to break out any minute. Meanwhile he would mind his own business while mulling over what Mickey had just told him about the two guys from Boston. The barkeep dropped off his beer. It was another ten minutes before he placed the bowl of Irish stew in front of him along with two pieces of white bread and a thick pat of butter. The stew was mostly potatoes, but it helped fill the void in his stomach. The bread did its best to soak up the alcohol.

It was going on eight by the time the mill shift crowd thinned out, leaving a low din in its wake. Flannery mopped the bar at their end where quite a bit of beer had been spilled. He then hauled out a bucket of sand and spread some on a spot by the door where one of the drinkers had thrown up his nightly supply of liquor. When that unpleasant deed was done Mickey returned to remove Doherty's scraps.

"Hey, Mickey. What else can you tell me about those two Boston guys?"

"I didn't tell 'em nuthin', Doherty. Honest I didn't."

"I know. I'm not saying you did. I just need to know a few things, like what they looked like and why you thought they were a couple of hitters. That's all."

Flannery let out a sigh of relief. "Do you think they was lookin' to make trouble for you and Timilty?"

"I don't know. Tell me more about them; that might help me figure it out."

"Like I said there were two of them. One was older, maybe in his forties. He wore one of them tweed caps and had a face that looked like a potato." Mickey chuckled at his own clever description of the man. "He was all red-faced with some scars. It was hard to get a good look at him 'cause he had his cap pulled down low. He was the one with the heavy Boston accent that did most of the talkin'."

"And the other one?"

"Taller and younger. Black Irish. He wore a fedora but had a lot of dark hair that stuck out on the sides like he needed a haircut. Had a black mustache and them killer type eyes. You know, like you see on bad guys in the movies. He kinda reminded me of Jack Palance in *Shane*."

"Why do you think they were hitters?"

Mickey took a few seconds as if to recall why he used that word to describe the two men. "The older one with the potato face, he was wearing a tight jacket and I could see the bulge under his arm. When he leaned forward across the bar I thought I heard somethin' hard hit the wood. I can't say for sure that they was packin', but they look like the kinda of fellas who did."

"Thanks, Mickey. You've been a big help. How much do I owe you for the food and the drinks?"

"I done good, didn't I, Doherty?"

"You sure did. Thanks for having my back. If those two mamalukes come back, whatever you do don't tell them anything about Gus being here, okay?"

The bill was $2.50. Doherty left a fiver on the bar and told Mickey to keep the change.

When he got back to the apartment he was surprised to see the lights on and even more surprised to see Rachel lying on the couch watching TV. He coughed to let her know he was there in case she didn't hear him unlocking the door. He took the easy chair that sat adjacent to the couch. "What're you watching?"

Rachel didn't bother to look in his direction. Her eyes were locked on the TV screen. "It's a new series called *Twilight Zone*. It's kind of like science fiction mixed with the paranormal."

"Paranormal? I'm not sure what that means."

"Shhh. I tell you what's going on when they break for a commercial."

Doherty used the occasion to light a Camel and kick off his shoes. He was tired and a little bit drunk. Even though he tried to get a good look at Rachel he could only see her face bathed in the blue light reflected from the TV screen. Finally the show was interrupted for a commercial.

Rachel turned in his direction and explained, "This episode is about a man who works in a high-pressure ad agency in New York. He's under a lot of stress at work with his boss always hounding him to 'push, push, push harder'. One day he yells at his boss and calls him fatso and storms out of the meeting room. At the end of that day he is taking the commuter train home to his house in the suburbs. He falls asleep and when he wakes up he's in another time and place and there is a different conductor on the train wearing an old fashioned uniform. He looks out the train window and it's the late 19th century. It's a warm July day and he sees this small town called Willoughby with an idyllic village square filled with happy people. He gawks at it from the train wishing he could be part of this peaceful world. He gets up from his seat but then the train starts moving and he soon wakes up in the present. This town he dreamed of looks like the exact opposite of his miserable life. That's all I've seen so far."

When the story returned Doherty decided to keep quiet and watch it along with her. He suspected that after what happened to Rachel last spring she wished she could escape to a place like Willoughby.

The program resumed and the harried guy is at home with his wife. He is trying to explain to her how miserable he is at work and dissatisfied he is with their exorbitant lifestyle that he has to work so hard to maintain. He tells her he just wants a life where he can be the 'full measure' of the person he wishes to be. Then he tells her about his dream of the stop at Willoughby; she responds that he's a boring man who can't deal with real life. Throughout the show the fellow keeps pressing his hand against his chest as if his high-pressure life is causing him to have heart pains.

In the next scene he's at work and the phones on his desk are ringing off their hooks. Meanwhile his secretary comes in to tell him the boss needs to see him immediately. The guy is so overwrought that he goes into the bathroom and smashes a mirror. When he comes out he calls his wife and tells her he can't take it anymore and needs her support. Instead she hangs up on him.

Next the man is riding home on the train wondering what he's going to do and how he'll be able to face his shrewish wife. This time when he falls asleep he decides he'll get off when the train stops at Willoughby. Soon he's awoken by the conductor wearing the old-time uniform bellowing, "Next stop, Willoughby." The man is beckoned by the conductor to get off the train at this stop. He does disembark and everyone in the town knows his name.

All of a sudden it's nighttime and snow is falling. Someone is swinging a lantern while the conductor, the one from the present time, is telling him that the poor fellow jumped from the moving train while saying something about a stop named Willoughby. The man's dead body is then loaded into the back of a station wagon and when its rear door is closed it has a sign on it that says "Willoughby and Sons Funeral Home". The show ends with a poetic commentary by the host about how we all wish we could sometimes escape from the pressures of modern life.

Rachel stood up and turned off the TV. She looked at Doherty for the first time. She had a stunned look on her face and all she could say was, "Holy shit."

Doherty didn't say anything. He just sat in the easy chair pulling slowly on his cigarette. Finally in a low voice he said, "What are you doing here? I thought you left for good."

"I don't know, bubbie. I tried to stay away but I couldn't. My parents were driving me crazy and I had nowhere else to go. I hope you don't mind." They stared at each other for a long time without saying anything.

"What have you been up to lately?" Rachel asked, breaking the spell.

"I've been working a case. As you probably remember, I was hired by Gus' business partner, Johnny Briggs, because Gus had gone missing. Briggs was anxious for me to find him because Gus' absence was bad for his business."

"Did you find him?"

"Yeah, I found him all right. Unfortunately two people connected to his being missing were killed along the way."

"Jesus, Doherty. What the hell have you gotten yourself into?"

He spent the next half hour filling Rachel in on what had transpired so far including his dealings with Maureen Donovan and Jimmy Ricks, as well as how he'd purloined the sex movies from Frankie DeAngelo's apartment. The movies, he explained, seemed to be what everyone was after and the key to solving the murders.

"So Tango was able to successfully introduce you to that pimp in Providence because they were like brothers under the skin?" Rachel said, her voice dripping with sarcasm.

"It all went down fine for Tango. Turns out this pimp had seen your friend's group perform at some Negro clubs in South Providence and liked his music. At no time was your jazz musician buddy in any kind of trouble. I was, but not him." He hoped that would satisfy her.

"And this girl from Cranston that got killed, why was it you had to see her so many times to get information you could've gotten in one visit?"

"I only went to her place three times - and she was already dead on the third visit," he added coldly, hoping to ward off the inevitable.

"Did you sleep with her?" Doherty didn't answer. He lit another cigarette and sat stoically waiting for Rachel to fly into a fit of anger.

"You don't have to say anything. I know the answer already."

"Jesus, Rach, you and I've been acting like brother and sister for nearly six months now. What did you expect me to do, wait the rest of my life for us to get back together?"

"I suppose you're now going to launch into some bullshit about how a man has his needs."

"No, I think I'll go to bed instead. I'm dog-tired."

After he left the room he could hear the television spring back into action. He washed his teeth, relieved himself in the bathroom and then stripped to his skivvies and got into bed. After all that had happened in this case, the last thing he needed was a lecture on infidelity from Rachel. People were dead and he was partially responsible for that, or at least for not doing all he could to prevent their deaths from happening. And now there were two thugs from Boston nosing around his town asking questions about him and Gus.

Doherty was dead asleep when Rachel slipped into the bed beside him. She reached down and did the very thing she knew would arouse him. When he rolled to his back she climbed up and straddled him. He tried to speak but she covered his mouth with her hand. "Fuck me," is all she said.

"Rachel I don't…"

She slapped him across the face. "I said 'fuck me' you sonofabitch!"

"I don't like that language when…"

She slapped him again, harder this time. "Just do your fucking job, if you still can."

Reluctantly Doherty did as she requested. Their coupling was crude and lacked all sense of affection. It was purely a physical act. When it was over he was drained and embarrassed. All he could do was smoke a cigarette and try to shake off his self-loathing. Rachel rolled onto her back and stared at the ceiling. He tried to make a weak attempt at conversation. He then reached out and touched her but she didn't respond to that either. Eventually they both fall asleep.

When he awoke in the morning the other side of the bed was empty. He pulled on his shorts and padded through the apartment. There was no sign of Rachel anywhere. A fresh pot of coffee was warming on the stove. Doherty poured himself a cup and wandered back into the living room. It was only then that he saw an envelope taped to the TV screen. He pulled out a cigarette and sat down in the easy chair to read it.

I am sorry things had to end this way. I know you did the best you could. I guess it just wasn't good enough. No matter what happened between us I would've always felt damaged being with you. Once I thought I could have fallen in love with you. Now it's too late for that. Please don't try to get in touch with me. Consider this sayonara.
Love, Rachel
P.S. You can keep the TV

Chapter Thirty-Two

In the morning Doherty got the Chevy out of Belanger's garage and headed north toward Providence. While nestling a cup of coffee between his legs he tried to review the events of the previous night, especially his last hours with Rachel. He couldn't decide if he was relieved or disappointed that their ongoing melodrama appeared to be over for good. He'd gotten closer to her than any woman in quite some time - and now she was gone.

The rape she suffered at the hands of Stanislaw Krykowski had thrown their relationship into a tailspin that it would never recover from. Even if it was unconsciously so, she would always blame Doherty for what happened that night. When she showed up at his door a few weeks after the assault he was hopeful they'd be able to move on. But for Rachel there was no moving on, at least not with him. Leaving their relationship behind was her only route to salvation. He'd miss her, even though he understood why she needed to leave.

The main branch of the Providence Public Library was located within the downtown grid on Empire Street across from the Majestic Theatre; the same theatre where Doherty'd seen *North by Northwest* last spring while waiting to make his first move on Krykowski. The library was also not that far from the Shepard Building where the Polish Nazi had worked as a shoe salesman before his untimely death.

The library was a large brick building, constructed sometime around the turn of the century. It was an impressive edifice in a city that had many notable buildings to its credit. As he mounted the stone steps that led into the entry-way, Doherty was a bit overwhelmed by the enormity of the structure. The one story West Warwick library in Crompton was miniscule in comparison.

He asked at the checkout desk where he could find old newspapers and was directed to the circulation department on the second floor. After ascending another staircase he found that department located at the front end of the building sandwiched between two large windows that provided nice views of the city's center. Glancing around the second floor he noticed that there were stacks of books everywhere. He wondered if every book ever printed could be found in this library. If not, it certainly contained every book he might ever want to read.

A youngish woman wearing a blue headband and black horn-rimmed glasses attached to a chain dangling around her neck was working the circulation desk. She might have been attractive if she ditched the glasses and the headband. But this was a library and not a nightclub. She was here to do her job not look good for men like him.

"Can I help you, sir?"

Doherty had been framing his questions all the way into town, but now found himself at a loss for words. Eventually he stammered, "I was wondering if you carried copies of old newspapers here?"

She smiled, more at his unease than at him, and said, "We have copies of the *Journal* and the *Bulletin*, as well as the *New York Times* and the *Boston Globe*. I'm afraid if you're looking for anything except the *Journal* or the *Bulletin* older than two years you'll have to search them on microfilm."

"Micro?"

"Microfilm. They're like filmstrips. You put them in a special filmstrip machine located in a viewing carrel. Most our microfilms contain a full year of a paper's text as well as pictures, comics and other graphics," she explained hoping she wasn't losing him along the way.

"Do have real paper copies of the *Boston Globe*?"

"We do. But in the case of the *Boston Globe* we only have paper copies from the past two years. Anything before that would be on microfilm. I believe we have microfilm copies of the *Globe* going back to the middle of the last century."

"How would I find specific issues that I'd want to look at?"

"We have individual indexes for the Providence papers, the *New York Times* and the *Boston Globe*. For any other papers you'd have to search for them in the Readers Guide to Periodical Literature. Perhaps if you told me what you were looking for I could better help you."

Doherty looked around the library and wondered why someone who was as voracious a reader as he felt so uncomfortable in this large book depository.

"I'm looking for some articles about a Boston politician. Ideally, I would like to find some pictures of him if I could." He considered making up some cock and bull story as to why he needed to do this, then decided not to since the reference librarian probably wouldn't care anyway. It was her job to facilitate his search, not question it. Besides it was none of her business why he needed to find some pictures of Kevin O'Shaughnessy.

The woman pointed to her left and said, "Second shelf down on that bookcase. That's where you'll find the *Boston Globe* index. The latest ones are in soft cover. Anything from a year ago and back will be in hardbound collections. If you know what you're looking for just go right to your subject. Everything is alphabetized and after each entry you'll see a bunch of numbers, mostly referring to the paper's volume etc. What you really want to look for are the dates. The number after the date refers to the page."

Doherty thanked the librarian and headed over to the shelf she'd directed him to. It took him a while to locate the *Boston Globe* index. As she described them, the last two volumes covering 1958 and 1959 were collected in slim paperbound versions with green covers. The ones from before that were in thick, dark blue, hardbound tomes, each covering a five-year period.

He started with the latest copies and worked backwards. If O'Shaughnessy was as secretive an operator as Judge DeCenza had indicated, it might prove difficult to find anything of value in old *Boston Globes*. In fact, there were no references to O'Shaughnessy in any of the 1959 papers, or in 1958 for that matter. He had to go all the way back to 1956 to find two small references. One was accompanied by his name in italics. He took the volume back to the reference desk to ask what an italicized citation meant.

"That means there's a picture or some other kind of visual reference," the woman with the blue headband explained.

Bingo, he'd hit on what he was looking for. He took out his notepad and wrote down the two citations from 1956. After doing so he resumed his search.

In time he found three more references to Kevin O'Shaughnessy, two from 1954 and one from 1953. One of the '54 citations was also in italics. He took down a few more volumes and ploughed through them all the way back to 1950. There were only two other references to O'Shaughnessy and neither was marked by italics. Nevertheless he chalked down the dates in his notes.

When he returned to the reference desk the girl was helping someone else so he waited patiently. When it was his turn she smiled and said, "Did you find what you were looking for?"

"I think so," he replied, then told her of the dates from 1956, 1954 and 1953 he wished to look at."

She shook her head. "Like I explained before, I'm afraid the papers you wish to see are only available on microfilm. I can send someone to get them for you if you want. It will take about five minutes. Once they're here we can set you up on at a viewing carrel. However, I should warn you that newspaper pictures don't show up very well on microfilm. They tend to be a little blurry."

She asked Doherty to fill out a form on which he wrote down the specific dates of the papers he wished to view. She also wanted to know if he had a library card. When he told her he only had one for the library in West Warwick she showed marked disappointment.

He hoped the blurred images in the papers' photos would be good enough, even though he worried their poor quality might frustrate him in his search. Besides he didn't have any other options short of driving up to Boston to look at the actual papers in the *Boston Globe* archives, if such a thing existed.

It was closer to ten minutes before a young man, a boy really, wearing a sleeveless V-neck sweater over a short sleeve white shirt and baggy pants arrived at the desk with the requested filmstrips. His hair was a bramble of reddish curls and his glasses were held together at the nosepiece by a strip of adhesive tape.

"Dennis will help you get started at a viewing carrel," the girl said.

He followed the boy to the back corner of the second floor to a projection unit with a chair attached. Once Doherty was seated in the carrel Dennis showed him how to spool the microfilm through the viewing machine. The machine itself reminded him of the peep shows he'd viewed as a kid on the midway at Rocky Point. His uncle had taken him there a few times. While he watched short filmstrips of old time baseball stars like Babe Ruth and Lou

Gehrig through the viewer, his Uncle Patrick looked through a similar viewer at peep shows of women wearing little or no clothing.

When Dennis leaned over Doherty's shoulder he could smell peanut butter on the kid's breath. Once the strip was looped in properly, he turned on the light and a large projection of the front page of an old newspaper immediately came into view. Before leaving the kid showed Doherty how to adjust the focus and how to turn the crank to move the paper along from one date to the next. He warned Doherty not to crank too quickly as he might break the filmstrip if he did.

After the boy left Doherty consulted his notes and then spun the mechanism that advanced the microfilm to the date he sought. He was careful to turn the crank slowly as the kid had suggested. What he was viewing reminded him of instructional filmstrips on personal hygiene, the care of equipment and even battle tactics he'd been shown while in the service.

In time he arrived at the first reference from 1956 and scanned the articles on the designated page until he found an appropriate one. It wasn't very helpful as O'Shaughnessy was mentioned only as a part of a group of financial donors to an orphanage in Dorchester, Massachusetts. It was the second citation, the one that had appeared in italics that caught Doherty's attention. A group of men, all with Irish surnames, were standing behind his eminence Richard Cardinal Cushing, the head of the Boston archdiocese. Everyone knew that Cushing was the most important prelate and Catholic leader in New England.

He tried to zero in on O'Shaughnessy's mug, but as the librarian had indicated, newspaper pictures did not transfer well onto microfilm. After much squinting he left the microfilm where it was and returned to the desk to ask the librarian she had a magnifying glass he could borrow.

She smirked as she handed him a small plastic one. "A lot of our elderly readers ask for these. Some of them can barely read a word without one."

"I'm not quite in that category yet," Doherty said defensively "You were right about the newspaper pictures not showing up very well on the microfilm."

He returned to the carrel and used the glass to eyeball Kevin O'Shaughnessy as best he could. He might be the guy who was in the skin flicks with Gus' daughter, but he couldn't tell for sure from this picture. If O'Shaughnessy was a close acquaintance of the Cardinal, he was definitely someone who wouldn't want his bare ass to be seen in public on a stag film – especially one that so blatantly degraded a Catholic schoolgirl.

The third 1956 reference had to do with O'Shaughnessy endorsing some-one running for Congress from the district that encompassed most of the city of Boston. No picture accompanied this article. Satisfied that 1956 had been thoroughly examined, Doherty ran the filmstrip all the way through and re-turned it to the round plastic case labeled *Boston Globe, 1956.*

Then following Dennis' directions he carefully spooled the 1954 *Globe* papers into the microfilm machine. The paper's layout was slightly different than the '56 version, though the search process remained the same. The first article merely contained a reference to O'Shaughnessy being present at some testimonial dinner in Boston for an outgoing councilman. There were pictures accompanying the article but none of the captions contained O'Shaughnessy's name. When Doherty scanned the pictures with the magnifying glass he could not locate anyone who looked like the guy standing behind Cardinal Cushing in the more recent issue.

The second citation proved to be the mother lode Doherty'd been look-ing for. The article was about a political breakfast held each St. Patrick's Day in South Boston. Apparently it was a big event up in Beantown where a lot of politicos took good-natured, cheap shots at one another while celebrating a day for the patron saint of Ireland and his exiles abroad.

The article began on the front page and spread over two pages into the City section. Numerous pictures accompanied the piece, including one large, reasonably clear one of O'Shaughnessy standing with a group of men that in-cluded Boston Mayor John B. Hynes and the young senator, John F. Kennedy. He skimmed the articles looking for O'Shaughnessy's name. Most of the sto-ries focused on the ribald comments made by city councilors and other Boston politicians. Kennedy was cited for his lackluster performance that the reporter said would not help enhance his campaign to be the Democratic nominee for vice-president in 1956.

Finally he found two references to O'Shaughnessy made by a couple of different Boston pols. One referred to him as the Lamont Cranston of Massachusetts politics given that people knew his name but seldom saw him; they only knew where he'd been by the trail of dollar bills he left behind. It was a common reference to the Lamont Cranston who was the invisible crime fighter The Shadow on the radio show of the same name. The second jab at O'Shaughnessy was by another pol who called him a Robin Hood in reverse – a man who stole from the poor and gave to the rich. According to the article each comment elicited only a smattering of laughs since many of those in attendance had no idea of who Kevin O'Shaughnessy was. The paper identified him merely as a prominent Democratic fundraiser.

But there was no doubt that the man in the large photo was a younger and slightly less corpulent version of the guy in the skin flicks. If O'Shaughnessy was a shadowy figure as the *Boston Globe* reporter indicated, exposure of those films would certainly wrench him out of those shadows. Frankie DeAngelo had already paid dearly for his role in the scam with his life. And so had Maureen Donovan. Their deaths must've sent shock waves through Jimmy Ricks' world. He was well protected, but not so protected that a couple of well-paid bulldogs from Boston couldn't reach him. Aside from Ricks himself only Doherty and Gus knew just how precarious the pimp's position was.

Chapter Thirty-Three

In the morning Doherty checked into his office at a quarter past ten. Agnes was nowhere to be seen so he slumped into his swivel chair and assumed his usual position with his feet atop the desk in their accustomed spot. He popped out a Camel and tapped one end on his desktop to repack some loose tobacco. By the time he'd torched it with his Zippo he could hear Agnes' heavy breathing as she ascended the stairs. In another couple of weeks it would be too much of a struggle for her to haul her pregnant belly up to the second floor. He shouldn't be so concerned since she wasn't supposed to be in his employ anyway. But with Rachel gone and Agnes about to follow, there would be no one to do the clerical work for Doherty and Associates.

He heard her struggling to get her coat off. Once that was done she stuck her head inside his space. As usual she commented on him sitting in the dark, even though he'd told her a dozen times that it helped him to think. She eased into his office and settled herself into his client's chair. She let out a big sigh as if sitting down was an ordeal in itself. For her sake he flipped on the green-shaded desk lamp.

"It won't be long before you can't make the stairs," he said, trying hard not to be unkind.

Agnes looked at him, then turned away. "The doctor says exercise is good for pregnant women. He's always tellin' me how Indian girls would have their babies out in the fields and then go right back to work."

"Was he referring to Gandhi Indians or Sitting Bull Indians?"

"Huh?"

"Never mind."

In a feeble attempt to get things back on track he proceeded to tell Agnes about Rachel Katz's fond farewell. To maintain a modicum of good taste he left out the sex part. Despite his growing closeness with his secretary, Doherty never shared anything about his sex life with her. He never shared it with anyone except his barber, Bill Fiore, and when he did it was only to toss him a few bones to give Bill an occasional cheap thrill. Besides, he suspected Fiore's sex life was a lot more exciting than his. Most men didn't talk about stuff like that with one another unless they were bragging. And when they were bragging it usually meant that most of what they were saying was a load of bullcrap.

"How's the Timilty case goin'?"

Once again Doherty had to consider how much to share with Agnes. She knew Gus pretty well and had a very high opinion of him. He didn't want to say anything that would damage that impression.

"Well, there are two people dead and I can't raise Gus on the horn no matter how many times I try ringing him up. Right now I'm kind of stymied until I can get ahold of him."

"Why don't you try goin' by his place? With two murders already maybe he's just bein' extra cautious about answerin' the phone."

Doherty hesitated before responding. "Well, you see, the thing is I don't exactly know where Gus is living these days."

"Jeez, boss, what kinda friend are you? You don't even know where your best buddy lives."

"Gus tends to move around a lot," he lied. "So I'm not sure where he's putting his head down this month."

"Does that mean until he contacts you you're at a dead end?"

"Not exactly. One other person I could speak to about this is my Uncle Patrick. But he doesn't come around that often, as you could tell from his visit the other day."

Agnes shook her head accompanied by a look of mild disgust. "Then what're you gonna do, boss, sit around here on your keister and wait until the phone rings? You already said two people are dead on account of this case. A real private eye would be out there beatin' the bushes, lookin' for the killers."

Doherty had to smile. "Well aren't we in a feisty mood today. Must be the hormones from your pregnancy."

Agnes stood up abruptly, or as abruptly as she could in her present condition. She put her hands on her now substantial hips and gave Doherty her best schoolmarm look. "The detective I know wouldn't be sittin' in his smelly office all day feelin' sorry for himself just because his girlfriend walked out on him. If he had a case to work, he'd be workin' it. You admitted yourself that you're somehow connected to those two murders. You can either go to the police and spill what you know or you can get out there and solve them yourself." Agnes turned and retreated to the front office, dramatically slamming the door as she did.

After she was gone Doherty lifted the receiver and dialed Gus' number for the twentieth time. As if a miracle had been brought on by Agnes' angry outburst, someone picked up on the other end. Nothing was said though he could hear breathing.

"Gus, it's me, Doherty. Say something will ya."

A groggy voice replied, "Yeah, I hear you. Talk to me."

"Jesus, Gus, where the hell have you been? I've been calling you non-stop for the last two days. "

"I had to lay low. I picked up the scent of two torpedoes on my tail. My landlady told me they came by my place twice. She could tell by their looks that they weren't the Fuller Brush men. I tried to make myself scarce until I had to come here to pick up a few things. You're lucky you caught me this time."

"We need to talk, Gus. And I mean soon. I think I've picked up some clues as to what's going on, but I don't want to talk about it over the phone. The two guys you just mentioned were in Paddy's the other night asking about you and me. Mickey Flannery correctly clocked them as a couple of hitters down here from Boston. I've got a pretty good idea they're after those films. And I also have a hunch who they're working for."

"If we meet, it's gotta be some out-of-the-way place where nobody we know would see us," Gus said, his voice shakier than Doherty'd ever heard it. "To be honest with you, right now I'm running a little scared. Whoever's tailing me has to know something about my daughter's role in this business."

Doherty considered the suggestion and then gave Gus directions to a place where no one would ever expect see them.

George's Tavern was no busier than the night Doherty had his last sit- down there with Jimmy Ricks. He was already nursing a double shot of Jameson when Gus slid into the booth across from him. Timilty checked out the seedy ambience of George's and said, "Where'd you find this place?"

"It's where Ganetti set up my meet with Ricks. He thought it would be a better spot for me than having to go into darktown to the Club Mocambo."

Gus laughed. "I'm just trying to visualize a cool cat like Jimmy Ricks in this gin mill."

"To tell you the truth, I don't think Ricks appreciated the ambience."

The owner and bartender, George DiMucci, came to the booth to see what Gus wanted to drink.

"Where's your no-neck friend Gio tonight?" he asked Doherty in a way that told him that maybe Ganetti's men weren't all that welcome in his bar.

"I don't know," Doherty said not wanting to be reminded of his debt to the Ganetti family. In order to change the subject he said, "George, I'd like you to meet my friend Gus. Gus, this is the owner, George DiMucci. George used to be a boxer. Fought under the name of Tiger DiMucci. Once went the distance with Kid Gavilan. Isn't that right, George?"

Gus looked up from the table and offered his hand. "I figured you were a fighter from looking at the pictures on the walls. What were you, a middleweight?"

George laughed, "I started out as a welter but had to move up to middle when I couldn't make the weight no more. I put on a few pounds since I stopped fightin'," he said as he patted his now substantial stomach that spilled over his pants. "I once sparred with Tony DiMarco. You heard of him haven't ya?"

"Sure, George, sure. I saw Tony fight a few times," Gus said. "I remember one of his fights at the Boston Garden against Gaspar Ortega. It was a real bloodbath."

George smiled again. "Yeah, Tony could always take a punch. I hit him wid my best shots when we was sparrin'. His head felt like a rock. After I hit him he just looked at me and smiled."

"Tony's still fighting, isn't he?"

"Yeah, he's still in the ring. Last time I saw him I tolt him to stop fightin'
before his brains turned to scrambled eggs. But he don't listen to chumps like
me. That happens to a lotta guys, you know. I gotta think them Basillio fights
took a lot outta him." George began to back away but not before Gus ordered
a Bullmills on the rocks.

Gus then turned his attention to their predicament. "So what've you got
that you couldn't tell me on the phone?"

"I could've told you everything on the phone, but Agnes had just given
me a lecture about sitting around on my ass when I should been out fighting
crime. I thought it would be a good idea to leave the office and get out into the
field. Along with her large stomach, her pregnancy seems to have given her a
set of balls as well."

Timilty smiled at Doherty for the first time since he sat down. "You better
be careful, pally. It won't be long before the tail is wagging the dog at Doherty
and Associates."

"Not going to happen. She can barely make it up the stairs as it is. I give
her another week or two before she tells me she's done working till after the
baby's born."

"Say what you will, you're gonna miss her when she's gone."

"Yeah, I know. Plus I got more bad news in terms of my operation. Rachel
picked up and left yesterday morning. This time I think it's for good. She
hasn't really gotten over the attack by Krykowski. Although she never put it
into words, I know she blames me for what happened. It's probably for the best
that she finally hit the road."

"You're gonna miss her too, pally. First Millie, then the girl that got shot in
Cranston, and now Rachel. And pretty soon Agnes. You don't have a very good
track record in the female department."

Doherty lit up a Camel and took a swig from his glass. "Well maybe it's
better that way. My life in this business keeps getting more and more dangerous as time goes on. It used to be so much easier when I was just hunting
down guys who skipped out on their wives. Now it's like a murder drops on
my doorstep every six months. At this rate I should've stayed with the cops."

"And been a gofer for the DeCenza machine. I don't think that would've
suited you in the long run. Look at it this way, pally. You're now in the big time.

Consorting with men like Frank Ganetti Jr. and Jimmy Ricks." Gus did not even trying to hide the smirk on his face.

"You can add to that list my Uncle Patrick and his boss Kevin O'Shaughnessy."

"*The* Kevin O'Shaughnessy – the big Democratic money man up in Boston?" Gus was obviously impressed.

"So you've heard of him."

"Hey, pally, I'm in the investigations business. It's my responsibility to know who's who and what's what."

"Well according to my uncle right now Kevin O'Shaughnessy is also the unofficial New England treasurer of the Kennedy-for-President campaign."

Gus shook his head. "Man, you really are getting up in the world, aren't you?"

"And you too my friend."

"Me? How do I fit into all this?"

"That's why I asked you to meet me at this fine establishment. You see I spent some time yesterday at the Providence Library looking at photos in old newspapers. *Boston Globes* to be exact. And guess what I found?" Doherty didn't bother to wait for Gus to answer. "The guy who Ricks and DeAngelo caught on film doing it with that young girl. Sorry, I mean with your daughter; he's none other than Kevin O'Shaughnessy – in the flesh so to speak. My suspicion is that it's his zealous pursuit of those embarrassing films that's led to the deaths of Maureen Donovan and Frankie DeAngelo. For obvious reasons he's desperate to get his hands of those films before anyone else sees them."

"According to my Uncle Patrick, Kevin O'Shaughnessy has spent his entire life building up a reputation for probity and secrecy. Now with the Kennedy campaign getting under way and him playing a major role in it, the last thing he needs is for some smut films, which he happens to star in, getting out to the public. Apparently Ricks and DeAngelo weren't satisfied plucking some low hanging fruit. They made the mistake of trying to shake down somebody who may be even more ruthless than them."

"Damn," Gus said, clearly impressed. "I guess that's why Ricks seemed so nervous when I met with him. He indicated right off the bat that he already knew about DeAngelo's untimely death."

"You met with Ricks?"

"I told you I was going to track him down. I went right to the Club Mocambo to confront him. Some of his bloodhounds thought they'd scare me away, but Jimmy called them off before any damage was done."

"What did he have to say?"

"Well at first he was full of his usual bravado. Said he wasn't worried about no two-bit gunners from Boston coming down here to jack him up. He thinks the Federal Hill people will protect him because his operation is so indispensible to them. He didn't say *indispensible* because I don't think he knows what that word means. But that was the gist of what he had to say."

"Do you think they'll protect him from O'Shaughnessy's thugs?"

"I don't know. What I do know is that the Providence wise guys have certain arrangements with their cohorts in Boston. They coordinate a lot of their operations with the Italians in the North End. What I don't know is what kind of deals they have with the Irish mob up there. O'Shaughnessy isn't a gangster, but you can be sure as shooting he has some connections with them. I'd lay odds that those two guys who've been sniffing around looking for you and me aren't exactly his *political* operatives. On the other hand, they could be free-lancers; you know, guns for hire."

"Where does that leave Ricks?"

"If these guys have been sent here by some Irish gang that has an *understanding* with our local organization then it means the Federal Hill people might be willing to throw Jimmy to the wolves to keep the peace. However, if these guys are operating on their own strictly at the behest of O'Shaughnessy, then certain gentlemen down here, like your friend Frank Ganetti, aren't gonna be pleased with them encroaching on their turf."

"What do you think that means for us?"

Gus leaned forward and said in a low voice. "It means if we're forced to smoke these guys to get my daughter back, then no one in Rhode Island, except maybe the cops, is gonna give a shit."

Doherty signaled George the bartender for another round. He then looked Timilty square in the face and said, "Jesus Gus, are you suggesting that we kill these guys if we get the chance?"

Gus leveled an equally determined look at Doherty. "I will do whatever it takes to make sure my little girl is safe. If it means I have to shoot these two dirtbags then I'll do it. I'm certainly prepared to do them before they do us."

"I hate to spoil your little hunting party, but your daughter didn't exactly look like an innocent little girl when she was cranking off O'Shaughnessy in those skin flicks. It was pretty clear from the way she acted for the camera that she was in on the deal with Ricks and DeAngelo from the start. For chrissakes, Gus, you told me yourself that you haven't had any kind of relationship with her since she was a kid."

Their conversation was interrupted when the former boxer dropped off two new drinks at their table. With only a few customers in the place he lingered for a minute hoping to reopen the conversation about his boxing career. Gus gave him a go-away look and George reluctantly returned to his post behind the bar.

"I have a better idea, Gus. One that doesn't involve any more people getting killed." Timilty nodded for Doherty to continue.

"Why don't I reach out to my Uncle Patrick? I'll offer O'Shaughnessy a deal through my uncle. First I'll ask him to call off his goons for both us *and* Jimmy Ricks. Once that's settled I'll offer to swap the films for your daughter. It'll be a straightforward transaction that should please everybody. There'll be no good reason for them to keep your girl once O'Shaughnessy has the films. It's not like she's going to blab to the papers. And if she did why would they believe the word of a whore involved in a shakedown operation against that of a man with O'Shaughnessy's reputation. No offense, Gus, but she does make her living as a sex piece for some important people. I have a hunch there are a few prominent men in our own state who'd prefer that she keep her mouth shut."

"And as far as Jimmy Ricks is concerned, he never did draw down any cash from this particular blackmail scheme. If they decide to murder him anyway just for payback, then that's between them and the people who are supposedly Ricks' protectors. But if I was O'Shaughnessy I wouldn't do something stupid like that. Especially now when he's playing such a big role in trying to make Joe Kennedy's kid president. I mean just having a father like Joe will be scandal enough for the young contender."

Gus seemed satisfied with Doherty's proposal, up to a point. "What happens if they don't go for the deal? Suppose O'Shaughnessy decides he needs to tie up *all* the loose ends."

"I don't think that's going to happen," Doherty said, hoping he was right. "If things don't go as I suggest then I guess we'll be forced to do it your way."

When they departed George's Tavern Gus agreed to call Doherty sometime in the next twenty-four hours. Otherwise he would sit tight until Doherty had a chance to put his plan in action.

Chapter Thirty-Four

The next afternoon Doherty took the short walk down Brookside to Democratic Party headquarters in the old Plaza Hotel. He may have been on a fool's errand, though he was convinced only the good offices of Judge Martin DeCenza could lure his Uncle Patrick back to West Warwick. It was barely four o'clock, yet with standard time returning the previous weekend it was already getting dark. He could see from the street that the lights were on in the party's second floor offices.

The frosted glass door stenciled with the lettering for the *Democratic Town Committee* was unlocked when he arrived. He thought more appropriate lettering would read *"Judge Martin DeCenza's Personal Fiefdom."* In any case he decided to keep his smart-alecky mouth buttoned up today, at least to the extent that the Judge's behavior allowed him to.

DeCenza was sitting in his glassed-in private office conferring with his right hand man, Angel Tuohy. Neither of them noticed Doherty until he knocked on the office door. When they spotted him Touhy rose quickly to greet him, as was his role. Meanwhile the Judge leaned back in his swivel chair and gave Doherty a knowing smile.

Touhy opened the door about a foot and said, "What do you want?" in a less than friendly voice. Doherty thought the Judge's henchman would have to clean up his act some if he intended to run for state rep.

"I'd like a few minutes with your boss," Doherty answered, putting emphasis on the last word as a way of reminding Touhy exactly what his position was relative to the Judge.

Angel looked over his shoulder at DeCenza who barely moved while keeping the sly smile on his puss. "The Judge is a busy man. If you want to meet with him you'll have to make an appointment."

Doherty looked beyond Touhy and said, "He doesn't look all that busy to me." The silly game of cat and mouse was getting tiresome. When Touhy looked back at the Judge the great man offered a slight nod. With that DeCenza's man swung the door open to let the supplicant in. As he passed within inches of Touhy, Doherty flashed him a knowing grin. It did not go down well with the doorman.

The Judge leaned back in his chair and gave Doherty a good going over. Finally he spoke. "For a man who has shown utter disdain for all things political, Mr. Doherty, you're making a habit of coming up here to see me. I presume you're here to ask for another favor."

Doherty dropped into a chair on the other side of the large desk without it being offered. Taking offense Touhy took a step closer to their visitor.

His boss raised his hand. "It's all right, Angel. I believe Mr. Doherty is accustomed to taking liberties where none are offered. You do know that was a sign of rudeness, don't you?" the Judge asked his visitor.

Instead of answering DeCenza's inquiry about his manners, Doherty used the occasion to light up a cigarette. His actions were intended to make everyone in the office feel uneasy.

"Are you here on a personal matter, Mr. Doherty? Is Harry giving you a hard time about loitering in his barbershop? Or perhaps you want to ask me to give a job to another one of your disabled war buddies."

Doherty took his time replying to the Judge's queries. He could sense Touhy nervously shuffling behind him. He wouldn't give DeCenza's boy the courtesy of turning in his direction, letting him know he was even conscious of his presence.

"Actually I'm here on a matter of a political nature and one that you might be interested in."

"Well that is a surprise," the Judge said, now clasping his hands behind his head and rocking back in his chair. "I thought you found politics, how did you describe it, 'as a dirty business from start to finish'."

"I don't believe those were my exact words. In fact, I don't suppose politics are tainted by corruption everywhere like they are in our little state. I'm sure there are places in America where politicians serve the public good with honest intentions."

The Judge continued to rock back in his chair. He let out a little chuckle at this last remark. "I wouldn't be too sure about that, my boy. Nevertheless, could you please get on with your business. If you've come to talk politics, then I would be happy to give you some time. Otherwise Angel and I have important affairs to attend to."

Doherty calmly smoked, being careful not to jump into things too quickly. He knew the Judge appreciated subtlety and was determined to play at his pace.

"It's my understanding that you had some unpleasant dealings in the past with my Uncle Patrick McSweeny." The Judge's expression did not change though his eyes grew noticeably darker.

DeCenza nodded his head. "Is that what you're here to talk about? Events that happened years ago."

"Perhaps. Suppose we start with you telling me about those past disagreements between you and my uncle?"

DeCenza was quiet for an uncomfortable amount of time. Long enough to make Tuohy nervously shuffle his feet as if waiting for a high sign for him to usher Doherty out of party headquarters.

When the Judge did speak it was in his usual controlled manner. "Years ago Patrick McSweeny was part of a Democratic reform committee that organized itself here in Kent County. Their stated mission was to 'clean up corruption in the party'. At the time I believe their real goal was to remove me as party leader. Word around town was that your uncle fancied himself as my logical replacement as county chairman."

"Well, whatever their mission was, apparently they weren't very successful."

The Judge shook his head and even stole a glance at Touhy. "No, not entirely. I survived their insurgency. But in order to do so I had to dump a couple of my chosen candidates from the ballot. Good men, I might add. Men who'd been loyal to me for years. I was also forced to jettison some of my allies on the county committee. Believe me it was a bitter pill to swallow after all I'd done for the party here in West Warwick and other parts of the county."

"What happened to my uncle's plan to unseat you?"

The Judge's mouth drew into a tight-lipped grin. "Your beloved uncle deserted the reform committee shortly afterwards to chase bigger game up in Boston. First that sonofabitch gave me a near heart attack and then he up and left the area as if none of his actions had any consequences."

"So I take it there is no love lost between the two of you."

The Judge waved his hand as if what happened in the past no longer mattered. Doherty wasn't buying it. He couldn't help but detect an unmistakable bitterness in the Judge's voice. He was the kind of man who preferred to get even rather than get mad.

"Did you get your people back into their positions after my uncle left the area?"

The Judge shook his head. "Not entirely. It turned out this reform committee was here to stay even without McSweeny as their leader. My willingness to bargain with them gave these reformers a false sense of empowerment – a sense they have not given up on to this day. To pacify them I must periodically put one or two of their favorites on the ballot as candidates for some lesser offices. They're grateful knowing that if these men have my backing they're sure to be elected."

"And did you have to do the same with the party committee?"

The Judge actually smiled at this point. "I gave them representation and let them feel as if the county committee has some real power in the party." At this point the Judge rocked forward in his chair and leaned across his desk. "In the end, however, any real decisions made about the Democratic Party in our county are made right here in this room. Isn't that right, Angel?" Touhy grunted in agreement. "I hope that doesn't offend your tender sensibilities, Mr. Doherty."

"Not at all, Judge. Knowing where the power lies in this town is why I'm here today. I was hoping to enlist your help in a little scheme I'm cooking up involving my uncle." The prospect of such familial conflict clearly piqued the Judge's interest.

"You see it's like this: As you know my uncle is deeply involved with the campaign to make young Jack Kennedy president of the United States."

"Yes, I believe you passed that information on to me the last time you were in here. I've also heard this from some of my other sources as well. As for me, with Stevenson not running this time around, I'm considering supporting Senator Humphrey. Though that's neither here nor there at this stage of the campaign."

Doherty began again. "Well, you see, my uncle is working directly for Kevin O'Shaughnessy, who you yourself identified as an important fundraiser and inside operator in Democratic politics out of Boston. According to Patrick, O'Shaughnessy is already shoveling a lot of money into primary states; money that comes directly from Joe Kennedy and other well-heeled Irishmen who want to see one of their tribe finally make it to the White House. My uncle, along with some other interested parties, has been traveling the country over the past few months to advance the Kennedy name in states where presidential preference primaries are being held next year."

"Yes, I'm aware of that. None of this is new to me," the Judge said feigning boredom.

"Without getting into details, I have some information that could cause O'Shaughnessy *and* my Uncle Patrick a great deal of embarrassment. I would like to use this information to leverage some concessions from them."

DeCenza now sat up, apparently interested in what Doherty had to offer. After all using such knowledge to bend people to his will was what the Judge was best at.

"If I remember correctly you do have an uncanny ability of using embarrassing information to get certain parties to accede to your wishes. Indeed, that was something I learned firsthand last year."

DeCenza was obviously alluding to Doherty's knowledge of a crooked real estate deal that the Judge had been involved in that gave Doherty some very useful influence with him. Influence he was hoping to cash in on at this time.

"Given what you know why don't you just sit down with your uncle and parlay with him face to face? Frankly I don't see how any of this concerns me. Unless, of course, you're willing to share this knowledge with us."

Doherty had to smile at this last remark. "Well I would Judge if I trusted you. But you see, I don't. Not entirely anyway. The problem is that my uncle knows I'm up to something. Lately he's been nosing around town trying to find out about some recent cases I've been working. As a result I believe he'd be reluctant to sit down to talk turkey with me right now. In fact, I'm pretty confident either he or O'Shaughnessy have sent some very unpleasant men down here from Boston to put pressure on me and a colleague of mine. I'm fairly certain these men may have already murdered two people to insure that this embarrassing information never gets out to the public. Based on what they've already done, it looks like they'll stop at nothing to make this so."

The Judge slammed his hand down on the desk. "Damnit boy, you didn't say this had anything to do with murder! Whoever these men are they better not drop any bodies in my town. And if they do I will hold your uncle personally responsible."

Doherty wasn't sure what that threat meant nor was he about to ask.

"Getting back to the business at hand, here's my plan: I'd like you to invite my uncle down here to meet with you. Tell him you've had a change of heart and would like to contribute a substantial amount of money to the coffers of the Kennedy campaign. You might even throw in that you'll make some of your operatives available to them if necessary. He will avoid meeting with me, but not with you. Especially if he thinks there's cash in the offering."

"I still don't follow. What exactly is in this for me?"

"We, meaning you and I, will meet with my uncle at which time I will try to negotiate a deal with him. I'll let him know what I have on O'Shaughnessy and while doing so will drop hints to the effect that you too are privy to this information. If nothing else that will cause him to believe you have something on him he will never be able to get out from under. Call it payback, if you wish, for his role with that reform committee. In the meantime I will try to extract something from O'Shaughnessy that is of grave importance to my current client. That's about all I can share with you at this time."

"Is that all you wish me to do? Set up a meeting."

"Yes. All you have to do is arrange this with my uncle, preferably here at your office. By meeting here rather than at my place I can be sure there will be no foul play. I strongly suggest when you call him you don't let on that I'm going to be part of the conversation. I don't want him to find out beforehand that I'll be here. I know he will agree to meet with you because all he and O'Shaughnessy are seeing these days are dollar signs."

"What do you think, Angel?" the Judge asked his man.

Touhy shrugged his shoulders. "I dunno, Judge. I don't see enough upside for you."

DeCenza put his fingers to his temples and appeared to be lost in thought. After a few moments he looked up at Doherty and said, "I'm inclined to agree with Angel. You're going to have to give me something more substantial before I acquiesce to this scheme."

Doherty knew he could use Johnny Briggs or Gus to hide behind client confidentiality, yet wasn't sure that would get him any closer to the deal he had in mind. If his Uncle Patrick had the least suspicion that Doherty knew O'Shaughnessy was complicit in some murders, he wouldn't be able to look his nephew in the eye let alone parlay with him. Much as he hated to admit it, he needed DeCenza to act as the go-between or else it would leave the door open for possibly more murders. And Doherty and Gus could be the next on their list.

"Let me put it this way, Judge. Once I reveal to my uncle what I have on O'Shaughnessy, it could very well lead to the end of that man's career in politics. And if O'Shaughnessy goes down I have no doubt he'll take my uncle with him. All their work for the Kennedy family will go up in smoke. Patrick's career as a big time political fixer will be finished. Would that be enough to satisfy your thirst for revenge?"

DeCenza moved his gaze from Doherty to Touhy. He didn't see what transpired, though something of importance passed between the Judge and his man. DeCenza was exercising patience as a means of keeping Doherty on edge.

"I will attempt to set up this meeting as you've requested. I cannot guarantee that your uncle will attend, though from what you've told me his role in the campaign will more or less compel him to. Especially if Mr. O'Shaughnessy recommends that he does. And," he said pointing a finger directly at Doherty, "I fully expect that what you have on McSweeney and his boss will doom the two of them. In fact, I will insist upon it. This transaction must be done quietly and with no evidence of my hands on it. I have no desire to cause any undo damage to the Kennedy campaign. Although I do not think young Jack Kennedy is prepared to be president, I will not stand in the way of a Catholic and an Irishman striving for our nation's highest office."

Chapter Thirty-Five

Angel Touhy arrived at Doherty and Associates on Friday afternoon shortly after the private eye returned from his lunch at the Arctic News. Doherty was sitting behind his desk smoking a cigarette when he heard the loud knock on the outer door. Agnes wasn't in today and too lazy to answer it himself, he merely yelled for his visitor to "come in." When he saw it was Touhy he didn't even bother to take his feet from the desktop.

The Judge's man stood in the doorway in a topcoat and well creased fedora. He didn't say anything and neither did Doherty. His visitor was waiting until he caught his breath after climbing the stairs.

"Why don't you sit down and take a load off?"

Without bothering to remove his hat Touhy dropped into the client chair on the other side of the desk. Doherty offered him a smoke but the big man didn't accept. Instead he pulled out a pack of his own and lit one up. He must not've wanted to accept anything Doherty was proffering.

"The meeting is set up for four o'clock tomorrow afternoon. The Judge says you should come a little early in case your uncle has a change of heart when he sees you there."

"Tell the Judge I'll be on time." Doherty waited to see if Angel had any other messages to deliver. His guest said nothing more. He sat calmly smoking his cigarette as if he had all the time in the world.

Doherty broke the silence. "I hear tell you might be running for state rep next year. How's that going?"

Touhy looked at the bare wall above Doherty's head and didn't respond. The quiet in the room made things awkward. So much for small talk Doherty thought.

"I'm thinking about it," Angel said, as if it were his decision to make. If Judge DeCenza decided Angel Touhy was going to be his man in the state assembly, then Angel was going to be him whether he liked it or not. Knowing the way the Judge operated, it was either that or Touhy would be out on his ass, no longer playing an integral part in the DeCenza machine.

"What's there to think about?" Doherty said sticking the needle in a little deeper.

"I dunno. I kinda like being in charge of the water department. I got a nice car and I get to travel around the county on a regular basis. It's a sweet deal. I feel at home here in West Warwick."

This was the first inkling Doherty had that Angel Touhy was wary about venturing onto a big stage like at the State House. It wasn't the rep part that troubled him. Judge DeCenza would tell him how to vote on any matters of importance. It was consorting with people on a regular basis who were smarter than him.

Doherty gave Touhy his most cynical look and said, "Can we cut the crap, Angel. Everybody knows your real job around here is doing heavy lifting for the Judge. You try doing that kind of shit up at the statehouse, the people there'll cut you down to size in a minute. Besides, getting out of town might do you some good. Give you a chance to get out from under the Judge's shadow and do something on your own. I hear he keeps you on a pretty short leash down here."

"You'd like that wouldn't you." Angel said with a sneer. "It'd open up a spot for your blind boy to take over at the water department."

Doherty dropped his feet to the floor and stood up behind his desk. He pointed at Touhy and said, "Willy Legere is not my *boy*. He got hired because he's a responsible and efficient young man doing good work. He's blind because he got that way serving his country overseas during the war. Not like some other people I know around this town." Doherty heard that during the war the Judge had arranged for a young Angel Touhy to get a soft office job with the navy over in Newport."

"He's still blind, ain't he?"

"What does that have to do with the price of fish? Eyesight or no eyesight he can do the job can't he. To my way of thinking, probably better than you."

Touhy stood in order to meet Doherty eye to eye. "I don't know what you got on the Judge that made him hire that boy, but I don't like being his nurse-maid, driving him everywhere whenever the boss says I gotta." Touhy adjusted his hat and started for the door.

"Hey, Angel, good luck with your campaign."

The big man turned and flipped Doherty the middle finger. Indeed he would have to buff up his act if he was going to represent their town in the legislature.

Doherty was ensconced in DeCenza's office the next day at a quarter to four, along with Touhy and the Judge waiting for his Uncle Patrick to arrive. The Judge offered drinks all around. They each opted for a few fingers of Crown Royal. Both Doherty and Touhy took theirs straight up while the Judge diluted his with water and ice. Little was said of the impending confab as they drank their whiskey and the two younger men smoked. A little after four they heard the tapping of Patrick's cane as he mounted the stairs to party headquarters. Angel pulled back the blinds to look out onto Brookside Avenue.

"Is he alone?" the Judge asked.

"He's got a driver," Angel answered. "But it looks like he's gonna stay with the car."

When Patrick McSweeny knocked on the glass door to the office the Judge indicated that Touhy should answer it. Always the dutiful servant, Angel did as he was told. Patrick looked even older to Doherty than he had when he visited with him recently. He shuffled across the big room, placing a good amount of weight on his walking stick. Touhy took his arm just in case Patrick had second thoughts once he saw his nephew was there. When he did notice Doherty, the look on McSweeny's face could best be described as mildly alarmed.

As if to cut off any forthcoming confusion, DeCenza circled around his desk and gripped his guest in a warm two-handed shake. "So good to see you again, Patrick. It's been too long." He almost sounded sincere; projecting such feelings was DeCenza's stock-in-trade.

Without taking his eyes off his nephew, McSweeny replied, "And you too Martin. You're not looking any worse for wear."

"Oh, you know how things are: you win some, you lose some and the years go by nonetheless."

Touhy brought a chair over and set it down in such a way that Patrick would be facing both Doherty and the Judge. Angel remained standing behind their guest, indicating that if he had any plans on leaving prematurely that was not an option. DeCenza hadn't bothered to introduce Doherty's uncle to the next state rep from West Warwick.

"Can I get you something to drink?" the Judge asked McSweeny holding up his own glass of brown liquor to indicate what was available.

"You know what I would love. How about a coffee milk? You know, I miss them so much and you can't get anything like it in the Boston area." They all knew Rhode Island was about the only place in the region where one could get a coffee flavored milk.

"Angel, will you ask Donna to run up to Smith's or some other place and get Mr. McSweeny here a coffee milk." Turning his attention back to Patrick he said, "I know how you feel. It's even getting hard to find coffee milk down this way. Thankfully my cousin's dairy is still producing it."

Patrick took in the group, not at all sure why his nephew was there, though too polite to ask. He nervously tapped his cane on the floor. "So Martin, I understand you've had a change of heart and would like to make a significant contribution to the Kennedy-for-President campaign. I don't know if you've ever met the young man; he is quite impressive you know. And that wife of his, she looks like a movie star."

"Yes, and I understand the young man also has a proclivity for the real Hollywood starlets - much like his father did," the Judge responded. It was a mean comment; one that Patrick might've been offended by if he didn't believe some substantial money would be changing hands before the afternoon was over.

The girl soon returned with the coffee milk and handed it through the door to Touhy who then conveyed to McSweeny. The tan colored substance was in a pint bottle shaped like a smaller version of the quart ones that milkmen still delivered to the doors of many townspeople. The red DeCenza Dairy logo was etched onto the glass. The Judge grabbed a glass from his liquor cart and handed it to his guest for his milk.

McSweeny poured some of it into the glass and placed the half empty bottle on the Judge's desk. He then held the glass out and said, "Perhaps a little snoot wouldn't hurt." He patted his stomach adding, "I've got to be careful of the whiskey these days on account of my ulcer." The Judge added a shot of Crown Royal to his guest's milk.

It was Doherty's turn to jump into the conversation. "To be honest with you Uncle Patrick, we didn't ask you down here to discuss the Kennedy campaign. In fact, right now the Judge is thinking of supporting that Humphrey fellow." Patrick was clearly uneasy and swung his head around among the three men. "You're here because I need to talk to you about Kevin O'Shaughnessy."

Patrick quickly regained his usual geniality, however fake it was. "I will remind you young man that Mr. O'Shaughnessy is the very salt of the earth. Why just yesterday he..."

"I suggest you cut out the blarney while we talk? Two people are dead on account of your so-called salt of the earth and I don't intend to be the third."

"Why, Hugh," Patrick said trying to act surprised. "Do you think I would let anything happen to my own flesh and blood?" It was a question that did not deserve an answer.

Doherty turned to DeCenza and said, "Listen Judge, I think this will all go down much better if I talked privately with my uncle. I know this is your office and..."

DeCenza raised his hand. "Think nothing of it, my boy. Angel and I will retreat to the outer office until you two are finished with your business."
With that the Judge and Touhy took their drinks and left Doherty and his uncle alone. Tuohy, however, remained just outside the door in case Patrick had any thoughts of exiting before things were concluded to Doherty's satisfaction. His uncle poured some more coffee milk into his glass and got up to add another belt of whiskey to it. This time it was more than a snoot.

"I don't know how we have come to this, boyo." Patrick said as he patted Doherty's knee. "We used to be so close; you were like a son to me."

Doherty allowed himself a brief smile. "Yes, I was. And you were always a better father to me than Peter Doherty. Unlike him, at least you were sober most of the time."

"And your mother, your mother was..."

"Please Uncle Patrick, whatever you do, do not sit here canonizing my mother. She did the best she could under difficult circumstances. But remember, it was always me that was sent down to Paddy's or some other saloon in town to pull my old man out before he spent his whole paycheck on drink. I shed no tears when he passed and neither did she."

Patrick was at a loss for words. One of the world's quintessential blatherers was closed-mouthed for once in his life.

"What are you doing being in business with a man like Martin DeCenza?"

"I could ask the same thing about you and Kevin O'Shaughnessy. I only asked the Judge to set up this meeting to lure you down here. That's all I wanted from him. And obviously it worked because here you are. In light of recent events I knew you wouldn't agree to meet with me directly." He still wasn't sure how much his uncle knew about the murders he was certain were carried out by thugs working for O'Shaughnessy.

Patrick sipped his liquor-spiked milk and smiled knowingly. "You may think that's all there is, but you'll see soon enough. With Martin there will always be future bills to pay. You get him to do you a favor and you will be indebted to him forever. Trust me, I know whereof I speak."

"I wouldn't worry too much about me right now. I'm not as naïve as you may think. But that's not why I hoodwinked you into coming all the way down here to West Warwick. We have some important business to discuss. I want to talk to you now as my uncle, not as a bag man for the Kennedy campaign."

Patrick sat back and lit a partially smoked stogie. It soon filled the office with an acrid smell that Judge DeCenza wouldn't be happy about. He assumed that was his uncle's intention. "Okay, speak your piece. How much are we talking about?" He removed his billfold from his breast pocket as if he could settle all accounts by simply spreading some green around.

"This is not about money. Not yet anyway. As you may or may not know, two people have been murdered down here by men I'm positive are working for your beloved Kevin O'Shaughnessy. I have reason to believe these people were killed because O'Shaughnessy is anxious to secure some films; sex films to be exact that he is an unwitting participant in. I'm pretty sure at the time these movies were made he had no idea he was being filmed. I believe the men who made them tried to blackmail your beloved Mr. O'Shaughnessy afterwards."

From Patrick's expression, Doherty was thinking that his uncle did not know about the films, or at least did not know they were what O'Shaughnessy and his thugs were after.

"I see," he said with a touch of disappointment in his voice.

"One of the people killed was a scam artist who was trying to shake down O'Shaughnessy in return for not taking the films public. I believe in the legal circles this kind of action is called extortion. However, the other person killed was nothing more than the dead guy's neighbor whose apartment may have been broken into by mistake. She was an innocent bystander and, I might add, the single mother of an nine-year old boy who is now parentless."

"Jesus, Joseph and Mary!"

"To make matters worse, I've been informed that the men I suspect are the killers have been nosing around Rhode Island lately looking for me and our mutual friend Gus Timilty."

McSweeny looked confused. "Why in God's name would they be after you two?"

"Probably because they think we have the films."

"And do you?"

Doherty didn't answer. Instead he said, "Why don't we bargain first before I put all my cards on the table." Patrick reluctantly agreed.

"We believe O'Shaughnessy and his people have something we want. If he does and is willing to trade it, we will gladly swap them the films in return."

"And what exactly is it you think Mr. O'Shaughnessy has?"

Doherty leaned forward and said in a firm voice, "The girl who was in the movies with him. It's evident from watching them that she was part of the set-up. She is very young, probably under legal age. Given his current position with the campaign these films made O'Shaughnessy a perfect mark for blackmail. It's our belief his people snatched up the girl as insurance against that eventuality. Obviously we would like her to be returned in one piece. I'm proposing a simple transaction: we give his people the films and they give us the girl. And one other thing: O'Shaughnessy has to call off his hound dogs. I don't want to be looking over my shoulder for the rest of my life."

"I don't understand what part you wish me to play in this unpleasant business."

"We want you to be the messenger. All you have to do is arrange a time and place for this exchange to be made."

"Why me?" Patrick asked nervously.

"Because you're my uncle and both O'Shaughnessy and I trust you. I assume you have his ear and he'd be willing to listen to you. I always have, at least until recently."

Patrick nodded, clearly seeing the reasoning behind his nephew's offer. "Where are these incriminating films now?"

"That's my business. I don't trust you that much."

Patrick let out a belly laugh and patted Doherty heavily on his knee. "Why you dirty politician. I guess I taught you better than I thought. What about Martin?" he said nodding in the direction of the outer office. "How much does he know about all this? "

"Only as much as I've been willing to tell him. Up to this point he knows nothing about the films, O'Shaughnessy's role in them or the girl."

"Listen, sonny, no matter how this business plays out, I'd be careful about what you share with those two out there." They had a good familial laugh over this piece of advice.

With some effort Patrick drew himself up and laid a hand upon his nephew's shoulder. "I will do all that I can to make this thing happen. You have to understand, Kevin O'Shaughnessy is a very powerful man and he might not ..."

"Like doing business with a couple of shanty Irishmen from West Warwick."

This caused Patrick McSweeny to emit another hearty belly laugh. "I will use my great powers of persuasion to get the man to see the error of his ways. If anyone can do this, boyo, it's your uncle Patrick."

"I know; that's what I was counting on."

Chapter Thirty-Six

Patrick called the next afternoon to say that he'd arranged for the exchange to be made midnight Monday at an abandoned lot behind the drive-in movie screen in the shipyard area between Cranston and Providence. The other party insisted that Doherty come alone. Few other details were offered except to say that the two men hunting for him and Timilty would no longer cause them any harm once the deal was consummated.

As soon as he got off the phone with his uncle Doherty immediately rang up Gus. As before there was no answer. It left Doherty with a dilemma: should he go to the meet alone and hope that he could pull it off by himself or should he try to stall O'Shaughnessy's goons until he heard from Gus. The other problem was that he had only one of the missing films. He had given Gus the other one after the night he rifled the office of Doherty and Associates. To make matters worse Doherty wasn't at all familiar with the shipyard area. Despite Patrick's admonition that he come alone, he knew he'd feel more secure if Gus were there to have his back. After all it was Gus' daughter that he was supposed to be rescuing.

He was rolling the details of the proposed exchange around in his head when Gus finally called him at home Sunday night. He said for safety's sake he was still staying away from his apartment and was calling him on a pay phone. Doherty didn't know where Timilty was holing up and didn't bother to ask. The less he knew about Gus' whereabouts the safer he would be if anything went south over the next twenty-four hours. He filled Timilty in on the arrangement his Uncle Patrick had passed onto to him. Gus was quiet at the other end for so long that the operator came on the line to tell him he had to put another dime into the phone box if he wanted to continue the call.

"I don't like it," Gus said. "It could be a trap."

"I don't think we have much choice if you want to see your daughter alive again. Keep in mind these guys have already committed two murders in pursuit of those films."

"You're right about that. Give me some time to organize a plan. In the meantime why don't you get the movie you have and I'll dig up the one I lifted from your office. I'll pick you up around eleven tomorrow night. I think it'll be better if I drove."

"Patrick said they insist I come alone – with the films."

"Don't worry, you'll be alone, at least as far as her abductors are concerned. Let me handle this my way. I know the old shipyard area pretty well. It's important that we do this right so that nobody gets hurt. You just be ready with your film in hand."

After Gus hung up Doherty took his .38 out of his dresser drawer and spent the next half hour cleaning and checking it yet again, loading and unloading it as he did. When he shot Krykowski it was only in the gut, which didn't kill him. One of the Nazi hunters used Doherty's gun to finish the job. It was the last time it'd been fired. He hoped there would be no reason to use it again tomorrow night.

In the morning Doherty walked from his office to the Centreville Bank. Nina was at her desk behind the low restraining wall. When she saw him she flashed a smile that had a bit of a come-on to it. He told her he needed to visit his safe deposit box once again. For a second Doherty considered asking the bank clerk if she'd like to go out on a date with him. He discarded that notion, electing for the time being to concentrate on his business with O'Shaughnessy's thugs. Still, it didn't prevent him from checking out her shapely gams as she led him into the vault where the safe deposit boxes were stacked.

They each used their keys to liberate his box. He then took it into the small sitting room where he extracted the movie case that contained the more incriminating film of O'Shaughnessy. He dawdled for another five minutes to give Nina the impression that he was perusing some other items in the box. Before leaving he slipped the film into the briefcase he'd brought with him.

He returned to her desk and Nina accompanied him back to the main vault. The empty box was returned to the lower level where it resided. He locked the outer plate with his key and watched as she bent down to do likewise with hers. As she did he once again checked out her physique, finding it a lovely sight indeed. He reconsidered his thought about asking her out, but again chose to put that on the back burner for the time being. When she was done she pulled her dark hair away from her face and gave him a lovely sidelong glance. He couldn't wait for another excuse to visit the vault with her.

The rest of the day went by about as slowly as it could. Doherty caught himself constantly watching the clock in his office as it made its slow orbit around the dial. Fortunately Agnes came in after lunch to finish up some paperwork. He told her he'd finally caught up with Gus and hinted that the Timilty case was just about closed. She looked at him skeptically, but thankfully didn't ask any more questions about the two murders. He'd solved those cases too, though not to anyone's satisfaction. After the deal went down tonight he thought about turning O'Shaughnessy and his hoods over to the police. Of course, if he did he'd then have to explain his role in it. That would surely complicate matters for him, as well as for Gus and his Uncle Patrick.

He told Agnes he would write up a detailed report on the Johnny Briggs case, even if it was only for their files. He'd keep his agreement with Briggs that the deal remain on the QT, at least until Gus was back on the job. He'd already decided to add an extra hundred bucks to the final bill for his *troubles*. Although she wasn't pleased when he was less than forthcoming with details, Agnes was wise enough to accept it when he was reluctant to share anything more. In most cases it was to protect her from harm, or the police if they came snooping around. She didn't say anything even though he could sense her displeasure with the way he was handling things. He figured her pregnancy hormones were resting today.

At four he closed up shop and went for a long walk through town, giving himself a chance to dope things out. Luckily he didn't run into anyone he knew so he was left with his own thoughts – and fears. He grabbed a coffee at the Donut Kettle and then took himself home for some grub and perhaps a short nap before Gus swung by to get him.

Back at the apartment he tried wrestling with the Faulkner book again, but the author pinned him two out of three falls. He gave it up halfway through the part where the son who went from Mississippi off to Harvard drowns himself in the Charles River. So much for an Ivy League education.

He spent some time trying to recall what he knew about the shipyard area. He'd only been up that way twice. The first time was when he was a young teen and his Uncle Patrick took his mother, his sister and him out for dinner at Johnson's Hummocks, Providence's most famous seafood restaurant. It was a big place that sat across from the shipyard construction facilities on Allens Avenue. The occasion was his mother's birthday and Patrick had invited them out to celebrate. He hadn't bothered to invite Doherty's father, as his uncle was not on speaking terms with Peter at the time. It was one of the few occasions outside of church when he'd seen his mother get dressed up. Most days she wore only a housedress until later when she took the part-time job at Pasquale's bakery after his father died. On those days she wore a mustard colored uniform to work.

For her birthday she dragged out a fancy dress from her closet that she hadn't worn in quite some time. It was a little tight, as his mother had put on more than a few pounds since she'd last worn it. When she asked Doherty and his sister Margaret how she looked, neither of them had the heart to tell her it was too small. They both lied and told her she looked terrific. That elicited a seldom seen smile. For the evening out his mother even put on some lipstick and fancied up her hair as best she could. Her brother Patrick did his best to treat her like she was 'queen for a day'.

The only other time he'd been to the Shipyard was when he was called for his induction physical. The draft board was housed in a small building that had once been a commissary for men who built ships there before the war. After Pearl Harbor there was so much activity at Rhode Island's main shipyards, a much bigger commissary was built to accommodate the thousands of new workers hired on.

At the induction center he and a lot of other men were put through their paces to see if they were fit enough for duty. By then Uncle Sam wasn't too particular about who was being called up for service. In '43 the army needed all the cannon fodder it could get. It was embarrassing how emaciated many of the inductees looked when stripped to their skivvies and shoes. Doherty had to remind himself that the Depression had taken its toll on nutrition even among draft age men. Many of his fellow inductees would've been rejected by the military a year earlier. But the country no longer had that luxury given how the war was shaping up.

The shipyard was located at Fields Point, which stuck out into the upper part of Narragansett Bay. Kerwin's Beach, a popular swimming spot for city dwellers, had been located there before the Maritime Commission took over the area as an emergency shipyard. Half the land was in Providence and other half in Cranston. Once it became clear that the country was probably going to war, over a million yards of landfill were trucked in from nearby hills to cover the beach. This greatly increased the size of the yard by extending the point further out into the bay.

The expanded shipyard operation ran into trouble from the very beginning. First the shop set up to hammer out and shape the plates for the proposed ship hulls caught on fire. Then the company brought in by the government to run the shipbuilding operations proved to be in over its head. Knowing Rhode Island, they'd probably gotten the original contract simply by greasing a number of palms. Eventually the work was turned over to the Kaiser Corporation of Kaiser Aluminum fame, which was successfully running similar operations on the West Coast. Before long there were nearly 14,000 men, and later women, building ships in the yard. Along with Quonset and Davisville and the naval operations over at Newport, the Kaiser plant at the shipyard was one of Rhode Island's most important contributions to the war effort.

In order to facilitate the operation, miles of new roads were laid into and through the shipyard area so that materials could be hauled from one gigantic shed to another. A couple of dozen Liberty ships, frigates and cargo vessels went right into the water from Rhode Island's shipyards. Doherty read that in the end sixty-three ships were added to our naval forces from this operation alone. Big shots like President Truman, Navy Secretary Forestal and members of Congress toured the facilities in the latter stages of the war when the construction sites were still in full operation. Then at the end of 1945, just like that it was all over. The war ended and 3000 shipyard workers suddenly found themselves without good paying jobs.

After that the area became a virtual vacant lot - at least until last year when a large drive-in movie theater was erected on part of the land. It was a mammoth enterprise that could accommodate 1700 cars. Along with the theater it featured a sunken playground for kids, a Ferris wheel, a merry-go-round, a miniature golf course and small train track that encircled the entire layout. There were rumors that the owners were entertaining thoughts of putting on live concerts at the park with big name talent. Doherty wondered if Elvis Presley would perform there after he finished his stint in the army.

Aside from this entertainment complex the rest of the shipyard area remained a vast wasteland. Unless the state could attract a container port to the site, it would continue to be nothing more than a vacant tract of land with weeds growing through the concrete. As with the shuttered mills in West Warwick, there was no way enough industry could come in to fill this enormous land mass.

Although some government agencies, both state and federal, made rumblings about using the shipyard area for other purposes, as of now it was like a lot of other facilities hastily built during the war to turn out the weapons necessary to defeat the enemy. When the war ended they were no longer needed and were quickly abandoned.

Doherty must have dozed off because the next thing he knew there was a loud knock at his door. When he opened it Gus was standing in his hallway wearing a dark windbreaker and work pants. He looked more disheveled than usual. Doherty quickly grabbed a jacket, his .38, the film canister and a thermos of coffee he'd prepared.

Along the way to the shipyard Gus speculated that the place would be as dead as a doornail on a Monday night, especially now that the drive-in was closed for the season. Doherty told Gus that he was expected to make the exchange at a vacant lot behind the big movie screen. Once there his instructions were to park and blink his headlights twice. His counterparts would then do the same. After that the swap would be made as planned.

The large sign for the drive-in theater was dark when they pulled off Allens Avenue and headed in the direction of the theater. It wasn't hard to find, as it was the biggest structure in the area. Despite being closed until spring, the marquee still advertised the last two pictures that had played there. They were both science fiction movies, typical drive-in fare. One was called *Journey to the Center of the Earth*, and the other *Island of Lost Women*. Gus drove slowly along the outside of the chain-link fence that encircled the drive-in complex. Before they reached the appointed meeting spot he stopped the car abruptly.

"What're you doing, Gus?" Doherty asked nervously.

"I'm getting out here. You're going on alone."

"What do you mean? Where are you going?"

Gus set the brake and slid out of the driver's seat. He told Doherty to take the wheel. "They asked you to come alone, so you're going on from here by yourself. I don't trust these bastards and we're not going in there naked. You go transact the deal while I take up a flanking position."

"Listen Gus, I don't really feature heading around back on my own."

Timilty reached onto the floor by the back seat and handed Doherty the other film canister. "Here's the one I took from your office. You have the second one with you and your piece, right. Is it loaded?"

"Of course it's loaded."

"You sense that things are starting to go down Queer Street, you open up on these guys. Whatever you do, try not to hit my little girl, okay."

"Jesus, Gus. I don't like this. I don't like it one bit."

Timilty didn't answer. He quickly walked away into the night. Doherty placed the film Gus had given him on the passenger seat along with the other one. He checked his watch. It was three minutes to midnight. He waited another five to allow Gus time to get to wherever he was going. Then he slowly drove the Mercury around the outskirts of the drive-in lot and pulled behind the big screen.

The screen blocked out the moonlight casting the whole area into darkness. He could barely see the other car facing him about a hundred yards away. He drove slowly in its direction. About halfway there he stopped and flashed his lights twice. In a short while the other vehicle flashed its lights back at him. Doherty pulled ahead another twenty yards before cutting the engine. He left his headlights on. He wanted to be able to see who he was dealing with. He assumed that one way or another he wouldn't be there long enough for the lights to drain the car's battery. Before getting out he slid his right hand into his jacket pocket to check his pistol for about the twentieth time. It was easily accessible with a bullet in the chamber.

The other car likewise kept its lights on. He slowly got out of Gus' Merc and stood beside it holding the films by his side. The air was thick with a heavy mist. Three figures climbed out of the other vehicle and moved slowly in his direction. There were two men; one was tall, dressed in a long black topcoat and a fedora pulled low over his eyes. Doherty couldn't see his face very well under the brim. He was escorting, pushing really, a young blond girl ahead of him, his hand firmly grasping the back of her neck. She was wearing a thigh length woolen jacket and a skirt.

The other guy was short and had on a rain jacket and snap brimmed, wool cap. The three walked slowly in Doherty's direction. As they did his hand automatically went to his pocket where it nestled on the grip of the .38. As a sign of good faith he moved away from the car and headed toward them. When they were within twenty feet of one another everyone stopped.

The short one stepped out front. Just as Mickey Flannery had said, the guy had a face that looked like a potato. It was a mass of acne scars and real scars. From what he could see of the other one, he did indeed have stone cold, killer eyes. He was holding the girl's neck so tight that she was having trouble moving her head. Even at this distance he could hear her breathing heavily. She might have been a looker under other circumstances, like on film. Right now she just seemed young and scared.

"You got what we come for," short one said, a hint of Irish brogue in his voice. It was not the kind of charming lilt his uncle often put on. This one was full of menace.

"I got what you want. First tell your friend there to take his stranglehold off the girl's neck."

"You ain't exactly in a position to be makin' demands," the one doing the talking said. "Where's your buddy Timilty? We thought he'd be comin' to get his little whore." The big guy eased his grip on the girl's neck though he didn't let go of her completely. He smiled a sinister grin at Doherty.

"Gus couldn't make it. Monday nights are when he stays home to take a bath."

"Smart guy, huh."

"Let the girl go and I'll give you the films."

There was an uncomfortable silence. Doherty carefully held up the canisters so they could see he wasn't raising a gun He knelt down and placed one of them on the ground and kicked it across the gap between them. The one with the cap bent down and picked it up. He pried open the lid and looked inside. There was a film in it, which appeared to satisfy him.

"Don't worry, it's the film you want. Now why don't you let the girl go?"

"What about the other one? We was sent to collect two of them."

"Let the girl go first and I'll slide it over. What've you got to lose? There are two of you and only one of me." The goons looked at each other. The one with the cold eyes now had a shit-eating grin wrapped across his face. He let go of the girl's neck and she moved a few feet in Doherty's direction then stopped.

"Christina, it's okay. I'm a friend of your father. Come over to me. She took a few more steps yet seemed too scared to move any closer.

"How about the other film, buddy?"

Doherty placed it on the ground and slid it in their direction without ever taking his eyes off them. His right hand stayed firmly gripped on the .38 in his pocket. The one in the tweed cap inspected what was inside the second case and nodded to his partner. Then as quick as a flash the big guy stepped forward, grabbed the girl by the hair and pulled her back to him.

"Looks like there's been a change of plans," he said with a smile. These were the first words out of the bigger man's mouth.

Doherty went to move forward but stopped when he saw Gus emerge from behind their car.

"I don't think so," Timilty said just before blasting a slug right through the back of the big guy's head. The sound was deafening. Blood splattered all over his daughter's shoulders and hair. She began to scream hysterically.

The little guy went for his piece but was having trouble getting it out of his jacket. In that instant Doherty ran forward and hit him flush on the jaw with a right hook. He went down and was scuttling on the pavement like a crab, still trying to get his gun out when Doherty stomped down as hard as he could on his forearm. He heard a bone crack. The man screamed in agony.

"Jesus, you sonofabitch, you broke my fookin' arm!" Doherty was about to inflict some more damage when Gus grabbed his coat.

"Take Christina back to the car. Now!"

Doherty looked at the grimace on Gus' face. "You heard me, take her to the car."

"But, Gus."

Timilty clearly was in no mood for an argument. Instead he walked over to the guy writhing on the ground holding his broken arm. He pointed his pistol at the man's face and said, "Are you two part of some gang up in Boston or are you freelancers? "

"My fookin' arm is broken," the guy moaned.

"I don't give a shit about your arm. Now answer my question if you want to stay alive. Are you part of a gang?"

The man shook his head. "No, me and Damon work alone. We ain't with nobody."

"Now tell me what you did to my daughter?" The man didn't answer so Gus leaned down and pointed his gun about five inches from the guy's pain-ridden face. "What did you two scumbags do to my daughter?" Doherty was trying his best to edge the girl away from the scene but she wouldn't move.

"They fucked me!" she screamed. "They both did, over and over, again and again." Doherty wondered why this would offend Gus given that Christina made her living as a prostitute and by appearing in skin flicks.

Gus leaned closer to the man and said, "Do you believe in God?"

"What?" the guy responded through clenched teeth.

"I asked if you believe in God?" The man didn't answer.

"Are you a Catholic?"

The man mumbled. "I was raised one, but I don't have no use for that church shite no more."

"So you don't believe that Jesus is your lord and savior?"

Doherty couldn't figure out what his old pal was up to.

The injured man looked quizzically at Gus. "What the fook's with all these questions? If you're gonna shoot me just do it already."

"I wanted to know if you believe in God, because you're about to meet him." Gus stepped back a few feet and shot the man on the ground right through his forehead. Then for good measure he put two more slugs into his chest. He walked over to the body of the tall one lying inertly nearby and pulled off two rounds into his midsection for good measure.

Gus came back to where Doherty was standing with his arms around the whimpering, blood splattered girl and said, "Now will you please take Christina to the car while I clean up this mess." He had a look on his face Doherty'd never seen before. It sent a chill up his spine.

Timilty dragged each of the dead men to their car. Once he'd retrieved the keys from the ignition he popped the trunk and dumped their bodies inside. Doherty could tell that the effort took a lot out of Gus. When that was done he retrieved the two film canisters still resting where the smaller man had dropped them. He signaled Doherty to follow him in his car.

They drove to the remotest part of the abandoned shipyard near the water's edge. Gus locked the car and walked toward the bay and tossed the keys into the blackish water. Returning to his car with the films tucked under his arm he climbed into the back seat with his daughter who was now quieter but still visibly shaken. He requested, though it sounded more like an order, for Doherty to drive them back to West Warwick.

Along the way Gus did his best to comfort his daughter while Doherty tried to dope out what payback there might be from this double shooting. The fact that the two dead guys were lone wolves and not part of some Irish mob in Boston could mean there would be no repercussions from any local parties for tonight's events. However, there was always the possibility that Kevin O'Shaughnessy might choose to send some other hitmen down to Rhode Island for retribution.

When they got back to West Warwick, Gus handed Doherty the two film canisters suggesting that he do with them whatever he wanted. Otherwise he made no comment about what had transpired at the shipyard. While parked in front of his apartment building Doherty left the car running and climbed out without saying a word. Gus came around to the driver's side, his shirtfront and jacket stained with the blood of the two dead men. No words were exchanged. He simply took the wheel and drove off with Christina remaining by herself in the back seat.

Chapter Thirty-Seven

Over the next few days Doherty did his best to put the events of that night behind him. Needless to say, it wasn't easy, or even possible. He picked up a case of a woman whose husband ran out on her after she discovered he'd emptied out their Christmas Club account at the local Hospital Trust Bank. With a little nosing around Doherty located the husband hiding out at a cousin's in Coventry. The wife could have easily found him herself. Doherty suspected she wanted to get a private eye involved to put a scare into her timid spouse.

After some inane conversation in which the poor fellow admitted he took the money to get back at his wife because she constantly browbeat him, Doherty convinced him to return home before she filed for divorce on the grounds of abandonment. He explained that a divorce proceeding would cost him a whole lot more than the $328 he'd taken from their account, three hundred of which he'd subsequently pissed away betting on a *sure thing* at Narragansett Park that finished out of the money. The most convincing part of his argument was when he told the husband that the only grounds for divorce in Rhode Island were physical abuse, adultery or abandonment. Although he didn't know for sure if this were true, Doherty assured the runaway husband that once he squandered the money at the track and afterwards left the house, his wife could argue that he'd willfully abandoned her. If he went home now, Doherty explained, he would not have been gone long enough for it to qualify for abandonment.

He could tell by the look on the guy's face that he didn't quite follow this explanation. But he decided to return home anyway because the cousin's wife didn't want him staying with them any longer. Doherty never discovered how things panned out. He was grateful for the fifty-buck finder's fee he collected up front from the distraught wife since this was the only money he'd taken in since Johnny Briggs' visit to his office. At some point he would bill Briggs for the additional expenses incurred while tracking down Gus.

Every day Doherty scanned the morning *Journal* and the evening *Bulletin* to see if the bodies from the shipyard shooting had turned up. After Gus shot the two men, he'd stripped them of identification before stuffing their bodies into the trunk of their car. All this was done while Doherty watched from Gus' car with the daughter slumped against his shoulder whimpering the whole time. He knew he should've been more consoling to her while Gus disposed of the evidence; he just didn't have any consoling left in him after what he'd witnessed.

A week after the shooting there was still no news of the dead men in the local papers. Doherty took on another job, which was just as well, believing that work was the best tonic for the time being. This case involved an auto body shop owner from Warwick who wished to hire Doherty to find a former employee who had absconded with a little over $2000 he was given to take to the bank.

Doherty dug up some old sources in the auto repair business, including Armand from Packy's Garage where he'd purchased his '55 Chevy. Nothing panned out until he took a short walk around the corner from his apartment to talk with the fellow who owned the automotive paint store that fronted his building on Main Street. The guy was in the process of relocating his operation to Cranston. After some small talk about the move he asked him if he had any knowledge of someone who was trying to set up a new body shop in the state. The paint store proprietor informed him just that week he'd been contacted by a guy from Foster looking to establish a line of credit for his recently opened shop.

With this news in hand Doherty drove west out Route Six to that town. He'd never been to Foster and certainly didn't realize there was a North Foster, a South Foster as well as a Foster Center. It got him to musing on why there wasn't an East Warwick to go along with his hometown of West Warwick. He'd never been out to Foster, which seemed like the country compared to his usual turf. It was bigger than he expected so it took him a lot of time and some questions at a couple of local gas stations before he found the shop he was looking for.

It was nothing more than a one bay garage that didn't even have a hydraulic lift to raise cars up high enough for someone to work on them from underneath. A newly hand-painted sign hanging over the open bay read Art's Auto Body. There was only one man in the place so Doherty assumed he was the Art on the sign. The garage only had one dented car in the bay and one in the driveway. That seemed to be the full extent of Art's business at the moment.

They would've shaken hands but the body man's were laden with grease. He was youngish and from their brief conversation didn't strike Doherty as being particularly bright. As a cover for his search he made some inquiries about getting a few dents straightened out on his Chevy. Art was more than happy to have his business, explaining that he'd had just opened his shop and was grateful for all the work he could get.

After some casual talk about auto body operations in that part of the state, Doherty asked the proprietor where he had worked before opening up his own garage. The stupid bastard gave him the name of the place in Warwick where he'd stolen the two grand. When Doherty heard this it was all he could do to keep a straight face. After some more small talk he told the fellow he would bring his car around the following Monday, which was the first day he could afford to take it off the road. He hinted that he was a traveling salesman, though he never said so directly.

As soon as he returned to the office he phoned the client in Warwick and told him where his two thousand dollars had gone. The man said he'd contact the Foster police as soon as he got off the phone. A week later the owner of the shop in Warwick sent him a check for a hundred dollars to go along with the initial fifty-dollar retainer. The envelope included a note saying that he only got a fraction of the original two thousand back, but was taking his former employee to court in hopes of putting a lien on his house and future earnings

A few days after that case was closed Doherty read in the *Journal* that two decomposing bodies had been found in the trunk of an Oldsmobile 88 sitting in a tow yard not far from the shipyard section of Providence. According to the article, the vehicle had been removed from a barren stretch of land in the old shipyard when it failed to be picked up after sitting there for two weeks. It was towed to the junkyard where it sat unclaimed even though the license plates indicated it was registered to a Reginald McDonough of Charlestown, Massachusetts.

Apparently the junkyard proprietor had contacted the Boston police, who in turn tried unsuccessfully to locate McDonough. The yard owner was informed that if the car wasn't claimed within a month the Providence police would impound the abandoned vehicle and sell it at auction, giving the junkyard a commission on the sale. However, before the future of the car could be settled one of the yard workers at Scannelli's Salvage detected a rank odor coming from the vehicle. The trunk was pried open and that's when the two decomposing bodies were discovered.

The paper described the two men as having met their demise by being shot multiple times at close range. The initial assumption was that one of the bodies belonged to the aforementioned McDonough. As of yet the Providence police were unable to identify the second victim.

It took almost a week before they positively identified one of the bodies as McDonough's and the second as Damon Armagh, also of Charlestown. Apparently investigating their demise was not a high priority for the Providence Police Department. Speculation was that they were victims of a mob shooting here in Rhode Island, not an uncommon occurrence in the country's smallest state. Another theory was that they were shot someplace in Massachusetts and their bodies were transported in their own car to Providence so as to be far away from the original crime scene.

In follow-up stories it was noted that both victims had long criminal records for such things as grand larceny, breaking and entering, assault and battery, assault with intent to kill and other lesser charges. In the case of McDonough, there was a conviction for attempted murder that had earned him a ten-year stretch in the Massachusetts state prison at Walpole. He served six of the ten before being paroled. Otherwise both men had done shorter stints behind bars for lesser crimes. It was also revealed that the two had once been members of the Seven Hills gang in Charlestown. However, according to a Boston police spokesman, neither man has been affiliated with that crime organization for a number of years.

When the police searched McDonough's apartment in Charlestown they found an arsenal of weapons, an extensive stash of unopened cigarette cartons and over ten thousand dollars in cash hidden in a lockbox secreted behind a painting in his bedroom wall. As far as the cops could determine, Armagh had no known current address and evidence showed that he might have been living with McDonough at the time of his death. Several people who had prior dealings with the two men in Charlestown were questioned. No one had much more to say about them than "good riddance." Others simply reverted to Charlestown's well-known *code of silence* and said nothing. In the end their deaths were written off as two persons who would be missed by no one.

Chapter Thirty-Eight

It was raining heavily when Doherty woke the next day. Not wanting to expose his good cordovans to the large puddles that were forming on the sidewalks and in the gutters, he rummaged through his hall closet looking for an old pair of galoshes. It was only then that he noticed the movie projector he'd rented from United Camera collecting dust in the bottom of the closet.

After several viewings of the two stag films, he'd stowed the projector and forgotten about it. He removed the heavy device and set it up on his kitchen counter where he used a damp cloth to remove the accumulated grime from the machine. After dressing he put the projector into a plastic garbage bag to protect it from the rain and lugged it down to Belanger's garage.

It was coming down in buckets as he made the slow drive across Cranston onto Broad Street in Providence, where he turned left and headed toward United Camera. People on the street were attempting to shelter themselves under umbrellas or hats they'd pulled down low to protect them from the downpour. Several women he passed along the way were wearing those fold-up plastic things a lot of females use to cover their newly permed hair. Some pedestrians were valiantly trying to shield themselves from the weather by holding newspapers over their heads; papers that quickly turned into soggy messes.

He parked in front of United Camera and hauled the Bell and Howell into the store. The fellow who had helped him with the initial rental was nowhere to be seen. Two clerks were occupied helping other customers; otherwise the store was devoid of activity on this miserable day. When one of the clerks finally came around the counter in his direction Doherty hoisted the projector out of the plastic bag and gently rested it on the glass countertop. He explained that he'd been forced to keep the projector longer than he anticipated and would be willing to pay any additional fees if necessary. He thought about making up some story about how he had to do a work-related film presentation. He quickly reconsidered deciding that too many words would only serve to draw suspicions as to what the projector was actually used for.

The clerk peered over his glasses at the machine as Doherty pretended to look at expensive cameras in the lower part of the display case. The man then ran the projector's cord to a socket under the counter and turned on the machine to make sure it was in working order. While he did this Doherty couldn't help but think of everything that had occurred since he first rented the device.

He informed Doherty that he would have to check their records and would be right back. To amuse himself Doherty wandered around the store looking at the mountains of photo equipment a person could buy if photography were his hobby or profession. As someone who'd never had anything more sophisticated than a Brownie Hawkeye, it was all pretty overwhelming to him. Taking up photography as a pastime, he surmised, could easily become an expensive avocation.

The man returned a few minutes later and told Doherty there would be an additional charge of ten dollars for the extra time he'd kept the projector. The fellow seemed almost apologetic. Doherty didn't hesitate and passed him two fives, glad to be rid of the machine on which he'd viewed films that brought so much grief to so many people.

Gus' office was only a few blocks up the avenue from the photo store. Instead and turning around and heading back to West Warwick, against his better judgment Doherty drove there as if drawn by a magnet. The Briggs and Timilty Investigations Agency was located on the second floor above a variety store and an insurance broker's office. Once inside the door of their offices, he was greeted by a young woman with a hatchet shaped face and a no nonsense demeanor. She was good looking in a sharply angular sort of way. Her dark hair was pulled up on her head away from her face so that it wouldn't interfere with the business at hand. A pencil was stuck through her hair bun. Doherty asked if Gus Timilty was in.

"Do you have an appointment?" she answered in a businesslike tone.

"No, but he and I have been working on a case together. I thought I'd drop by to tie up some loose ends." He flashed her his PI license to support his claim.

"Just a moment," she said as she pressed some buttons on the phone.

"A Mr. Doherty is here to see you, sir," she said. He heard a squawk from the other end that no doubt belonged to Gus.

She replaced the phone and said, "You may go right in. It's the third office on the left," she added indicating a narrow corridor behind her desk.

He slipped around the secretary and walked in that direction. The door to the first office was open and a skinny man was sitting at a desk with his face hovering about five inches above an adding machine as he punched some numbers into it. The door to the second office was ajar and from the looks of things there was no one inside. Timilty's door was closed. Doherty knocked before walking right in without waiting for a response.

Gus was sitting behind his large desk with his chair turned in the direction of the window behind it. When he turned around Doherty saw that he was well-coiffed and nattily dressed in a blue blazer, a red plaid tie and white oxford shirt. Gus was looking much more professional today than the night he blew away those two thugs. They nodded a greeting at each other as he took the chair in front of Gus' desk and immediately struck up a Camel.

The office had a large window that afforded them a nice view of Broad Street. "Looks like it's raining cats and dogs out there," Gus said.

"Yeah, it's a mess. I had to return the projector to United Camera and thought I'd drop by to see how you were doing. I was hoping that while I was here I could pry a little more cash out of Johnny Briggs for my expenses."

Without hesitating Gus reached into his desk and extracted a thick envelope. He took some bills out of it and counted out ten twenties and handed them across the desk. "This should cover your costs."

Doherty picked up the cash and stared at it for a few beats. "What is this, hush money for me to keep my mouth shut?"

Gus smiled but it was a hard one, not a friendly one. "Let's just say it's an added bonus for your *troubles*. Briggs wasn't going to give you anything more because he's still pissed off about the business he lost while I was out doing … doing what I was doing."

"Does this mean you're back on the job now?"

Gus shrugged. "Hey, pally, what the hell else am I gonna do? This is the only life I know."

"What about your daughter? How's she getting on?"

Gus' expression changed immediately. He got up from behind his desk and shuffled over to a coffee pot and poured himself a cup. "Would you like some coffee? I don't have any cream or sugar, but you take it black anyway, don't you?"

"Yeah, black's fine." Gus handed him a cardboard cup, took one for himself and sat back down in a heap behind his desk.

"You haven't answered my question, Gus."

He raised his head; a mournful look now graced his face. "She went back to Jimmy Ricks."

"Are you kidding me? After all..." he didn't bother to finish the thought.

Timilty shook his head sadly. "I couldn't really keep her. My place was too small and she didn't feature sleeping on a foldaway couch every night. She kept talking about how good her life was when she was working for Ricks. I tried to explain to her how women in that business ended up. I even mentioned her mother, which probably wasn't such a good idea. For some reason she blames me for what happened to Loretta. Like it was my fault that her old lady was a junkie. Anyway when I went back to work I couldn't exactly keep an eye on her. One day I came home and she was gone. Took all the new clothes I'd bought her and left. Didn't even leave me a note."

"How'd you find out she was back with Ricks?"

"I asked around. Then to satisfy myself I went over to the Club Mocambo to talk to the man himself. He almost apologized for taking her back, but not quite. Told me he couldn't turn her down 'cause she was his best earner. I did get him to promise there'd be no more movie making. He said he'd already told her that. According to him she was disappointed - thought she was going to end up in Hollywood after her turn in sex films. Ricks also agreed to keep her off the hard stuff. Said he'd only let her smoke some reefer now and then when she was with a big shot client. She must've told Ricks what I'd done, which was why he was being so cooperative. I guess you could say I saved his life."

"Sounds like a fairy tale ending."

Gus looked profoundly sad. "I didn't know what else to do. I mean she and I hardly know each other. And after what happened that night I could tell she'd never feel safe living with me. You know yourself from the war, that kind of shock can stay with a person for a long time."

"In some cases for life."

Doherty stubbed out his butt and stood to leave. There was nothing more to be said.

"You don't think there's gonna be any fallout from what happened over at the shipyard, do you? According to the papers it sounds like nobody's gonna miss those two."

"I don't know, Gus. I haven't heard anything. If I do I'll let you know."

They shook hands like friends, though both knew what happened that night had changed their relationship.

"I'll see you around, pally."

"Yeah," was all Doherty said before leaving. At least now he was two hundred bucks ahead of the game.

Chapter Thirty-Nine

He could hear the thump of His Uncle Patrick's cane on the stairs long before he reached the second floor. Luckily it was Agnes' last week of work so she would intercept him before he came into Doherty's office. Through a half opened door he could hear his uncle breathing heavily as he sat in the chair facing Agnes' desk. Once he was able to catch his breath his uncle asked Agnes about her pregnancy. The two of them spent some time sharing health complaints as Doherty readied himself for an expected confrontation with his uncle. In time he walked out to greet Patrick, who today looked no worse than usual even with O'Shaughnessy's two thugs now dead.

"Ah, there's my nephew," he said with his usual bonhomie. Patrick didn't bother to rise from his chair to shake hands. In return Doherty offered a weak greeting.

"Why don't we go into my office and talk," he said without much enthusiasm. Agnes gave him a disapproving look for his rudeness; a look he purposely ignored.

It took some effort for Patrick to raise himself and shuffle on his cane into the inner sanctum. Doherty didn't bother to offer any assistance. Once inside he closed the door behind them.

"What do you want, Patrick?"

His uncle looked disappointed. "Why you dirty politician, is that any way to greet your closest living relative?"

"My sister Margaret is my closest living relative," he said contradicting his uncle.

"And she lives where, boyo – a thousand miles away out in Michigan."

"Actually it's Minnesota. Now could you please tell me what the hell you're doing here?"

His uncle looked angry, or as angry as a glad-hander like Patrick McSweeny would ever allow himself to look. Nothing was said for a few moments, leaving both of them feeling uncomfortable. He'd never known his uncle to be at a loss for words.

"Do you think I could have a wee bit of a snoot?"

Doherty pulled a fresh bottle of Jameson out of his desk drawer, grabbed some cardboard cups from the shelf by the coffee pot and poured each of them a couple of fingers.

"Are you here on another mission for your pal O'Shaughnessy?"

Uncle Patrick sipped his whiskey and then shook his head in what looked like mock sympathy. "Ah, I'm afraid poor Mr. O'Shaughnessy has had to take an extended leave from the campaign. Ill health I've been told. Me thinks this could mark the end of Kevin's lifelong role in politics. They say he's decided to take an open-ended trip to dear old Ireland. Apparently he wishes to visit some of his elderly relatives while they still walk the earth. There's even been talk around the campaign that he might take up permanent residence in that country of his ancestry."

"Well wouldn't that be dandy. He gets off scot-free while four people lie dead, thanks to him."

Patrick offered up a sinister smile. "Don't kid yourself, boyo. The Kennedys were never going to let such a scandal get within ten feet of one of their most important moneymen. He's been dispatched across the sea just like Joe dispatched his mentally troubled daughter Rosemary to an institution because her presence diminished his family's image."

"So what does O'Shaughnessy's departure mean for you, Uncle?"

Patrick smiled again, this time in a more pleasing fashion. "You might say that Mr. O'Shaughnessy's misfortunes have proven to be a bit of a windfall for me. Since his departure I have moved up a few rungs on the campaign ladder. I will no longer have to travel to such hillbilly bastions as West Virginia or freeze my arse off in Wisconsin. I will leave those unpleasant duties to lesser men while I simply receive and dole out funds for the campaign from the comfort of my office in Boston."

"And in the meantime O'Shaughnessy pays no price for the murders left in his wake."

"Well, with those two unsavory characters from Charlestown neatly dispatched, I assume by yourself and Gus Timilty, there really is no one left who can tie the other deaths to O'Shaughnessy. It's unfortunate that Kevin has such deviant proclivities when it comes to the fairer sex," Patrick added here, turning the conversation in a wholly different direction.

"It's a condition that I've been aware of for quite some time. In fact, several weeks ago when I found out about the films I suggested to certain people that he be jettisoned from the campaign so as to avoid bringing any undue embarrassment to our operation. The only problem was how to get rid of him. You see Kevin O'Shaughnessy has been such an important powerbroker in Massachusetts politics for so long it was assumed he was invulnerable."

"Then how was he done in like he was?"

This elicited a knowing grin from his uncle. "Once I made the acquaintance of those two low-rent hustlers in Providence and heard about their blackmail scheme, it took only a little persuasion on my part to convince them to set up poor Mr. O'Shaughnessy on film. I could tell they would be perfect for the kind of enterprise I had in mind. The surprising thing was how cheaply we were able to enlist that pimp and his sidekick in our plan. I suppose it was the promise of extorting some serious money out of Mr. O'Shaughnessy at the other end that roped them in. Unfortunately when they tried to put the bite on Kevin he unleashed his hound dogs. I suspect those Providence fellows didn't quite know what hit them. The only problem is that somewhere along the line the films disappeared and no one can locate them. You wouldn't happen to know where they are, would you?"

Doherty didn't answer the question. He was still rattling around in his head the idea that it was his Uncle Patrick who made the arrangements with Ricks and DeAngelo to entrap O'Shaughnessy on film in such a compromising manner. Arrangements that ultimately resulted in DeAngelo's heinous murder.

Patrick reached into his coat pocket and extracted a thick envelope. "I have here five thousand dollars in cash we would be willing to pay for those films. I was hoping you might be able to locate them for me."

"And whose money is that you're waving around? Joe Kennedy's? Kevin O'Shaughnessy's? Or your own?"

Patrick smiled weakly. "Let's just say certain parties would like to have possession of those films as insurance against any plans Mr. O'Shaughnessy might have of coming back to Boston. They would also like to guarantee that he will not do anything to negatively affect the campaign. I'm sorry, nephew, but it wouldn't be in anyone's interest for me to tell you where this money comes from."

Doherty considered the proposition for a minute before opening his locked file cabinet. He extracted one of the film canisters and tossed it onto the desk.

"I'll tell you what I'll do, for old time's sake. I'll give you this film while I keep the other one. That way you'll have what you need to hang over O'Shaughnessy's head and I'll have what I need."

"I don't understand. Why would you need to keep the other movie?"

"Because I'd like to guarantee that if anything were to happen to me or Gus Timilty, the other film would have a very public viewing; one that would no doubt cause great embarrassment to the Kennedy campaign as well as Kevin O'Shaughnessy. Let's just say if either Gus or I were to accidentally die in a car crash or slip on a banana peel and crack our skulls, the film would automatically become public property. Do you understand what I'm saying?"

Patrick let out a joyful laugh. "Well, sonny, it looks like you may have learned a lesson or two from this old sod after all. Perhaps my well proffered advice over the years has not gone for naught." Patrick quickly scooped up the film canister. He slipped some cash out of the envelope and dropped the remainder on Doherty's desk. "In exchange for this highly prized movie I will leave you with $3000. My benefactors will not be entirely pleased with this turn of events, but I will do my best to make them see the light."

"I guess that concludes our business," Doherty said with finality.

Patrick stood with the aid of his cane. "Not entirely. You'll still have to deal with Martin DeCenza. You see, I deduced from that sham meeting you had him set up with me in return you promised him your actions would result in my political downfall; something the dear judge no doubt has dreamed about for years. But you see, my boy, just the opposite has occurred. I am more highly placed than ever. I don't think Martin will look very kindly upon you for failing in your joint effort to bring me down."

"Well, you let me worry about Judge DeCenza. We've had some run-ins in the past. Not fulfilling his fondest wishes happens to bring me a great deal of pleasure."

Patrick smiled and the old glint that had been missing came back into his eyes. "Well, boyo, maybe we aren't so different after all. They say that blood is thicker than water. And I must say, you certainly have a strong dose of the McSweeny blood in you."

"On a more pleasant note, I'm planning on having some of your cousins over to my place in Boston for Thanksgiving dinner. Now that this rather unsavory business is concluded I was wondering if you'd like to drive up and join us."

It was Doherty's turn to smile. "I think I'd rather stay home and eat a Swanson's frozen dinner."

Patrick shrugged. "Suit yourself." Then without shaking hands his uncle shuffled out of the office, tapping the floor with his cane while the film canister was awkwardly tucked under his arm.

Chapter Forty

As soon as his uncle left Doherty hightailed it down to the Centreville Bank with the other film and the three grand. Fortunately Nina was at her post, where she gave him her extra sweet smile. Doherty found her looking as fetching as ever today.

Without his asking she said, "I suppose you'd like to get into your safe deposit box again." He simply nodded assent, accompanying it with a smile of his own. Once they had extracted the box from its casing in the big vault he moved toward the little conference room.

"Nina, I was wondering if you'd join me in here for a few minutes." The dark haired bank clerk looked at him quizzically then looked back at the outer office. "It is a little irregular. Though I suppose I could for just a few minutes."

Once inside the small space they took seats on either side of the plain aluminum table.

"I want to ask you a favor. I'd like you to be a cosigner on my safe deposit box."

Nina gave him a funny look. "But we're not married or even related. It's usually a wife or a relative that asked to do that."

That made Doherty laugh. "Well I suppose we could go out on a date first to see how that works out."

"Are you asking me to go out with you?"

"Only if you agree to be a cosigner on my box."

"Well that's about the most unusual pick-up line I've ever been pitched." Nina reached across the table and took one of his hands. "What is this all about, Doherty?"

He extracted the film canister from his briefcase. "I have here something that could cause a number of very important people serious embarrassment. Personally I have no desire for this film to ever leave my safe deposit box again. You see, for the time being having this film in my possession affords me protection from the wrath of some very powerful individuals. If anything were to happen to me I'd like you to take it out of the box and bring it to the *Journal-Bulletin* office in Providence. Once there I would like you to give it to somebody of authority in the newsroom."

"There is a letter here that I will leave in the box with the film. It explains everything you'll need to know including who's in the film and the names of two writers at the *Journal* that would be the most appropriate contacts. In addition it identifies a friend of mine named Gus Timilty, who also needs to be protected by this film. You don't have to tell anyone at the newspaper how the film came into your possession or what's on it since I'm not even going to tell you that. If you agree to sign on to my box no one will ever know that you have access to it except for you and me."

"Boy, you sure know how to charm a girl, don't you." Nina said while her face betrayed uncertainty about the whole affair.

Doherty appreciated her good humor. "Frankly I don't think anything unpleasant is going to happen. This film is what you might call an insurance policy. I can guarantee that nothing bad will ever happen to you if you agree to be my co-signer," he added, though he couldn't be sure this was entirely true.

Nina smiled her lovely come-on smile. "Hey, what the hell. Life working in a bank can get pretty boring. This is the most exciting thing that's happened to me since I got my cat. I'll agreed to be a cosignatory on your box only if the offer for the date is for real."

"It'll be my pleasure. Dinner and a movie? I hear that picture *Some Like it Hot* now playing at the Palace is real laugher."

Nina stood up and ran her hands down her sides to straighten out her skirt. "Let's go sign the papers before I change my mind."

"Oh, and one other thing, Nina. I have three thousand dollars in cash here. I'd like you to deposit it into my business account and then take out fifteen hundred of it in the form of a cashier's check. Can you do that while I wait?"

When Nina returned they signed the appropriate papers to put her down as a co-owner of the safe deposit box. After that she accompanied him back into the vault to lock it up. When that was done she handed him an envelope with a bank check for fifteen hundred dollars in it. Before he left they agreed that he'd pick her up after work on Friday.

The next day he drove into South Providence hoping to catch Gus at his office at Briggs and Timilty. Fortunately the big man was in. This time the secretary escorted him to Gus' lair where his old pal was sitting at his desk reading the morning *Journal* with a cup of coffee by his elbow. Something had changed in Gus' demeanor toward him since his last visit, though his old friend tried to cover it with a welcoming smile.

"I had a visit from my Uncle Patrick the other day and he left me a present. I thought half of it should go to you," Doherty said as he slipped the bank check out of his pocket and handed it to Gus. Timilty looked at the figure and then whistled through his teeth.

"Dare I asked where this came from and what it's for?"

"You can ask but I can't tell you, mostly because Patrick himself was pretty vague about the source. Suffice it to say, it appears to be a payoff for our role in getting Kevin O'Shaughnessy dumped from the Kennedy campaign." Doherty then proceeded to tell Gus how his uncle had maneuvered the once powerful Boston wheeler-dealer out of the Kennedy operation and out of the country as well. In addition he filled him in on how he gave one of the films to Patrick in exchange for three thousand dollars and kept the other one as a form of insurance for the two of them.

"I've arranged for that film to be made public in the event that anything untoward were to happen to either of us. Aside from that it's better that I don't give you any more details about this arrangement. Suffice it to say the mechanism I set in motion should keep us out of harm's way. And if it doesn't then certain parties on the other end will pay dearly for their actions."

Gus gave Doherty an uncomfortable smile. "You're being awfully mysterious about this whole business."

"Yeah, I know. And that's the way I'm going to keep it."

"Does that mean we're okay about what happened that night at the shipyard?"

"I don't know, Gus. I'm going to have to think on that for a while."

That was the last Doherty saw or heard from Gus Timilty for a couple of weeks. Then one day out of the blue his old mentor called him at the office.

"I just thought I'd let you know that I gave a grand of that money from your Uncle Patrick to Christina. I told her I hoped she'd use it to get out from under with Jimmy Ricks. At the time she seemed overjoyed at the prospect."

"Then what happened?" Doherty asked knowing there was a 'but' to the rest of Gus' explanation.

Timilty laughed softly. "She took the dough and bought a bus ticket to California. She left me a note saying she was going out west to try her hand in the movie business. She said Jimmy Ricks was not happy about her departure."

"Well she does have some experience in that line of work."

"Screw you, Doherty."

"Likewise I'm sure."

With that his oldest and dearest friend rang off. He didn't know if he'd ever see Gus Timilty again. He would've missed him more if things with Nina weren't going so well.

THE END

ACKNOWLEDGEMENTS

I would like to thank David McKenney of the Brewer Yacht Sales, Inc. of North Kingston, RI who gave me a brief tour of the boatyard at Wickford and a little information about the surrounding area. I would like to acknowledge the help Zack Stedman, the General Manager of the Bonnet Shores Beach Club, who caught me nosing around the property in the off-season and rather than sending me packing took me on a tour of the facility. He even showed me some vintage photographs of what the club looked like around the time *The Missing Films* is set. Another thank you goes to Ara Gechijian of New England Photo in Arlington, Massachusetts for his insight on how movie cameras and projectors worked in the late 1950s.

I would also like to thank Tim Cranston of North Kingston for providing me with some historical information about Wickford Village, which incidentally is where I lived for the first two years of my life. Needless to say I don't remember living there, though I do remember later visiting family friends who still resided on Green Street in what had once been government housing. I should mention here my old crew from Cranston days with whom I had lunch at the Twin Willows in Narragansett, Rhode Island several springs ago. That day inspired me to set a scene at the *Willows*. I would like to give a shout out to Sandra Moyers, who edited an Arcadia History publication titled *Images of America: Cranston Revisited,* which helped me to revisit the Cranston of the late 1950s. Finally I want to recognize all the bad boys who lived in the Village near the Print Works in Cranston with whom I got into much mischief in my younger years.

For background information on the 1960 Rhode Island senatorial election I consulted G. Wayne Miller's biography of Claiborne Pell, *An Uncommon*

Man: the life and times of Senator Claiborne Pell. For information on the murder of Amasa Sprague and the subsequent trial of the Gordon brothers, I used fellow ARIA member Paul F. Caranci's book *The Hanging & Redemption of John Gordon* as my main source.

Of course, no acknowledgements would be complete without thanking my wife and best friend, Jeanne Berkman, for her help in editing this book and giving me the appropriate criticism when it was most due. I thank her most heartily for her suggestions, even when I didn't follow them.